FOR
*Peter and Paul and Christopher*

# THE
# WICKER
# MAN

# THE
# WICKER
# MAN

A NOVEL BY

Robin Hardy &
Anthony Shaffer

PAN BOOKS

First published in the United States in 1978 by Crown Publishers, Inc.
First published in the United Kingdom in 1980 by Hamlyn

This edition published 2000 by Pan Books
an imprint of Macmillan Publishers Ltd
25 Eccleston Place, London SW1W 9NF
Basingstoke and Oxford
Associated companies throughout the world
www.macmillan.co.uk

ISBN 0 330 39018 X

9 8 7 6 5 4 3 2 1

A CIP catalogue record for this book is available from
the British Library.

Typeset by SetSystems Ltd, Saffron Walden, Essex
Printed and bound in Great Britain by
Mackays of Chatham plc, Chatham, Kent

Man is born to believe. And if no church
comes forward with its title-deeds of truth,
sustained by the tradition of sacred ages and
by the conviction of countless generations to
guide him, he will find altars and idols in his own heart
and his own imagination.

BENJAMIN DISRAELI

# Introduction

THIS BOOK, THE NOVEL OF *THE WICKER MAN*, THE
script for which was written by Anthony Shaffer, is a
curious artefact. Many films produce literary spin-offs, but
more often than not these are hack jobs, souvenirs, vestig-
ial remnants of the days before videotape allowed enthusi-
asts to possess their own personal copies of films. Rarely, if
ever, do film novelizations add to or augment our appreci-
ation of the film in question. Which is why this book is so
unusual. In many ways it extends and amplifies the issues
on which the film meditates, fills in the gaps. In the process
it creates something that is often more compendious, more
nuanced, than the film which inspired it.

The novel's existence owes much to the savage treat-
ment its cinematic big brother received on its first release.
Made as a top-line feature, *The Wicker Man* ignominiously
ended up a B-movie, and a poorly distributed one at that.
Between being commissioned and finally arriving in cine-
mas, *The Wicker Man* suffered a chain of calamity, not least
of which was a reshuffle at the upper echelon of British
Lion films. Peter Snell, the studio's managing director and
*The Wicker Man*'s greatest supporter, was replaced at the

top by one Michael Deeley as British Lion prepared itself to be absorbed by the EMI corporation. It is common for incoming studio bosses to treat the output of their predecessors with something less than reverence, and such proved the case here, compounded no doubt by the fact that *The Wicker Man* was a most difficult film to classify in terms of genre. Deeley pronounced the finished product execrable and refused it a solo release; after some drastic vivisection in the cutting room, it was paired off with Nic Roeg's *Don't Look Now* and sent on a despondent tour of the provinces.

At this point, most of those involved in any film would be prepared to write the thing off as having been born under a bad sign and leave it there. But Robin Hardy, *The Wicker Man*'s director (previously he had been involved with Anthony Shaffer in Hardy Shaffer Associates, a company which produced television commercials), was reluctant to see the film wither on the bough. He had also been involved in researching the pagan legend and lore which adorns Shaffer's script.

He eventually had the opportunity to put this learning to constructive use. In 1977, the film was discovered by a pair of New Orleans-based cineastes, who were developing a movie distribution venture. *The Wicker Man* became their pet project; they set about restoring the version which Hardy had made and securing for it high-profile exhibition on the west coast of America. Hardy, meanwhile, had added literature to the quiver of his talents, and he set about adapting Shaffer's script as a novel (Hardy says he had already commenced work on a *Wicker Man* novel prior to the completion of Shaffer's script). The resultant novel would not only help promote the resurrected film, it would sketch a richer portrait of Summerisle than was allowed in a 102-minute cinema feature. (The advance funds which Hardy received for the book also came in handy, and were ploughed into various legal skirmishes connected to restoring and re-releasing the film.)

Whatever its genesis, the *Wicker Man* novel will fascinate all lovers of the film, particularly those whose interest lies in the fact that *The Wicker Man* was among the first mainstream features to use religious faith as subject matter. Indeed, the novel seems to have been written to elaborate on such matters to an extent that would have been impossible in a commercial movie. It also has sufficient space to reveal how inspired Shaffer and Hardy were by the same matter as *The Golden Bough* (subtitle: *A Study in Magic and Religion*), James Frazer's herculean study of folk mythology that was published in twelve volumes between 1890 and 1936. The children who carry death out of the village; the rites of parthenogenesis practised over a blazing fire by Miss Rose's girls; the foreskins in the chemist's jar; the frog in Myrtle's throat; the pregnant women transferring their fertility to the apple blossom trees; the checklist of qualities (willing, king-like, virginal and foolish) which make Sergeant Howie 'the right kind of adult' to be sacrificed – all of these and many others echo the motifs explored in the pages of *The Golden Bough*. Hardy in the novel also transplants to Summerisle the classic myth which gave Frazer's book its title. In the sacred grove of Diana at Nemi, Italy, a grim figure was seen to patrol night and day. He was a priest and a murderer. To be succeeded he had to be killed, hence his anxious vigil. In this myth are the seeds of all Western cultural archetypes. In *The Wicker Man*, a similar scene is played out in a sacred grove near to Summerisle's castle.

Atop the foundations of Shaffer's script Hardy built a roccoco edifice adorned with religious detail and debate. We discover more about the troubled background of Sergeant Neil Howie. He had failed in his attempt to become a priest, daunted by the challenge of preaching his minority faith, Episcopalianism, in the staunchly Presbyterian Highlands of Scotland. We see his broader range; Howie as a man and as a partner to the hapless Mary Bannock, and we see him as a figure more rounded, more formidable, than the pious, ramrod-straight cipher familiar from the film.

His jousting with Summerisle also has more impact than it has in the film, where considerations of audience tolerance limited their exchanges to something only slightly more than bickering. When we consider Lord Summerisle here, we might even say the novel is more effective than the film. It had been Shaffer's intention in writing *The Wicker Man* to argue that no brand of religious faith has a greater claim to authenticity than any other; all religious faiths are merely social constructs – culturally determined ways of living. The corollary of this is that all faiths are equal. The battle between Howie and Summerisle should for both men be from a standing start.

In the film, however, Howie has an added advantage: he isn't played by Christopher Lee. No audience watching *The Wicker Man* would be unaware of the baggage Lee brought to his role: he had played *Dracula*, Frankenstein's Monster and *The Mummy*. From the outset the assumption would have been that Summerisle was on the side of wrong. So the film became unbalanced in favour of the Christian consensus, becomes a conventional battle between good and evil. In the novel, Summerisle is shorn of such associations; the battle is more ambivalent, more unsettling – and, in the end, perhaps more in keeping with the treacherous moral landscape Shaffer initially envisioned.

Allan Brown
Glasgow
February 2000

## CHAPTER I

# Saturday –
## the 28th of April

HOWIE WATCHED THE BIRD CLOSELY THROUGH HIS BIN-oculars. The eagle rose from her nest with hard strokes from her heavy, damasked wings. The outer, primary feathers looked like thrusting fingers as they forced the air downward. Then the whole bird left Howie's field of vision.

He saw a single, startled eaglet left in the nest; its sharp, wobbly, little head craning to follow its mother's ascent. Surprised to see only one chick, he focused hard on the nest, looking for any sign of another. Howie was rewarded by being able to glimpse just the upper edge of an egg, half concealed by the eagle's down its mother had left around it, keeping it warm.

Neil Howie took the binoculars away from his eyes and stared at the mountainside below the eagles' eyrie. Treeless and bleak, the rolling foothills of gaunt Ben Sluie stretched like an ocean swell of purple heather towards the craggy, limestone face of the mountain. Beyond was a strip of indigo sea capped by the fleeced heads of waves, choppy in the easterly wind that blew from mainland Scotland, whose hilly coast was the merest smudge on the horizon. Interrupting the gentle undulations of the heathered hills was a single pile of huge, oblong rocks perched on one of their summits. They looked like the tumbled pillars of an ancient edifice but seemed, on closer inspection, to be so eccentrically shaped as to have been, quite by hazard, strewn there through some geological accident. Here two rare golden eagles had chosen to nest.

Howie wished, as he vainly searched the landscape for what had startled the brooding mother, that they had chosen a safer place. Yet nothing seemed to be moving in the heather below the nest. Saint Ninian's Isle, in late April, was still fairly free of tourists and the area around Ben Sluie was six roadless miles from the ferry to the mainland. But Howie had been warned. There was someone abroad who planned to rob the nest.

'Still can't see anyone!' he said to Mary Bannock, his fiancée, who lay beside him in a thick patch of green, spring bracken, a safe distance from the eagles' eyrie.

'Will you look at her now, Neil? She's surely seen something to disturb her!' Mary's soft, Highland Scots voice was pitched deliberately low. Neil Howie had taught her, when they had started their birdwatching together, that the creatures were less likely to hear a human voice that used a lower register. Just as humans could not hear the higher notes of a songbird unless they recorded them mechanically and played them back at a slower speed. The eagle was too far away to hear her, of course, but speaking in low tones was a 'drill' they practised when out 'birding'. And birding was one of the activities that Mary and Neil most enjoyed doing together. Lying on the bed of bracken that served them as their own eyrie, they had laid out sandwiches and a Thermos. For, today, theirs was a waiting game.

Howie looked up at the eagle, soaring now on the warm air currents that rose from the earth after a day of sunshine, her head poised watchfully over territory she considered her own. He knew that someone must be there. For there was only one predator that could threaten a golden eagle on Saint Ninian's Isle, and that was 'man'.

'Aye, I think this is *it*, Mary,' agreed Howie slowly. 'Will you look carefully to the right of the nest there, love. In the heather. Take the foreground first, then the middle distance, then the distance ... working away from the nest, d'you see? I'll do the same on the other side. And keep your head down, love. If chummy's out there, I don't want him to see us!'

'Yes, Sergeant!' she said, and there was the faintest hint of rebellious sarcasm in her voice, but she did as she was bid using the shiny, new binoculars he had given her for her birthday. 'Her Neil', as she had thought of him since the day they had become engaged, was, after all, a sergeant of the West Highland Constabulary, responsible for one of the largest police precincts in Scotland and, in matters such as this, worthy of being obeyed.

Nor was her pride in him misplaced. At twenty-six his bailiwick consisted of one not-so-small town, Portlochlie, on the mainland, and some nine populated islands stretching westward far out into the Atlantic.

Mary searched the territory she had been allotted carefully, but could see nothing suspicious. The eagle was still hovering watchfully, but now quite high over the nest.

'If there was anyone hiding there in the heather, wouldn't she dive at him?' she asked.

'Not dive . . . you say "stoop",' corrected Howie without answering her question. He continued his meticulous search of the landscape.

She sighed. When he was after 'chummy', which she knew was police slang for the 'wanted criminal', he was as hard to distract as a hunting dog that thinks it has found the 'scent'.

'Maybe she's just searching for a wee bit o' food,' said Mary mischievously, adding, 'or maybe she's "searching for haddock's eyes amongst the heather bright . . . To make them into waistcoat buttons in the silent night"?'

'Lewis Carroll,' he said automatically, participating in another favourite game in which his schoolteacher fiancée won more often than not.

'It's my teatime, I know that!' said Mary, and she undid the plastic cup on the Thermos. 'And I think she's just after feeding her bairn.'

'No, her mate's away hunting for food. You're forgetting him,' Howie reminded her quietly. He shivered slightly. 'It's getting cold. She'll be wanting to get back to brooding that eaglet. You were right first time, love. Something . . . and someone, most like, disturbed her.'

Mary looked curiously at her Neil as he patiently searched the hills through his binoculars. She allowed herself the luxury, as she sipped some strong, sweet tea, to stare at his profile and love it, detail by detail. His tanned outdoorsman's face had planes and surfaces that reminded her of the physical map in an atlas. Ben Howie she'd nicknamed his rather prominent, aquiline nose – 'Ben' being Gaelic for mountain. She noticed that his eyes crinkled with the concentration of gazing through the binoculars, but they crinkled, she thought, into the same laughter lines that came with his frequent smile. She wanted to put her hand out and feel the soft, brown hair that curled slightly at the nape of his neck. She loved the eagerness and passion of her policeman who spoke in such a fatherly, husbandly way of eagles. Yet, it saddened her that they had now been engaged for three years and he had still not asked her to name the day. Still had not attempted to make love to her. She longed to ask him why but could never find the words. When it pricked her pride that he might not find her as attractive as she would wish, then she reminded herself of his Christian principles. How could she (and why should she), a well-brought-up Presbyterian girl, try to force this good, kind man into sex before marriage? Or so she persuaded herself. Even though the ache of this incompleteness in their relationship sometimes seemed intolerable.

His passionate nature Neil Howie showed her in so many other ways. In his love of birds. In the quiet, but incandescent joy his religion gave him. In the deep involvement with the quality of justice that he brought to his police work. Mary knew that these were not really separate facets of her Neil but logically, spiritually linked parts of the whole man. Knowing the law, in Christian Scotland, to be based on the teachings of Christ, he saw his work, in the police, as an opportunity to give a practical expression to his faith and convictions. What her Presbyterian church called 'bearing witness' and what his Episcopalian church called 'living your life in Christ'. His love of birds, for instance, he expressed practically, not sentimentally, and yet he had told Mary that birds, their lives, their beauty, and the many mysteries still attached to them (that baffled scientific explanation), all this was, to him, an endless reminder of the wonder of God's creation. Neil Howie used his knowledge of the creatures, and his power as a policeman, to watch over them and, wherever he lawfully could, to protect their environment.

He rested his eyes for a moment and took a sip of hot tea while Mary gazed watchfully towards the mountain.

'There's another bird!' she cried suddenly, entirely forgetting their voice drill. 'It's coming from Ben Sluie. Could it be the male?'

'It won't be any *other* bird. Not on an eagle's territory,' said Howie, searching the sky where Mary was pointing. Then he found the bird and refocused his binoculars fast.

'That's him all right. Och, will you look at the speed of him, Mary! But he's still quite high. Wait till you see him stoop. More than a hundred miles an hour they can do when they stoop. If chummy's out there hidden in one of those ravines in the heather, this'll be a grand way to winkle him out,' and Howie spoke as if he identified strongly with the male eagle about to stoop on the wrongdoer.

The female eagle was slowly descending towards her nest while her mate slowed his approach and hovered high over the eyrie. Then suddenly he seemed to fall out of the sky, diving tangentially towards a fold in the hillside below the pile of rocks and the nest.

'Dear God!' exclaimed a surprised Howie. 'The bastard's only a hundred feet from the nest. He must have . . .'

Howie had no time to finish his sentence, for a man stood up in the heather pointing a shotgun straight at the diving eagle. The two watchers could see the man's shoulder take the kick from firing the gun before they heard the shot. But the blast echoed all around the hills when the sound came, and it was followed by a second shot an instant later. The stone crags of Ben Sluie seemed to answer with a fusillade of echoes.

Then the diving eagle hit the man, knocking him out of Neil and Mary's sight.

'Mary, get, as fast as you can, to the telephone at Taskpool!' said Howie. 'Call the police station in Portlochlie and tell them I want two officers on the very next ferry. Tell them chummy's armed, right now. They'll get the magistrate's permission to use a gun, if we need it.' He saw her anxious face. 'But we won't, we won't! So don't worry!' he added urgently.

Mary hesitated. Howie was already sprinting out of the bracken and across the heather towards the spot where both eagle and man had disappeared. She felt she had to just 'register' his departing body in her mind's eye. The thick shoulders, tapering waist, and long legs of her Neil in his raw wool sweater and faded jeans. How absurd of him, she thought, to say 'don't worry'.

'Please take care!' she called after him and then started running down the long sloping plateau that led back to the ferry at Taskpool, which linked the barren scenic isle of Saint Ninian's to the busy fishing port of Portlochlie. Try as she would she could not stop the tears that kept coming to her eyes. She tried to remind herself that no criminal in his right mind risks shooting a policeman in

Britain. So universal is public approval of an unarmed police force that the criminal world would nearly always 'hand over' a cop killer. The nagging worry in the back of Mary's mind was that the people who rob rare birds of their precious eggs are not normal criminals. Some, she knew, did not even do it for profit (although a golden eagle's egg would be very valuable) but out of a collector's insatiable acquisitiveness. Such a person might not *act* as would an everyday criminal. This last thought made her run even faster, though her lungs were almost bursting with the effort.

Howie, meanwhile, was running with a trained athlete's sense of pacing himself. Although rugby football was his sport, Howie played on the 'wing' and was used to a couple of hours, at a stretch, of almost incessant running. He watched the place where the man had disappeared but he kept a careful eye on the terrain around him. If the man had killed the eagle, and it was almost inconceivable that he hadn't, why, he wondered, hadn't he reappeared?

Then he saw that the female eagle had left her nest again and was hovering above the spot where her mate had stooped. Instants later Howie had reached ground high enough for him to be able to see both the man and the male eagle.

The man had evidently only wounded the bird for he was kneeling on the ground using the butt of the shotgun in a desperate attempt to keep the great, fluttering creature away from him. But the eagle kept attacking again and again, his claws and beak outstretched, only to be warded off with another swingeing blow from the gun. He hasn't had time to reload, thought Howie, calculating that around four hundred more yards lay between him and the eagle's attacker.

Howie was sickened to see that the man had just broken the great bird's wing. Gamely, the eagle made another attempt to fly at the man's head but toppled pathetically sideways leaving his enemy a chance, at last, to stand up and fumble hurriedly for cartridges with which to reload his shotgun. He had just broken open the gun and was about to reload, when the female eagle stooped on him. She came so fast that only the sound of her wings made him start to raise his head before she had him by the shoulders, exactly as she might have grasped a hare or a lamb, her talons sinking straight into his flesh. The man shrieked, dropped his gun, and tried to shield his head against the she-eagle's hammering beak.

Howie had about two hundred yards more to go and used the distance to check the terrain ahead of him. He could see now that the bed of a stream had been used by the man to approach the eyrie. About a quarter of a mile away the stream disappeared over the hillside. Here, Howie knew, the hill descended steeply for another mile to the coast road that led to the small village of Talleter on the west side of the island.

The man struggling with the eagle had flung himself to the ground, twisting his body to try to make the bird get off his back. It was the right manoeuvre because, after a savage peck at his face, the she-eagle soared away heading straight for her nest. The man grabbed his gun, which lay still 'broken' but with one cartridge in the breech. He snapped it closed and was cocking it when, for the first time, he saw Howie.

''Ullo there!' gasped the man in a Londoner's sharp, nasal whine. 'That f—g bird f—g near killed me . . . Hey. What the f—!'

Howie had never paused for an instant in his run. On the contrary he had increased his pace as if he were coming around the goalposts for a touchdown. The man just had time to bring the gun up and try to ward him off, or perhaps even to shoot at him, when Howie left the ground in a flying rugby tackle that gripped the man's thighs just above the knees, and brought him to the ground with a bone-jangling crash. Howie had snatched hold of the gun, expelled the cartridge, and hurled the weapon away into the heather before the man could catch his breath. But he had no time to utter a word because Howie at once grabbed one of his wrists with both hands and spun him over onto his face, forcing his arm up his back as far as the shoulder blades. He ignored the man's shout of pain and looked over at the still fluttering body of the male eagle. The bird was clearly dead and mercifully so, considering the fearful injuries it had suffered.

'I'm a police officer!' Howie barked the fact in the man's ear. 'I'm charging you with killing a golden eagle and I'm cautioning you that anything you say may be taken down and used in evidence. Now get on your feet, man!'

\*

The last ferry left the small township of Taskpool on Saint Ninian's Isle an hour before sunset that evening.

Neil Howie and Mary Bannock stood on the tiny upper deck and watched the seabirds. Below, on the vehicle deck, the eagle killer sat in a police car, his head and shoulders bandaged and his wrists handcuffed.

'What'll he get, Neil?' asked Mary, referring to the prisoner.

'Probably just a fine if it's a first offence. Which I doubt. I'm sure he's working for some bloody collector down in London. It sounds daft but the firearm offence could be more serious for him if it turns out he hasn't got a licence. Of course he says he's lost it but that's easy to check.'

'What do they give you if you wipe out the last of a species?' she asked.

'The same!' answered Howie bitterly. 'I just thank God that someone in Talleter yesterday tipped us off about that bastard or he might have wiped out the whole nest. Of course, they probably didn't know he'd got a gun with him.'

Howie sloughed off his anger as he watched the water birds and went on: 'Och, don't let's think about him, Mary. Look at *him*. *He's* early!' He pointed to a bird perched on the big wooden posts which, clad with old car tyres, lined the ferry dock.

'I don't recognize him,' admitted Mary.

'A great shearwater, I think,' said Howie. 'Early for him to be hereabouts.'

On the trip across the five-mile strait to Portlochlie they enjoyed themselves identifying four different kinds of gull: the common gull, the blackhead, the greater blackbacked, and the herring gull. Although none of these gulls was rare, Howie always recorded the birds he'd seen during the day each evening before he went to bed. He made a point of noting what they'd been doing, whether preening, nest building, feeding, migrating, or whatever. It was a discipline that was not dissimilar to the notes he made each night in connection with his police work. He always categorized people he'd interviewed in a case. He tried to remember first impressions and record them. The eagle killer would be as dispassionately noted as his victim.

It was while he and Mary were identifying gulls that Constable McTaggart hurried up and put a letter into Sergeant Howie's hands. Hugh McTaggart was an unambitious officer who, although quite a bit older than Howie, had often been passed over for promotion. Partly, perhaps, because he made no secret of the fact that he preferred fly-fishing to police work.

'It's an anonymous letter for you, Sergeant,' said McTaggart. 'Came this morning. Sorry, I forgot it just now. What with all the excitement of getting chummy patched up. D'you know the doc told him he was sorry he could not let him bleed to death after he saw what was left of the eagle.'

'Is it just the usual filth?' asked the sergeant, wearily taking the letter from McTaggart.

'C'mon, Sergeant. You ken I'd have no bothered you with it if it was not important.' McTaggart was slightly aggrieved.

'Of course not, Hugh. Sorry,' said Sergeant Howie who had already started to read the letter attentively.

Dear Sergeant Howie,
    None of us have seen May Morrison's daughter,

Rowan, since last year. She is only twelve and has been missing from her home for many months.

She couldn't have left the island by herself. She's too young. Her mother won't say anything about it. Just to mind my own business. Well, I reckon it's all our business if a kid disappears, that's why I'm writing you this letter.

Signed,

A child lover on Summerisle.

P.S. I enclose a picture of Rowan Morrison.

He looked at the snapshot of a pretty auburn-haired twelve-year-old girl standing in front of a blossoming apple tree. It was a sunny, smiling face with the fair Scandinavian cast to the features that is often found in the outer isles where, in the dark ages, the Vikings raped and pillaged, leaving little but their blondness and a few place names behind. The envelope clearly bore the date stamp of Summerisle, the farthest west of the Outer Hebrides group of isles and, although populated, a private island that Sergeant Howie had never previously had reason to visit.

'Can I have a word with you, Sergeant?' McTaggart seemed not to want to speak what he had on his mind in front of Mary.

Sergeant Howie nodded and walked with McTaggart to the taffrail overlooking the vehicles in the centre of the vessel.

'Will you be flying there on Monday?' asked McTaggart, referring to the fact that Sergeant Howie would need to open up an investigation on Summerisle as soon as possible, but that the day he usually flew on his visits to the islands, in the police seaplane, was Monday and not, as the constable feared, on the morrow. Sergeant Howie absent on a Sunday invariably meant that McTaggart, being the senior constable, had to remain in charge of the Portlochlie police station.

'Monday?' Howie spoke sharply. 'The child's already been missing from her home for some time. It's an urgent case, man, no doubt about it. I'd go tonight if it wasn't too late already to be flying to the isles before dark. I'm sorry, Hugh, but you'll have to be on duty again tomorrow. Clock up a little more overtime. Reorganize the roster with the other lads till I get back.'

'Oh, bullshit, Sergeant! Lots of kids wander off. She's maybe fallen down some cliff. Why don't we radio them?' McTaggart was angry that the sergeant's zealousness was going to cost him a day's fishing.

'On Summerisle? You know damn well, Hugh, it's got no radio. No telephone. Just the packet boat calling once a week.' Howie spoke with a quiet, firm authority that closed the matter.

'What time will you be going?' asked McTaggart, resigned now.

'After the early service, around eight thirty,' said Howie, referring to his intention to go to the early Communion service at Saint Andrew's Episcopal Church. 'Have you ever been to Summerisle?' the sergeant went on, chatty now that he had quelled McTaggart's small rebellion.

'No. But I've tasted the famous Summerisle apples of course,' answered McTaggart thoughtfully. 'But it's strange, isn't it? All that fruit.'

'The whole place is a bit strange by all accounts. No

licensing laws. Dancing on Sunday. Oh, that'd appeal to a heathen like you, McTaggart.'

Sergeant Howie laughed as he said this for it was a joke between them that Hugh McTaggart resented all the Presbyterian-inspired Scottish laws relating to the Sabbath, mostly for the extra work it involved policing them. Privately, Howie agreed with the older man, but for different reasons. He could not think of the small-minded, mean-spirited horrors of the Scottish Sabbath as God-given. But to him the law was the law, however he felt about it.

McTaggart returned to the police car to keep his eye on chummy, and Howie rejoined Mary to watch the different birds that marked their approach to the mainland. Many were the birds you would expect to see around a busy fishing harbour, gulls and other scavengers. But Mary pointed to a kittiwake and reported having seen some eider ducks flying across the marshes to the south of the dock at Portlochlie, which they were now approaching. Her Neil politely asked her to describe the colouring of the ducks and then, before she had time to register her indignation at his disbelief, he became quite excited to see a bird he was sure could only be a rare ivory gull. It hovered above the ferry's wake but they could not easily see the underside of its wings. Howie decided to list it as a 'reported' sighting.

Meanwhile the ferry made its arrival at Portlochlie, distracting the couple's attention from the birds. The town lay to the north of the dock, a mixture of the whitewashed, terraced houses of the poor and the solid reddish granite buildings of the well-to-do. Howie watched the ferrymen getting the police car off first and saw McTaggart turn on the winking blue light on top of the vehicle and speed away to the local hospital to get chummy some further medical attention before locking him up for the night.

When all the cars had left the ferry, Neil and Mary noticed two cars waiting to come aboard. One of the deckhands went over to the leading car.

'There's no more tonight!' he said to the driver who had wound down his window.

'I told you that was the last one!' said an American woman's voice from inside the car.

While the deckhand went to break the bad news to the second car, Howie paused. He subscribed fully to the motto that a policeman is always on duty, but now he could see that he would have to perform a rather unpleasant duty that he knew the deckhand had shirked. The latter was already hurrying towards the Admiral Cochrane Public House that quenches the thirst of those who take the ferry between Portlochlie and Saint Ninian's Isle. Except, of course, on the Sabbath when the ferry doesn't run and all the pubs in Portlochlie are closed in deference to the edict of Scotland's Presbyterian majority.

'Good evening, sir,' said Sergeant Howie to the driver of the first car, a greying man of about fifty with a pleasant, tanned face. 'I'm afraid there'll be no more ferries till Monday morning!'

'You're kidding?' the American voice expressed disbelief. 'Forgive me, but why the hell not?' he added, getting out of his car.

'What's that he said?' asked the woman from inside the car. 'I can't get a word they say with these *accents*.'

'Zilch till Monday!' translated her husband patiently.

'We're going to have to shlep back into town here and find a hotel.'

'*What?*' came the American lady's voice pitched several semitones above the shrike in full song. 'Well you tell him we got reservations over on Saint whosit's island tonight!'

'Yeah, well we missed the last ferry, hon',' said the American hopelessly, looking rather appealingly at Neil and Mary as if he hoped they'd be able to produce some answer that would save him from his wife's wrath. But the lady herself was about to take charge of the situation, getting out of the car and staring across at Neil Howie rather accusingly.

'You in charge here?' she asked.

'No, madam!' said Howie civilly. 'I'm a police officer, off duty. But if I can help in any way?'

'Okay. How come there's no ferry till Monday?' she asked.

'Tomorrow's the Sabbath, madam!' said Howie. 'In Scotland we *observe* the Sabbath.' He spoke more like a tourist guide than a reproving Scot.

At the mention of the Sabbath the lady looked momentarily surprised but then fell silent, suddenly getting back into the car, leaving her husband to cope with the problem. A man and a woman from the second car came and joined the American. Both were young and looked English. They had heard the foregoing conversation.

'Know of a nice hotel we might get in?' asked the English girl of Mary.

'Here in town there's the Rothsay Arms, but it's really for "commercials". It's not very nice if you're on holiday,' said Mary. 'But there's the Highland Guest House, that's ten miles down the coast with a beautiful view of the island. They say the food's very good too.'

'*That* I'll believe when I *taste* it!' said the American lady from inside the car.

'D'you think they'll have room for us, too?' asked the American of Mary.

'Och, at this time of year I'm sure they will,' said Mary.

'You turn right at the main road,' said Howie directing them. 'Then keep going. It's almost ten miles. On the right-hand side, there's a big sign.'

The English couple went back to their car without further ado and drove off, but the American hesitated.

'Thank you for your help,' he said to Neil and Mary. 'Just one other thing. D'you think we'll be able to get a drink there? Our own Sabbath just ended and I wouldn't want to spend the next thirty-six hours without a drink if I can avoid it.'

'You better believe it!' came his wife's voice from inside the car. Howie smiled. He rather liked this man and was fascinated to realize that he was probably a Jew. You met very few Jews in the Highlands and they intrigued Howie rather as if they were a rare and precious breed of bird.

'The laws of Scotland,' he said, 'are particularly kind to bona fide travellers such as yourselves. The Guest House is fully licensed to sell you drink of any kind all day or night, even on a Sunday if you want. Let me make a call for you and tell them you're coming so they'll keep you some supper. What's the name?'

'Eisenbaum,' said the American. 'Jean and Paul Eisenbaum.'

Later, after Neil had telephoned the Highland Guest

House for the Eisenbaums, from the bar of the Admiral Cochrane, and had a drink with them and seen them on their way, they stayed and ate a pub dinner of game pie and pickles, washed down with bitter beer.

'Well, she certainly mellowed a bit after a wee drink,' said Mary adding, 'Jewish people fascinate you, don't they, Neil?'

'Aye. They do,' he acknowledged. 'Imagine believing you're God's chosen people and there being quite a lot of evidence to support the idea: Abraham, Noah, Moses, Jesus, Saint Paul, Karl Marx, Freud, Einstein to name but a few. Imagine having a book that is like a tribal diary trying to trace your ancestry direct to Adam and Eve . . .'

'Hey!' interrupted Mary laughing. 'Don't forget I belong to a fundamentalist religion too. You Episcopalians don't properly believe in the Good Book!'

'We don't take the Old Testament literally. But no more do most of you Presbyterians!' retorted Howie, amused. 'You all drink like fishes on the Sabbath, behind closed doors, and then go right out and vote for dry Sundays.'

'I do not drink like a fish on Sundays,' laughed Mary. 'And I voted for wet Sundays! But then I'm not very religious really, as you know. When we're married you'll have to have all the religion for both of us. Are you ever sorry you gave up the idea of being a priest?'

'No, not really,' said Neil Howie thoughtfully. 'But it would have been a challenge, here in Scotland, to be a priest of a minority religion like the Episcopalians. Mary, you know I think of the police now as my ministry. It doesn't rankle any more. That's the truth!'

'But?' Mary insisted. She worried that his failure to graduate from the seminary still hurt, even if he himself could believe that it no longer rankled.

'*But* it was the first, and, I hope, the last time I failed in what I set out to do. Did I ever tell you why I failed?'

'No,' answered Mary, who had never dared pry into this part of his life. She had sensibly waited till he would tell her about it of his own accord. And she had waited a long time. 'No, you never did,' she added simply, waiting.

'It was no any academic problem,' he said, a bit defensively. 'I did fine in the Latin and the Greek and all that. It was a matter of attitude. I think *today* . . . if I was being interviewed by the bishop today . . . I'd have passed.'

'Things have changed,' said Mary consolingly.

'Changed?' Howie was surprised. 'No, *things* haven't changed. *I've* changed. Being in the police has made me more, more . . .' He searched for the word and then he said, sounding still dissatisfied, 'more flexible.'

'More tolerant?' Mary suggested as being nearer to what he meant and came directly upon the residual seminarian in her Neil.

'No, you cannot tolerate what is not the truth. Not for yourself anyway. Nor can you really tolerate actions that go directly against God's *word*. I can't do that as a person any more than as a police officer I can tolerate people breaking the law of the land!'

'So what has changed in you?' asked Mary insistently.

'Och, I used to feel very strongly about the proliferation of daft religions here in Scotland. The "wee frees" down in places like Plockton with their three-day Sabbaths. The Baptists and your lot, love, who both believe they're "elect of God". That they're justified through faith, which would be fine, except that then they add that they believe God handed them out the faith like a club membership. So they're all members of the Elect Club and close the pubs and stop other people doing a stroke of useful work on Sundays. Daft of course. Harmless, you'd say, except that then they look down on everybody else who don't belong to their Elect Club, just like some people accuse the Jews of doing. But I say if the Baptists or your kirk of God had produced one man, let alone the Son of God, who could change the faith and the hope of the world, not to forget the course of history, they might have a reason to think of themselves as elect.'

'Was that part of your sermon in front of your bishop?' hazarded Mary.

'It was,' said her Neil, smiling ruefully.

'But did he disagree with you?' she asked gently.

'No. But we live in ecumenical times and he thought I was determined to declare war on the other churches; and so in a way I was.' Howie laughed out loud remembering what he had wanted to preach. 'Do you want to hear what I selected as the first goal of my ministry?'

She nodded, smiling her encouragement at him, waiting for it all to come out.

'I was going to preach that Scotland would be a happier place if it delivered itself into the love of God through the love of its fellow men. Simply that! Forgetting the fire and brimstone of the Old Testament. Forgetting the nitpicking over whether Jesus turned water into wine or grape juice and all that. What kind of a Redeemer can they be imagining, Mary, when they tell us that He came to a

wedding where the booze hadn't arrived so he took the
wellwater and turned it into some nutty fruit drink? To tell
a tale like that of Him is, surely, blasphemy?'

'You'd have made a lovely preacher, Neil,' said Mary,
'but I'm glad you're a policeman just the same. I don't
think I could have ever lived up to being your wife if you'd
been a priest. I'd have felt that I had to help carry on the
argument by your side. And it's not that I don't agree with
*most* of what you say, but I know that I could never say it
with quite enough conviction to convert anybody else.'

'In that case you'd have made the perfect, *average*
Episcopalian, Mary!' said 'her Neil', aware, even as he said
it, that he wished he hadn't.

Mary fell into a silence that she knew seemed like a
sulk but which she could not help, because she was on the
brink of tears. She so wanted to be what he required of
her. If only she could always know exactly what that was.
She didn't fear that he wanted to change her personality
and mould her, although subconsciously she knew it was
hard for him to avoid preaching and teaching. She had
read Germaine Greer and assumed that the goals of her
thesis were the *future*, but was by no means sure that they
*worked*. Not for her, anyway. She had explained to Neil
that she loved his enthusiasms, that they excited her. She
had hardly dared to say to herself, let alone to him, that
she, as a woman, waited with increasing impatience for
some of his passion to be channelled into loving her
physically.

In his car that they had left that morning in the parking
lot of the Admiral Cochrane, he now drove her home. She
sat beside him remembering the biblical description of how

the Virgin Mary 'pondered these things in her heart'. She did likewise.

The streets through which they drove were newly washed with rain. Worthy shops, selling no-nonsense goods, stood dark and innocent of neon signs along streets that echoed to the footfall of men wandering home from pubs. A few noisy youths streamed from the bus station after a trip to watch the home soccer team play away. Women were pulling their curtains, shutting in their aspidistras for the night, making private their disrobing themselves of the layers of wool that protected their pale Scots bodies from the uncertain climate. The lights of throbbing downtown Portlochlie were red, green, and amber only and presided over precious little traffic at this already ungodly hour.

He stopped outside her parents' detached home with its immaculate, rockery garden glinting in the streetlight. The street was entirely deserted except for a lone jogger. Howie noted this figure, as he noted anyone or anything remotely unusual that crossed his daily path. The eccentricity that caught his eye, in this case, had more to do with the man's dress than the fact that he should be jogging at all at this late hour of the night. A tall man, he wore a tracksuit, rather garish American-style sneakers, and a woollen balaclava helmet that left only his eyes open to the night air. To jog, to run in a woollen mask, the kind that night watchmen used on building sites in winter, was perhaps what really made Howie *register* the man. The night was cold certainly, but not *that* cold. And the man ran athletically, his long legs scissoring in carefully measured paces, using the balls of his sneakered feet. Didn't the wool curtail his breathing or had it some disguising purpose? Up to no good, Howie thought and realized guiltily that Mary was sitting beside him nursing her hurt at what he had said in the pub, damning her with his faint praise that she'd be an ideal, trimming Episcopalian.

Her home was already dark for her parents always retired after the ten o'clock news on television. He turned and looked at her face, rather pale in the lamplight, and found that she could not meet his eyes.

'A penny?' he asked, making an offering for her thoughts.

'Not worth that much!' she said in a small timorous voice.

But now she looked up at him and he recognized in her expression something that he knew to be more than caring and devotion. It was, for him, uncomfortably intense, this look of hers, because he understood it to be adoration, no less. He had always hesitated with Mary, pausing at the brink of what he felt. But now, in an instant of self-revelation, that he was sure was God-given, he realized how cold and mean and selfish he would be if he did not, at once, welcome all her love; if he did not take from her all that she longed to give and lavish on her all the love he was capable of giving. He realized that it was *he* who was afraid of being inadequate. That this was a kind of cowardice of the soul that he must learn, with her help, to conquer. Neil felt enormously contrite, and tender towards her now. To 'she' who didn't think her thoughts were worth a penny to him.

'Och, that's not true. Is it, Mary? Not true at all?' he asked gently, and suddenly, too moved for words, he put his arms around her body and his lips to her downy cheek and kissed her. To her dismay Mary found she could no longer hold back her tears and sobbed helplessly on his shoulder.

'Mary!' he said very quietly. 'I cannot bear for you to do that. Is it me that's making you cry? Listen, I think I know why . . .' He stopped what he was saying, realizing he had no right to assume he knew what was in her heart. It was an arrogant assumption. And yet he *thought* he knew.

'I think . . .' he started again.

'What do you think?' she managed to ask between sobs.

'I think that you think I'm waiting for you to become an Episcopalian before we marry!' he blurted it out.

'Is that what you think I think?' she asked incredulously.

'Maybe,' he said, feeling foolish, almost certain he had guessed wrong. Then he suddenly felt an altogether uncomplicated desire to kiss her lips, to warm her, to caress her till she was happy and laughing again.

She gave her mouth to his kiss not opening it too wide, fearful, as always, that if she gave him the feel of her tongue, as she longed to do, he would find her too abandoned and be repelled by her. Sweet though their previous kisses had been for her, this was more exciting than all those that had gone before. He opened her mouth and met her tongue with his. For the first time he seemed to want her in a tactile, sexual sense. His manly bear hug (that she enjoyed mainly because it was all she ever felt of his flesh) was now relaxed, and he was discovering her with his hands, was encouraging her to feel *his* body. Beneath his raw wool sweater she actually touched his hip and simultaneously felt his hand slide inside her thigh. She was at the point of trying to find the catch of his trousers when she felt his hand exploring upward. She slid her hips forward, opening her legs in encouragement, when suddenly he was quite still, and then withdrew his hand altogether.

'Please don't ever do that again if you're going to stop!' she heard herself saying sharply, involuntarily.

'Mary, Mary!' he was saying. 'Listen!'

'Yes?' she said, pulling herself back from him, quelling a desire to shout at him, 'For God's sake take me to bed and make love to me like a man.'

'Mary,' said her Neil. 'How soon can we get married? I want to worship you with my body. I want to give you bairns. I want us very much to be husband and wife just as soon as we can.'

'Why? All of a sudden *why?*' asked Mary, her eyes shining, but her voice still sharp, in spite of herself.

'Why? Because I love you. That's why!' he said reasonably, wondering, as nearly always, what she could possibly now be thinking.

'Och, you great lummox, you! Why could you not have said all that before?'

He was about to reply but she shushed him.

'The answer is yes. Married we'll be. As soon as possible,' she said quickly before he could change his mind or find some new rationalization for delay.

'When?' he asked, anxiously pulling his raw wool sweater down over his trousers to hide his all-too-evident desire.

'The week after next,' she said.

'Why not next week?' he asked, suddenly laughing, a surge of unreasonable happiness coming over him.

'Och, Neil, women have their reasons for these things. When you're an old married man you'll understand.'

'I see! Of course, love. Whenever you're ready.' He said this shyly, the imminent intimacy of marriage suddenly borne in on him.

'Well, there we are then,' she said happily, kissing his cheek and opening the car door. 'Tomorrow?'

'Tomorrow I'm flying to Summerisle immediately after Communion,' he said. 'It's a serious case by the sound of it. Could take a day or two,' he added, getting out of the car, about to see her to her door.

To Neil Howie's annoyance and surprise the tall jogger seemed to have been standing right behind his car and now darted off down the road. A peeping jogger, thought Howie wryly. Here was a hitherto unsuspected turn in Portlochlie crime patterns. And he dismissed the man, for the moment, from his thoughts as he kissed Mary goodnight.

'Take care,' she said simply, hating the idea of his flying the police seaplane around the islands, but determined not to show her anxiety.

As he drove home, he turned on the American Forces Network on his car radio. He liked their late night music and the messages for American servicemen from towns in the United States with fabulous biblical names like *Babylon*, New York, or *Bethlehem*, Pennsylvania. He wondered if they had attempted to install a hanging garden in the former.

Passing the Bull's Head tavern he saw that people were still inside drinking. Checking his watch, he found that it was after eleven o'clock, well past the legal closing time for all bars in Portlochlie. He sighed and, stopping his car, went inside the inn. An old man was playing the piano and singing 'The hole in the elephant's bottom!' Everyone else was almost immediately silent on Howie's entrance and gulped down their drinks (or left them undrunk) and made straight for the door. Howie came up behind the pianist and gently lowered the lid of the piano. The old man withdrew his fingers hurriedly. 'Long past "time", Dad,' said Howie, and closed the piano with a distinct bang.

'That'll be a summons before the magistrates, Jack!' he added to the landlord who hurried out from a back room. Howie could see that Jack was a bit drunk, like most of his customers. He didn't really feel sorry for him. In his opinion drinkers ought never to keep bars. Jack was said easily to drink the weekly profits of his bar.

Sergeant Howie went home to bed and dreamed of the golden eagle flying higher and higher until he seemed to melt into the sun.

*

At about the same time a three-masted schooner was preparing to leave Portlochlie harbour, her throbbing diesel engines virtually the only sound to be heard near the deserted quayside.

The crew of the vessel moved about the decks preparing the sails for use as soon as their ship should have cleared harbour. One seaman, however, stood by the gangplank as if waiting for some latecomer, peering into the gloom beyond the misty stretches of quayside illuminated by the harbour lights. A pair of sneakered feet appeared in the ambience of the lights, causing the seaman to visibly relax. And while he made his way to the bollards to prepare to cast off, the running man, whom Neil Howie had mentally filed as the 'peeping jogger', ran straight across the quayside and onto the deck of the schooner.

Five minutes later the ship was at sea heading west, her sails filling in a sharp offshore breeze but her diesel engines still running at full throttle. The schooner, whose name *Summerisle* was painted on her stern, seemed in a considerable hurry.

## CHAPTER II

# Sunday –
# the 29th of April

HOWIE HAD EATEN THE PRECIOUS BLOOD AND BODY OF His Lord Jesus Christ that morning. He knew, as he sipped the wine and ate the bread that symbolized His Lord's sacrifice, that the sure knowledge of His resurrection was, for him, the most moving and marvellous part of his faith. No fear attended him as he scattered the gulls fishing in Portlochlie harbour with his seaplane and then eased himself off the bumpy water to join his favourite creatures, the birds, in their own element, soaring high over the town and then heading west for the isles. Howie was happy in the faith that, even if his plane fell from the sky, and he were to be lost and obliterated in the ocean, His Lord's promise of resurrection would ultimately rescue him and give him everlasting life.

Sergeant Howie loved the islands, although the sight of them from his seaplane always gave him a feeling of sadness. He could see the ruined churches, the abandoned monasteries, and other evidence of the great migrations that had long since taken most of the original population to far-off Nova Scotia in Canada where, he had heard, they still spoke the Gaelic, a language now almost forgotten by the scattered farmers and the struggling fishermen whose clean white dwellings were dotted about below him. The migrations of people, unlike birds, were, alas, nearly always one-way.

If there had once been trees on the islands very few now remained. The isles were mostly very similar to Saint Ninian's, covered with heather and bracken on the hills, and peat in the marshy valleys. Sergeant Howie had, a few years before, been given a pamphlet by a local communist agitator whom it had been his duty to arrest for aggravated assault. The tract, which he read in order to acquaint himself more closely with the AntiChrist, contained a reprint of Karl Marx's famous article in the *New York Herald* about the Highland Clearances. It had told how the great acreages of common land that had once belonged to the Scots clans in their truly tribal days were enclosed in the nineteenth century for the convenience of the newly imported sheep, belonging to the Scottish lairds and the London bankers who backed them.

These same sheep were more valuable, by far, to the lairds than their own kith and kin, the clansmen, who had fought for their lordly families for centuries. Bailiffs pulled down the clansmen's simple cottages, and troops supervised the loading of these poor people onto the ships that were to take them to the new world. Not only the clansmen but the once plentiful trees too had fallen victims to the depredations of the sheep. The islands now were bald and barren save for the baaing of their fleecy inhabitants and the few sad people who had stayed to tend them.

'If Karl Marx had only surrendered to the socialist in Jesus,' Howie had told the bewildered pastor of Saint

Andrew's. 'What a glorious mission he could have had! A second Saint Paul!' enthused Howie, before dropping the unpopular subject.

As his plane flew over the island of Iona he could see below the restored monastery from which much of the Celtic West had been first brought the news of Christ reborn. Howie was proud, as a Scottish Celt, that this church had long preceded Rome in converting the heathen English. He consulted his map and set his course for the Outer Hebrides and beyond them, towards the island of Summerisle, named, he had heard, for the warm currents of the Gulf Stream that eddied around it.

Sergeant Howie was glad, at last, to have a chance to visit this most distant island in his precinct. You could, in the police, not afford to pay much attention to the gossip of travellers or the tall tales of fishermen and sailors. But the island certainly had a bad reputation. He didn't like the fact that the whole place was owned by Lord Summerisle. Howie disapproved of private islands. A laxness and untidyness in their relationship to the law tended to develop. That Summerisle needed the firm slap of a bit of rigorous police work, he had little doubt.

Nothing in the stories he had heard of the island adequately prepared him for his first glimpses of it from the air. That apples were grown there in great abundance, Howie, of course, knew, although it was surprising how many people didn't.

Most folk, elsewhere in the world, who had, at one time or another, tasted the 'Summerisle Famous' or the incomparable 'Summerisle Delicious', believed the name to be an 'advertising invention', probably the work of the Brothers

Lever or some such marketing conglomerate. The islanders were glad that this should be so. They had no wish for celebrity for their island, only fame for their apples.

The serried ranks of fruit trees on the eastern side of Summerisle were not entirely unexpected to Neil Howie, seeing them for the first time. But the beauty of the multicoloured blossoms standing out against the rich green of the orchard meadows seemed quite stunningly beautiful and reminded Howie, ever ready with biblical images, of a true land of 'milk and honey'.

This was an impression first gained as he flew over the cliffs that towered like the walls of an endless Gothic cathedral supported by hundreds of giant buttresses, some flying as they arched down into the turbulent Atlantic. Howie could see puffins, in their thousands on the cliffs, and gannets plummeting into the ocean, diving for their lunch.

The orchards themselves soon gave way to undulating hills, softly rounded and ancient and largely terraced with vines. As he flew over these hills and the neatly spaced white houses, many of them having extensive greenhouses and richly caparisoned kitchen and flower gardens, he could suddenly see the ocean once more and the entire west coast of the island, set like a crescent of emeralds at the centre of which nestled the pearly white, gabled houses of Summerisle Township. To his utter astonishment, the sergeant now saw that the whole of this curved, natural habour was lined with palm trees blowing gently in the warm wind from the far-off Gulf of Mexico. A haze of soft rain sheened the cobbles of the township while the sea still glittered in the afternoon sun. No greater contrast could be imagined than between this fruitful island and the other sad, ghost-ridden Hebridean isles he had left behind him.

It was as if he had flown off the edge of his 'known' world to some enchanted Arcadia.

He brought his single-engined seaplane in a long arc until, finding himself over an isthmus in the northern part of the island, he could see what his chart called Summerisle Castle, an impressive pile of Scottish baronial architecture whose coppered towers glinted a tropical green against the blue-grey ocean that besieged the isthmus. Then Howie turned his plane, banking fairly sharply into the wind, and made for the comparative calm of the leeward harbour. His aircraft's smooth, boat-shaped hull skimmed the choppy harbour waters like a big seabird, and then suddenly it settled, so that one almost expected it to furl its aluminium wings as it passed the three-masted schooner *Summerisle* riding at anchor.

Sergeant Howie peered out through the salt-sprayed perspex of his windows and could make out a main jetty with a neat white house marked HARBOUR MASTER. His view of the jetty was, for an instant, disturbed by a seabird taking off across his line of vision. It was a black-browed albatross. Quite rare in the Northern Hemisphere, it made him remember *The Rime of the Ancient Mariner*. How terribly unlucky it would have been for his plane to collide with and kill the albatross. He shivered at the thought, and then chided himself for his superstition.

A few men, fishermen certainly, stood quite immobile, staring at him from the quay. The chart had indicated the harbour to be heavily tidal, and he didn't dare bring the plane closer into the jetty. Howie switched off his engine, unlatched the cockpit roof so that he could stand straight, and dropped his anchor. Taking a loud hailer, he shouted at the motionless fishermen.

'I want a dinghy, please,' came Howie's voice, echoing and metallic.

No one moved on the jetty.

'Did you hear me?' he shouted, louder. 'I want a dinghy . . . please.'

At this moment the harbour master emerged from his house and ran to join the fishermen, doing up his jacket as he ran. At first he seemed, to Howie, to be consulting with the other men but then he faced the plane and, cupping his hands, shouted back.

'Hullo, sir. Lost your bearing?' His hoarse voice had the lilting accent of the islands.

'I don't think so. This is Summerisle, is it not?'

'Yes, sir,' shouted the harbour master, and the seemingly bewildered old fishermen nodded their agreement.

'Well, I'm right then,' yelled Howie. 'Send out a dinghy, please.'

'I'm afraid it can't be done, sir,' shouted the harbour master. 'This is private property. You can't land here without written permission.'

'I am a police officer,' said Howie, realizing they could hear him perfectly well and indicating his sergeant's stripes on his arm. 'A complaint has been received from a resident of this island that needs to be investigated.'

'A complaint, you say?' The harbour master's voice was disbelieving.

'About a missing child,' said Howie. 'That makes it a police matter. Private property or not. Send a boat, please.'

There was a brief colloquy on the jetty, then a single figure detached itself from the group and descended the steps to a boat moored to the wall. He cast off and headed towards the seaplane. Howie grinned mirthlessly and turned to replace the loud hailer in the seaplane and to collect his overnight bag. He was dressed as always for his visits to the islands in his blue serge sergeant's uniform with his peaked hat bearing the badge of the West Highland Constabulary topped by the crown, symbol that he acted in the Queen of Scotland's name.

The sergeant, while waiting for the dinghy to arrive, started to observe his surroundings. The extraordinary subtropical trees and shrubs he had already taken in. There was something else that was strange about the place but he was annoyed that, although sensing it, he still could not pin down what it was. Only as the dinghy carried him towards a growing crowd of fishermen on the jetty did it come to him. Beyond the noise of the sculls lapping in the water, beyond the cry of the gulls and the murmuring of the fishermen, there was *no* sound of twentieth-century life. No motor, no distant buzz saw; nothing of the sounds that emanate from modern man's machines, so that he is conscious of them only when they are suddenly altogether absent. Howie disembarked from the rowboat and ascended the steps towards the top of the jetty. The group of fishermen waited for him in a kind of phalanx, the harbour master at their head. Their weathered faces had, many of them, the flushed look of men through whom rivers of good whisky had flowed.

'Good day, sir,' said their leader, 'I'm the harbour master!'

Howie kept his distance from the contagiously liquored breath of the harbour master, but smiled at them all reassuringly. Seeing policemen so rarely, he thought, the very sight of one probably makes them nervous.

'Sergeant Howie,' he identified himself cheerfully, 'West Highland Police!' His attention was suddenly taken by something on the main harbour notice board. Beside the usual tide schedules and so on, there were some rather unusual posters. Well designed typographically, they appeared to be – if the copy was to be believed – encouraging travel or emigration. Two of them were respectively headlined, 'WANT TO TRAVEL TO THE WORLD OUTSIDE?' and 'WANT TO EMIGRATE TO THE USA OR CANADA LIKE YOUR FOREFATHERS?' But the 'travel' picture showed a Glasgow slum on a rainy day. The 'emigration' poster depicted a particularly insalubrious section of the Bowery in New York. In both cases the subheading was: 'Consult Lord Summerisle for free advice.'

Sergeant Howie could not resist looking at these posters in puzzled fascination for a while and then, hearing the habour master's voice, turned his full attention back to him.

'A missing child is always trouble,' the harbour master was saying.

'Yes. For everybody,' said Howie as they inspected each other again levelly.

'Perhaps you'd be so good as to explain matters to His Lordship,' said the harbour master nervously. 'He's most particular who lands here.'

'All in good time,' said Howie. 'We too have our own particularities.'

Howie produced the photograph of Rowan Morrison.

'Do you know her?' he asked. 'Her name is Rowan Morrison.'

The harbour master took the photograph and studied it.

'No. I've never seen her before. Have you, Barley?' he asked, passing it to one of the old fishermen, who shook his head, showing it to the others, craning their heads to see it.

'No. I canna say I have,' said Barley.

The photograph was passed from hand to hand. Heads were shaken, and they finally chorused:

'She's not from here!'

'What are you telling me?' asked Howie suspiciously. 'That this girl is not from this island?'

Hostile and incurious stares greeted his penetrating gaze as he seemed to challenge them to admit the girl was one of their own.

'That's right,' said the harbour master finally. 'She's not from here.'

'You get Morrisons on Lewis and a few on Mull,' said one old fisherman, trying to be helpful in suggesting the ancestral isles of the clan Morrison. 'I'd try over there.'

Puzzled but determined to test them further, Howie now produced the letter and, keeping his thumb over the absent signature, read the letter to them.

None of us have seen May Morrison's daughter, Rowan, since last year. She is only twelve and has been missing from her home for many months.

'The mother's name is . . . May Morrison.'

'Oh, May!' laughed the harbour master, wheezing. 'She quite slipped my mind. Yes, we've got May here all right . . . keeps the sweetshop up the hill, just opposite the Green Man Inn.'

'May Morrison,' said Howie coldly. 'You're quite sure?'

'Of course,' agreed the harbour master jovially, and all the others smiled too, glad, at last, to have been of help.

'I see. Thank you!' said Howie still annoyed with them but reflecting that all this fruit and isolation probably addled their brains. He must be patient and not play the 'big city cop'. He abruptly took back his photograph, which was being clutched by one of the fishermen, and put it, and the letter, back in his pocket. Then, turning his back on them, he started up the steeply graded High Street. They watched him go for perhaps ten yards. Then the harbour master shouted after him.

'But that's not her daughter!'

Howie turned slowly, looking back at the group of men, puzzled.

'No, that's not May's,' added another fisherman.

'Who is it then?' he asked.

Silence. Shrugs. Howie thought he heard a snicker, but it was just a man who was clearly the local halfwit, someone whom the others ignored. Howie turned away from them and continued up the steep High Street that led away from the jetty into the township. His face now was troubled.

It was not, he supposed, surprising that people seemed to stare at him as he walked up the cobbled street that was innocent of any cars whatever. The very absence of cars was one reason he had never had occasion to come here. Nothing that required a police-supervised licence seemed to exist in the township. There were no television or radio aerials. No electric or telephone wires either. He ignored the opening windows and doors as the people came, discreetly enough, to stare at him. Some of them smiled as they gazed; a few bade him 'Good afternoon.' Some kids ran excitedly about shouting:

'It's a *real* copper!'

Horse-drawn conveyances there were. Although Howie felt ashamed that he didn't know a brougham from a governess cart as his predecessors in the police must have done. How embarrassing it would be (he almost laughed out loud at the thought) to find himself in front of the Justice of the Peace here, whom he knew to be Lord Summerisle himself, and not to be able adequately to describe a traffic accident should one occur. He fervently hoped it wouldn't happen. Although in the broadening street in which he now found himself, there must have been fifteen horse-drawn vehicles either on the move or 'parked' (he wondered if that could be the right word).

He couldn't help stopping for a moment to admire the view that met his eyes as he reached the Green Man Inn. The remarkably well-proportioned buildings, all cleanly whitewashed, with window boxes brimming with flowers. The village green beyond, where daffodils and wild flowers grew in abundance. It was, for Howie, such an extraordinary contrast to the muted civic tidyness of his own native Portlochlie. Not even Howie, who loved his hometown with a fierce and proprietary pride, could have called

Portlochlie anything but merely pretty, yet this town was, for him, uncomfortably, extravagantly *beautiful!* There was something sensual about the way the flowers and the buildings seemed to lavish their felicities on the visitor's senses. It was unScottish. Howie found that disturbing and, in a way that he put down to the events of the night before, exciting. Perhaps, he thought, my love for Mary has heightened my senses. He blessed her for that.

The sweetshop was exactly where the old man had said it would be. That was a relief to Howie as he peered in its window. An assortment of magnificent chocolate confections met his gaze, as well as curiously lifelike and distended sugar babies. Behind, in glass jars, he could see amazingly large gobstoppers and bullseyes (much more like real *bulls-* eyes than anything to be seen on the mainland). Howie entered the shop to the accompaniment of a tinkling bell and found a small, buxom woman facing him over a counter covered with lifelike chocolate creatures. She wore a flowered overall around her generous person and laughing eyes moved in a rosy face. Howie found the clearly home-made sweets and candy so unusual that he could not refrain from an admiring comment.

'I like your chocolate rabbits!' he said, looking at what, on the mainland, would have been described as Easter bunnies.

'Those are hares,' said the little woman in mock indignation, 'not silly old rabbits. Lovely March hares. Can I help you?'

'It's Mrs Morrison, isn't it? Mrs May Morrison?' asked Howie. To his relief she nodded her assent. Perhaps this case was going to be a simple one after all.

'Oh, Lord!' she said excitedly. 'Did you come over in that aeroplane I saw flying round?'

'That's right!' smiled Howie.

'What? Just to see me?' She looked as if she wished she'd known he was coming and had not been caught in her second-best overall.

'Well, to check up on your daughter actually,' said Howie gently. 'We understand she's missing.'

Mrs Morrison was clearly amazed.

'Missing? My daughter?'

'You do have a daughter, don't you?' said Howie patiently. 'This is she?'

He pushed the photograph across the counter towards Mrs Morrison. She only glanced at it before shaking her head.

'Never!' she exclaimed.

Howie looked hard at her. Under his scrutiny she laughed suddenly, boisterously.

'I tell you no!' she added with emphasis. There was silence. And in the silence came the sound of a child's voice.

'Mummy!' called the voice, that of a little girl.

Howie started towards the door leading to the parlour. Mrs Morrison, still laughing, put her bulk in front of him and led the way.

'I think you'd better come with me,' she said and opened the door that led the way into her parlour. Sitting at a table was a small girl of about six years old. She had a pad of drawing paper in front of her and a dozen pots of poster paint.

'That's our Myrtle,' said Mrs Morrison to the confused

sergeant. 'She was six last birthday. Not a bit like the girl in your photograph. She must be at least twelve or thirteen surely?'

'Yes, but . . . Is she your only child, Mrs Morrison?' asked Howie.

'Yes. Our only child I'm afraid. That's sad for her, and sad for me, isn't it?' said Mrs Morrison giving Howie a sad-sweet smile.

'Say hullo, Myrtle. This is Sergeant . . .'

'Howie. Hullo, Myrtle,' said the sergeant.

'How do you do,' replied Myrtle, in a piping voice. 'Look, Mummy, I'm drawing a hare . . .'

Then, they heard the bell tinkling from the shop. Howie held the door closed, keeping Mrs Morrison in the parlour.

Howie had been trained to expect 'lines of inquiry' to sometimes lead to witnesses who told barefaced lies. More people told lies to the police than told the absolute truth. But the lies, in his experience, were not, as a rule, of the barefaced kind. More often the lie consisted of something being left unsaid. Here he felt sure that this was the case.

'Mrs Morrison, from information that has come into my possession, I have reason to believe you have *another* daughter,' he said, trying to see if *that* had been left unsaid.

'Do you now?' said Mrs Morrison, her laughing eyes hardening a little. 'Well, I should know best about that, shouldn't I?'

'And that she is missing,' insisted Howie.

Mrs Morrison looked at him pityingly and sighed.

'Do I look like a mother with a missing daughter? Come now, you're the policeman,' she said as politely as she could.

'Well, no, but . . .' Howie realized how true her observation was, aware that he must look foolish.

'But what . . .?' asked Mrs Morrison.

'I have to investigate,' said Howie, trying to recover his sense of initiative and control.

'Having come so far you mean?' The woman's question was pointed, but without malice.

'Please, Mrs Morrison, it's only that we have to follow up on information received.' Howie was embarrassed.

'From who?' suddenly Mrs Morrison was genuinely curious.

'I'm afraid I can't tell you that,' said Howie quickly. 'It's probably some crank. After all, if you tell me Myrtle is an only child . . .'

'Of course she is,' said her mother impatiently.

'Well, there you are,' said Howie. 'Would you have any objection if I talked to her for a moment?'

'Why should I?' said Mrs Morrison laughing again. 'You're not going to eat her, are you?'

Howie laughed politely and opened the door for her to pass through into the shop. Mrs Morrison smiled encouragingly at her daughter and went through the door. Howie closed it behind her and crossed so as to sit opposite Myrtle at the table. He could now see that the child was doing a drawing of a hare with huge ears and whiskers, which she was copying from a copper mould that had plainly been used to make the chocolate hares. She looked up and handed Howie a dripping paintbrush.

'Here you are,' said Myrtle kindly, 'you can fill in the ears in grey.'

Neat, dapper, Sergeant Howie was slightly put out to find his hand suddenly sticky with paint and quickly took the paint rag to clean himself. Carefully he selected a clean brush and started on the ears.

'Myrtle, do you know Rowan?' he asked.

'Of course!' said Myrtle.

Howie was startled by her answer.

'You do?' he echoed.

'Of course I do, silly,' said Myrtle tolerantly, as if to someone deficient of reasoning power.

'Where is she now?' asked Howie.

'In the fields,' said Myrtle enviously. 'She runs and plays all day. She is lucky!'

'Will she be back for tea?' asked Howie, now sure he was getting to the bottom of whatever mystery there might be.

Myrtle laughed uproariously.

'Tea?' she asked incredulously. 'She doesn't have tea.'

'Why not?' asked Howie meekly enough. 'Doesn't she like it?'

Myrtle stopped laughing abruptly and stared at Howie, amazed at his question.

'Hares don't have tea, silly!' said Myrtle emphatically.

'Hares!' Howie was totally nonplussed.

'She's a hare!' said Myrtle. 'Rowan's a hare. She has a lovely time.'

Howie sat thunderstruck. The door to the shop opened and Mrs Morrison reappeared.

'Did I hear someone mention tea? You will stay, won't you?'

'Thank you. That's very kind,' he said, thinking how hard it was to question children for whom the distinction between fantasy and fact was often so slight.

'Not at all. It must be thirsty work, asking all those questions,' said Mrs Morrison happily, pleased that he *seemed* satisfied after his interview with Myrtle.

Howie was served a Lucullan tea with scones and gingerbread men, clotted cream, and raspberry jam.

'What is that mess of raspberry jam?' quoted Myrtle, as she ate a huge mouthful of scone topped with cream and jam. She went on with her mouth full, imitating a grown-up's tone of voice:

'Hush, my child, that isn't raspberry jam.

That's old granddad run over by a tram.'

Her mother laughed and chided her.

'You didn't get it quite right, Myrtle,' she said, 'and you mustn't speak with your mouth full.'

'I've never seen a tram,' said Myrtle, as if that explained her lack of scansion. 'Have you, mister?' she asked Howie.

'Yes, in a museum,' he answered.

Then Myrtle was wildly excited and wanted to know all about trams. The sergeant humoured her and wondered about her childish story of the hare. The family clearly had hares on the brain. 'Mad as a March hare' was a phrase that flitted through his mind as he talked to the jolly, likable mother and her fey daughter and enjoyed the domestic scene. It crossed his mind to think how much he now looked forward to sharing a home, their own home, with Mary.

Then he had a second cup of tea and began to think out his next move. If there was an answer to the puzzle of a missing child whose alleged mother didn't appear to miss her, it must probably lie elsewhere on the island. A good place to start, the sergeant had always found in such investigations, was the local inn, centre of gossip and informal club to the community. He determined to spend the night there.

## CHAPTER III

## *Sunday Night –*
## *the 29th of April*

WHEN HOWIE LEFT MAY MORRISON'S HOUSE HE HESI-
tated at going straight to the inn. Although the early
summer evening was already drawing in, it seemed, from
his experience of these things, a little early for the bar
crowd to have forgathered. While the light lasted, he
preferred to look around the township to get his bearings.
An hour's stroll served him to commit the whole geography
of the place to his memory. Few people seemed to be about
and some young children, whom he stopped, and to whom
he showed Rowan Morrison's alleged photograph, ran giggling from him before he could get any sense from them.

He thought he noticed the movement of lace curtains,
the creaking and clicking of doors behind him, as if he
were being covertly observed. But it was, he realized, hardly
surprising in view of the unusual event his presence here
must represent. He concentrated on his surroundings.

In the little terraced yards that faced the setting sun as
it sank to its distant mission of awakening North America,
he noticed patterns of stones that he, at first, mistook for
the rockeries familiar to him, in the little gardens of his
neighbours, on the mainland. On closer inspection, how-

ever, these stones were clearly the carved heads of figures that seemed buried up to their necks in the island's rich loam. They gazed all in the same direction, as Muslims face Mecca, their stone blind eyes towards the sunset.

Howie remembered the tales of Celtic sailors setting out across that ocean even before good Saint Columba had come from Ireland to convert the Scots. Centuries before Christopher Columbus. His orderly, file-indexed mind noted the coincidence of similarity in the name of both saint and explorer as he made his way, in a reverie that was quite unusual for him, towards the Green Man.

The gloaming had turned to night as he arrived at the inn. It was a whitewashed seventeenth-century building, rather larger than those normally found in the Western islands. The bar was uncurtained and light streamed from it onto the green; laughter and the competitive shouting of bar conversation filtered through the windows. Howie paused and looked up uncertainly at the large inn sign. It bore the face of an earthy man from whose ears, nose, and mouth grew sprays of greenery, which entwined about him to form a screen from which he peeped out at Howie. The refraction of the light, from the bar, caused by the shifting figures within, made the eyes seem to move.

Inside the inn the scene was, at first sight, reassuringly similar to that in the bars he so carefully monitored in Portlochlie. Howie noted that here, as there, people lost the measure of the loudness of their voices as they drank. Their expressions, loosened into laughter or anger, lewdness or sullenness by the liquor, were different from the faces they wore each morning as they went about their appointed tasks.

He was not entirely surprised that, when they noticed his presence in the bar, the people were suddenly, all of them, quite quiet. His was clearly an alien spirit of authority and discipline, and he found familiar the feeling that they were constrained by his arrival in their midst. He greeted them courteously and they 'Evening'd' him back as they made a pathway for him to reach the bar. A florid man in his mid-fifties with a smiling, puckish face awaited him there expectantly.

'You the landlord here?' He asked this rather self-consciously of the puckish man, knowing that this question from a policeman to a landlord was usually the opening to an unpleasant conversation for the latter.

'Aye, I'm Alder MacGregor,' said the man, with a twinkling smile. 'And you must be the policeman from the mainland.'

'That's right,' acknowledged Howie. 'Howie's the name, Sergeant Howie of the West Highland Police. Now it's late and I'm quite obviously not going to get back to the mainland tonight. D'you think I could have a room for the night and a bite of supper? I mean, d'you think you could manage that?'

Alder MacGregor clearly welcomed the idea of Howie staying at the inn.

'Of course! Of course!' he said. 'My daughter will show you to your room.' At these words of welcome the faintest murmur was apparent in the previously silent bar. 'Willow,' shouted Alder MacGregor, opening a doorway behind him, from which there now came the sound of a girl's voice singing to the music of a fiddle, a tambourine, a squeeze box, and a drum.

At the sound of Alder's voice, this outer room also became silent. An instant later, Howie saw a magnificently built girl emerge. A blonde mane of hair framed a face of quite breathtaking sensuality. But the sergeant noticed her mouth most of all as she uttered the single innocently questioning word:

'Father?'

The 'F' in that word thrust out a quivering lower lip of such delicate succulence that Howie's body allowed itself to want that lip. Want Willow's mouth, want Willow's delectable person. As fast as Howie's body sensed this awful thought, almost as fast Sergeant Neil Howie, the affianced of Mary Bannock, put it, like Satan, behind him. Not for the first time that day he wondered if his awakened physical passion for Mary had not quite unbalanced the normally even tenor of his emotions. He reminded himself that it was Mary he *wanted*, not just a woman. And yet, and yet . . .

'This is Sergeant Howie,' he heard her father saying, 'a policeman from the mainland who will be staying with us tonight.' MacGregor turned with a ceremonious nod to Howie. 'This,' he added, rather as if he were presenting Helen of Troy to Paris, 'is my daughter, Willow!'

'Good evening,' said Howie with as much evenness as he could muster.

She smiled at Howie appreciatively as a good judge of horseflesh might size up a stallion for stud. For the first time in his entire life, Neil Howie felt as if a woman were measuring the build of him right through his coarse, blue serge uniform. As if she were weighing his 'testimonials' in the palm of her perfect hand. Totally off balance, he heard MacGregor speak again, as Willow, taking a door key from a hook, started to beckon to Howie to follow her through the crowded bar to the stairway.

'She'll show you to your room,' said her father.

But there was a great, sudden *roar* at this seemingly innocent remark. Howie, who had been about to assure Willow that he needed only to be given directions and had no need, yet, to go to his room, found himself pressed towards the lovely girl by the suddenly surging crowd. The old harbour master had spun her around and lifted one of her arms aloft as one might display a champion and to Howie's total disbelief, the whole bar started singing at him:

> *'Much has been said of the strumpets of yore*
> *Of wenches and bawdy house queens by the score*
> *But I sing of a baggage that we all adore,*
> *The Landlord's Daughter . . .'*

Although he had edged away from Willow, she and the men in the bar seemed, for the moment, to take no more notice of him. Only the laughing, darting eyes of Alder openly watched Howie's huge embarrassment with the puckish delight of someone presiding over a monstrously successful practical joke. The sergeant had so reddened that he looked as if he ought to, at the very least, undo his starched collar to facilitate the rush of blood to his face.

> *'. . . You'll never love another*
> *Although she's not the kind of girl*
> *to take home to your mother . . .'*

By the time the second verse had started, Willow was moving back towards the sergeant, her arms akimbo, her green eyes wide with invitation, her firm, unfettered breasts bouncing to the jig of the music under her thin, muslin blouse. He tried not to look at her but instead to assume a mainlander's ironical and detached interest at this bunch of wild and woolly islanders making an obscene spectacle of themselves, apparently for his benefit.

> '. . . Her ale it is lively and strong to the taste
> It is brewed with discretion and never with haste
> You can have all you like
> If you swear not to waste
> The Landlord's Daughter . . .'

Well, he was used to people trying to bait the police. He thought of hooligans at soccer games, demonstrators on picket lines, drunks at pub-closing time. He knew how to handle *them*. Go in and collar the leader. Get him under arrest and into a police cell double quick. But here he knew that tactic could not work. They were too many . . . and he was much too far from a police station. Plenty of time to get a whole posse of police over here to root out this sort of nonsense some other day, soon. But right now, he knew, like the good cop he was, that his priority was to find the Morrison girl, a task the impeding of which might well be the cause of this whole disgraceful exhibition. He wondered about that and his sense of humour came suddenly to his rescue.

'. . . And when her name is mentioned
The parts of every gentleman
Do stand up at attention . . .'

The men all thrust their bent arms in the air and
gripped them with their other hands at the elbow. The
classic old gesture was done in such unison as to seem
quite comical to Howie, who laughed in spite of himself.

A giggling Willow was standing so close to him now, as
the others started to dance about the room, that he could
smell the apple-sweet scent of cider on her breath; that
and a compelling musky smell that seemed to come from
her body. He turned his back on her only to see her
mocking face again in the looking glass behind the bar.
But his action seemed to have deflected her and she turned
to join the others in the dancing. The men fondled her as
she passed from one to the other, swinging and stamping
and clapping with them in time to the music.

'. . . Oh nothing can delight so
As does the part that lies between
Her left toe
And her right toe . . .'

Howie was disconcerted to find a rage mounting in him
as he watched Willow in the looking glass allowing these
drunken oafs to squeeze her buttocks and cup her sweet,
bouncing dugs in their horny hands. She was offering
herself to him and although he was determined to refuse
her, his body forced his envy of those who touched her in
a way that confused his mind. He tried to summon an

image of Mary Bannock to blot Willow's supple body from his thoughts. But he could not.

'Make you feel jealous, does it, Sergeant?' her shameless old pander of a father said to him, as he poured a couple of large tots.

Howie ignored the landlord's impertinent remark.

'Can I have my dinner *now*, please?' he asked.

'It won't be long, Sergeant,' said Alder, amused. 'Oh, don't let *them* worry you. Why don't you have a wee drink?' he added, offering Howie a tot.

Howie shook his head and lifted the hatch to put himself behind the bar, with Alder MacGregor, and away from Willow's ripe body that she kept pressing close to him, each time she swung by with one of the dancers.

He grabbed an ashtray and started banging it hard upon the bar. His face, meanwhile, glared around at the revellers in a determined bid to impose his will upon them and command their attention. Slowly the music and the singing and the dancing stopped.

'I think you all ought to know that I am here on official business.' He said it loudly, not shouting. The few remaining people who were catching their breath, giggling or still singing were now quite silent and curiously respectful in their gaze. Pleased at the effect of his words, Howie repeated himself in a normal voice, and as pleasant a tone as he could manage after the events of the last few minutes.

'I think you all ought to know that I am here to investigate the disappearance of this young girl, as the harbour master has probably already told you,' said Howie with a slight smile, holding up Rowan's photograph for them all to see. 'Her name is Rowan Morrison and we have reason to believe she has been missing for several months. I want you to pass this photograph among yourselves, and if you recognize her, or have any clue to her whereabouts, speak out. Is that clear?'

There were general murmurs of assent. Howie was gratified that Alder MacGregor made it his personal business to see that everyone in the bar examined the photograph. Perhaps, thought Howie, he's trying to make some amends for allowing that disgraceful scene with his daughter. In order not to seem to be invigilating their examination of the picture, he turned his attention to a rather remarkable group of photographs on the wall. They had the same shape as school-group photographs and each was dated with a different year and signed by the same local photographer – T. H. Lennox. They spanned at least two decades and were remarkably similar in composition. The setting, in each case, was the sanctuary of a church, piled high with luscious and perfectly formed farm produce – vegetables, fruits, and particularly apples. Standing astride the pile in each photograph was a pretty, pubescent girl of around thirteen. Last year's photograph was missing. The nail on which it had hung was there, and so was its faint outline on the wall, but that was all. As Howie took in these photographs, looking, in vain, for any girl with a likeness to Rowan Morrison, he could hear the murmured exchanges of those who were examining the photograph of Rowan.

'Not one of ours.'

'Never seen her at all.'

'Looks like the Mallory girl! Just the eyes, of course.'

Every man and woman from the drummer through to Willow were agreeing that they'd never seen her before.

Alder brought the photograph back to Howie with his discouraging news. The sergeant made a show of comparing Rowan to the girls in the photographs but he knew that none of them was she. Willow meanwhile whispered, with a sudden demureness which Howie could scarcely credit, 'Your dinner's ready, Sergeant.' She waited, her eyes slightly lowered, as Howie glanced at her in surprise. He was certainly hungry, but he had to file away the information about the photographs on the wall before he could permit himself to eat.

'What are these?' he asked Alder. 'Thanksgiving Harvest Festival ceremonies in the local church?'

'That's right,' confirmed Alder. 'As you can see there's one taken at the end of every summer.'

'What happened to last year's picture?' Howie slipped out the question as casually as he could.

'I'm afraid it got broken. We'll have to order another.' He seemed suddenly anxious to get back to his bar. 'Willow, show the sergeant to the dining room. His food must be getting cold.'

If Howie had not known that the people who now stood or sat convivially about the bar, as orderly as a church meeting, had only a few minutes before been behaving like savages, he would not have credited his eyes, or his memory. Even Willow, whose lovely arse had swayed invitingly before him when she had attempted to lead him to his room, now walked before him like a young debutante in a deportment class. But if Willow had become as

apparently demure as a Susannah walking away from peeping elders, no equally quick change was possible for Howie.
Indeed, now that he had time to distil his own reactions
to the game they had played on him he raged. True, he
was in control of himself, but he recognized his rage and
struggled with it.

Neil Howie hated their trivialization of sex, the turning
of what he saw as its sacred purpose into a vulgar game. It
had once been likened for him, this cheap prostitution of
the beautiful and the wonderful, to someone dumping a
cartful of shit in a room. Inevitably, the comparison had
been made by one of his teachers at the seminary but it
had never seemed anything but apt to Howie. He knew
that Willow had succeeded in stirring his senses and his
basest emotions, since he had for a moment desired her, he
who in no way loved her. This knowledge made him face
the fact that he had contributed in some small way to the
pile of shit in the bar. He had allowed these undisciplined,
provocative people to drag him, however slightly, for
however short a time, into sullying his own sense of the
purity of his love for Mary. That fact enraged him. Made
him intensely resentful of everyone who had conspired
together in the inn to do this thing to him. For a moment
he hated them for it. It took the pragmatic policeman in
him to make him forgive them for it, to recognize that
they almost certainly knew not what they did.

When Willow came to collect the plate from his main
course she found a rather disgruntled sergeant. He was still
trying to sort out, with his fork, something edible from the
unsavoury mess on his plate. A stringy lamb chop he had
eaten, but there remained four or five too-white, identically

shaped, clearly canned potatoes. Also a soggy mass of artificially coloured, equally obviously canned broad beans.

Willow had the grace to look a little embarrassed and wet her lovely lower lip with an enchanting little pink tongue. This was enough, she well knew, to take the mind of most males away from food. But not Howie's mind. For, in addition to feeling still hungry, he was faced with another puzzle.

'It's disgusting,' complained Howie, indicating he had had enough. 'The farmhouse soup was canned, and so are these potatoes and beans. Why?' he asked quite sharply.

'Well, I don't think they are, Sergeant,' said Willow defiantly, allowing her fragrant hair to brush his cheek as she leaned to pick up his plate.

'Broad beans in their natural state are not turquoise,' said Howie, pointedly holding one bean aloft on the fork. 'I simply want to know why?'

'Some things in their natural state have the most vivid colours!' said Willow salaciously.

'Why, in late April on an island famous for its fruit and vegetable produce, am I served canned vegetables? Aren't there any fresh?' Howie asked insistently.

'I wonder what you'll be wanting for "afters",' asked Willow evasively.

'Well, I suppose I can't go wrong with a Summerisle apple!' said Howie, cheering himself with the prospect of the island's speciality.

'Sorry, no apples,' said Willow.

'No apples?' Howie was astonished.

'I expect they're all exported,' said Willow lightly. 'You can have peaches and cream. They're nice.'

'Both from a can, I suppose,' said Howie, and saw in her smile that this was no more than the truth. 'All right,' he said, smiling back at her resignedly. He was thanking God as he watched her graceful body go and fetch him some cloying syrupy peaches and some soapy artificial cream that his Mary could, bless her sweet heart, cook. But, as if the landlord's daughter had divined this thought, she paused on her way to the kitchen, and looking back at Howie with her all-too-fathomable, green eyes, she said, 'Cheer up, Sergeant. Food isn't everything in life, y'know!'

A little later, Sergeant Howie decided to take some air outside the stuffy atmosphere of the inn before going up to bed. No sooner had he emerged from the inn onto the green than he heard the relative quiet of the bar burst into boisterous sound behind him. Wishing to have quiet so that he might further order the impressions of the last few hours, he struck out across the green towards the lights from the houses on the other side. As he walked he heard a voice singing softly in the velvety darkness:

> 'Ride a cock horse
> To Banbury Cross
> To see a white lady
> On a white horse
> With rings on her fingers
> And bells on her toes
> She shall have music wherever she goes.'

As the sound of the song died away, Howie became aware of other, different sounds in the darkness around him. Soft sighs and moans and occasional rhythmic laughter seemed to be all around him. Suddenly he found himself falling, having tripped over an identifiably human form lying on the grass. As a puzzled, alarmed Howie recovered himself, the moon slipped out from behind the clouds and illuminated the whole green. A dozen young pairs of lovers were coupling on the grass. It is true that they seemed partly clothed against the chill night air but Howie noticed with a fascinated horror that there was something curiously formalistic about each couple. In every case, the girl sat astride her young man, who lay on his back. The girls' feet were bare and the bells on their toes tinkled as they ground their young thighs to and fro, to and fro.

Seeing Howie in the sudden moonlight, they seemed, to the sergeant, like a herd of cows surprised in their field at night, staring but unalarmed. Their sexual rhythm was unfaltering like the chewing of the cud. But in one particular, they were starkly human and quite unlike the simple kine. Their 'ride a cock horse' was consciously ritualistic.

Howie seriously thought for a moment of arresting the lot of them, and the possible charges raced through his mind – 'indecent exposure in a public place' . . . 'a breach of the peace' . . . 'gross indecency' . . .

No sooner had the thought 'arrest them' come to his mind than he rejected it. Since every person present on the green, as far as he could see, was copulating there could be no reliable witnesses who could possibly be described as 'independent'. Nothing in his training had prepared him for such a situation except, perhaps, the regulations for dealing with a riot. 'Once you've read the "Riot Act" to warn the rioters to disperse you're entitled to arrest the ringleaders,' his lecturer at the Police College had told him. 'But if you're alone, laddie, forget it. Remember, a dead policeman serves no one's purpose if he doesn't serve to enforce the law.' While this mass insult to human dignity and decency, as Howie saw it, could reasonably be described as a kind of sexual riot there was clearly no practical remedy that he could apply to uphold the law of either God or Man.

In the moment that he recognized his impotence as a policeman to simply enforce the law he persuaded himself to view the phenomenon of what was going on around him with as much detachment as he could muster. He made himself look at the young people around him and recognize the humanity he shared with them in common. But that detachment could not survive the urgings of his own emotions. It made his mind swim to hold in his hate and detestation of what he saw. A virgin himself, he had never imagined that a woman in the throes of the sexual act would look or sound as did these young women.

The moans, the shrill cries, the unreal laughter, the grunts seemed to him like a barnyard caricature of what, in his attempt to ban in his own mind a puritan fear of sex, he had imagined as something that transfigured a woman, making her ethereally beautiful, making them both, man and woman, in the sanctified instant of procreation, marvellously at one with their Maker. For the second time that night he felt that these people were throwing shit at his dreams and his resentment was as terrible as, he realized, it was partly irrational. After all, he, who had no experience of the sexual act, possessed no patent of how it should look or sound or smell or feel. He, who despised 'electness', who knew that Jesus had forgiven and loved the Magdalene just as He loved everyone else, must force himself not to hate these young people for what, he realized, was his childlike, idealized image of man and woman's unique act. He longed to roar, 'Stop it. It looks ugly to me. And I was so sure it would look beautiful!'

Just then, a fair girl who had ridden her lover until the bells on her toes had rattled in a tintinnabulating rhythm, contrapuntal to the huge gasps that shook her body, now collapsed, crying with delight, on her lover's shoulder, and in her face he saw, looking down at her, unwilling voyeur that he was, a fleeting image of what he had imagined as the 'love of God' expressed in the sexual act. To see that look on Mary Bannock's face, to know that he had put it there, would surely be wonderful. Then, and only then, did Howie identify with the boy whose thrusting body had wrought that look in the happily weeping girl. To hear Mary moan and cry like that and still to drive her on and on was suddenly Howie's fantasy. But he wouldn't want to lie like a lummox on his back, like these lads, he thought. No, he would have Mary on *her* back, a plump buttock in each hand, and he would drive her into a delirium, so he would. He fought down the heavy breaths these images evoked and not without difficulty quelled the stirrings of his own sexuality.

Howie walked away remembering, for some apparently irrational reasons, 'those insistent feet' with which the 'hound of heaven' followed the poet 'down the labyrinthine ways'. Even as he escaped the sounds and images of the young people, who had scarcely seemed to notice him, certainly not to care about his presence, he started to search for some other meaning to what he had just seen. Why had *all* the women sat impaled upon their lovers? He dismissed, at once, the notion that what he had seen was in any way directed at himself, unlike the teasing song and dance in the inn. For how could they have known that he would leave the inn that night, at that time?

A small, chill fear beset him as he speculated on the fate of Rowan Morrison. Sex seemed the ruling passion of this strangely fecund island. The kidnapping of a very young girl, the supposed daughter of someone obviously not rich, could hardly have as its motive money. That she might be suffering some form of sexual abuse or bondage seemed, to Howie, more likely than not. He had seen the faces of all the young women on the green and they were certainly mature females, probably all sixteen or over, and their supine lovers seemed about the same age. From past experience he knew that the kidnapper of a child as young as Rowan, who was keeping her for so horrible a purpose, would most likely be much older than the youths on the green.

There was, now, as he walked almost silently on the soft grass, a new sound coming to him. A girl was weeping, somewhere quite close to him, and a little further away was another sound, so curious that it baffled Howie to identify it.

He could make out a stone wall in front of him. The dim pile of masonry that indicated the church was still some way away. As he peered over the wall, the sounds he had heard were at once explained by the sight he saw, yet to explain plausibly to himself *what* he saw was scarcely possible. He could only register it and gape. The wall enclosed the graveyard. A half-dozen people wandered about with watering cans sprinkling the graves, clearly the cause of the baffling sound. Sitting astride one of the nearby graves (a fresh one, judging by the lack of head-stone) was a young woman in exactly the same stance as the girls Howie had seen on the green. But there were no bells on her toes. Instead, using a little trowel, she seemed to be planting something between her bare thighs. The bizarreness of the people watering the graves seemed, in the scale of the abnormal that was crowding in on poor Neil Howie that night, almost commonplace. But the girl who sat astride the grave, only fifteen feet or so from the wall where he stood, was quite unconscious of his presence and certainly entirely unaware of the turmoil she had brought to the mind and spirit of the poor sergeant.

To his horror, he realized, after almost a full minute of watching her, that she was not doing at all that which his imagination had caused him to suppose. He had thought that she was forcing the loam from on top of the grave into her body. Whereas he could see quite plainly that what she was *really* doing was planting a little sapling in the earth between her thighs.

Instead of asking himself why a girl should, at this cool, damp time of night, be risking catching her death of cold as, stark naked, she planted trees on graves; instead of that his mind was suddenly obsessed with the idea of earth being the conduit of seed to the womb. A nightmare, Hieronymus Bosch idea he recognized it to be, forced, he supposed, to the surface of his mind from some cobwebby corner of his subconscious. Howie hated the egoism of introspection. He regarded it as self-indulgent,

undisciplined, and against God's good teaching, which was
to ignore self and look only to Christ as a means of self-
knowledge. For he believed that once Christ was within a
man He would banish all devils, and what else were such
images as these that his mind kept inventing but manifest-
ations of the 'evil one' within him? Each man, Howie felt,
must fight his own struggle against the devil inside him.
No one else could fight it for him.

It occurred to Howie, in a moment of quite extraordinary stress and fear, that God had led him to the island of
Summerisle, had shown him these terrible but exciting
images to test him. That after the night in which he had
triumphed over his own flesh and *not seduced* Mary, when
he knew it would have been so easy to do so, God had
decided, in His wisdom, to test him further.

If the obsessive idea of a woman packing her body with
earth seemed to linger long after he realized that it was
entirely in his mind, and no part of what he was actually
seeing, it was a measure, to him, once again, of how the
people of this island seemed capable of forcing him to join
them in giving vent to inner thoughts and feelings that
shamed him, that appalled him, that made him feel
covered with slime.

He longed to escape from the company and sight of
these people, to find some trees where the innocent birds
slept, except for the nocturnal owl whose clean, uncomplicated instinct to hunt was a law of nature that Howie
could understand. He turned and put the disturbing activity in the graveyard behind him. He put away from him
too, with some difficulty, the urge to simply find that
solitary wood, for which he longed. Instead he walked

briskly back towards the inn and his duty of preparing to inquire further into the disappearance of Rowan Morrison.

Although past eleven o'clock now, Howie was surprised and angered to find, if anything, more people in the bar than before. That they were relatively quiet, almost as if they'd been awaiting his return, was beside the point. He went straight up to Alder MacGregor and demanded an immediate explanation.

'It's past time, Landlord. Tell them to drink up and get out!' Howie didn't even pause for Alder's reaction but went to close the barroom door in the usual mainland manner for indicating legal Scottish closing time in a bar. But Alder was ahead of him.

'Sergeant, it's beyond your powers. We close here when we think fit.'

'You do *what?*' asked Howie sharply.

'Licensing laws are under the control of the Justices of the Peace, right?'

'Right!' agreed Howie. 'They can give permission for extensions for late closing. What about it? Is this a local holiday? Is that it?' he asked suspiciously.

'Not that I know of,' said Alder MacGregor, slightly bewildered. 'The point is that Lord Summerisle is Justice of the Peace here!' he went on.

'I know!' Howie was impatient to get to the door for people were still entering.

'He has extended licensing hours indefinitely. This whole island is his property, y'know,' said Alder Mac-Gregor.

'You mean you can stay open all night if you like?' Sergeant Howie was appalled.

'Sometimes,' agreed Alder MacGregor, enjoying the sergeant's astonishment. 'It depends how we feel. His Lordship don't care ... as long as everyone turns up for work, on time, next morning, that is.'

Howie managed to keep his cool. He was getting used to these shocks – storing up a list of things to report to the Chief Constable of the West Highland Police when he got back. They would need to send a task force of police to clean up this island when the time came. Meanwhile he must keep his mind clear for the Rowan Morrison case.

Alder MacGregor had returned to the bar to pour a round of stiff drams of malt whisky for the little band of balladeers seated in a little room off the bar. They had stopped their music and were being joined now by all the young people streaming in from outside. That here were the young lovers Howie had just seen on the green was clear from the fact that some of the girls were solicitously, shamelessly, thought Howie, brushing the grass from their menfolk's backs, as they entered the inn. It surprised him that so many of the younger people should crowd into this tiny room, their elders remaining dotted about the main bar. What really amazed him, however, was seeing the lovely Willow giving her father a daughterly goodnight kiss and heading for the staircase that led up to the bedrooms. She said, 'Goodnight, Sergeant' to him with only a trace of coquetry. 'My room is next to yours,' she added in even tones. 'Call me if you need anything in the night. Y'know it's sometimes hard to sleep in a strange room. So, if you need a hot water bottle or a cup of tea, don't hesitate to call, will ye?'

With which she was gone up the wooden stairs, her

splendid arse quite muted in its invitation. But still not the debutante's arse it had been at dinner time. He could see her reach the landing and go into a room directly above that into which the band and all the young people were now crowded.

Howie collected his own key and his overnight bag from behind the bar and went on up the stairs, finding his room easily from the number tagged to the key. It was, indeed, next door to Willow's room. Having undressed and washed himself briskly from head to foot, using the pitchers of hot and cold water he found thoughtfully provided on the old-fashioned marble washstand, he put on his thick wool pyjamas and after carefully folding his uniform, placed it under the mattress on the bed for overnight pressing.

Now came the ritual of writing up his daily report. He sat himself at a little table by the window and, taking out his notebook, started to list chronologically the increasingly strange events of the day and the night. Then he listed the birds he had seen, getting as far as the black-browed albatross, when he was interrupted . . .

Howie could hear something happening in the garden behind the inn onto which his open window faced. He looked out, craning only slightly to do so, and found he could see the open but curtained bay windows of what was apparently Willow's room next door. The light from the downstairs bar and the little room under Willow's bedroom flooded out into the night, illuminating a yard full of extravagantly large rhubarb plants with huge leaves.

Howie could discern two men standing there now, talking in low tones. One was a strikingly tall, dark-haired man in his mid-forties, wearing a crimson reddish dress

kilt, which Howie recognized as that of the clan Morrison.
Wearing no jacket, he stood out against the strange, giant
leaves in a ruffled, white evening shirt, a formal stock tied
carelessly around his neck. The figure beside him was that
of a kilted youth whose age was hard, in the dim light, to
determine except that Howie judged him to be a beardless
boy; a fact soon to be confirmed when he heard the lad's
newly broken voice. In one hand the youth grasped a tree
sapling. Howie noticed that he had the arched, trailing
branches of a young willow tree.

A flute and a drum started to play below in the little
room by the bar and Howie heard the curtains of Willow's
room open. Looking up at her window, he saw her there,
leaning languidly forward, her opulent breasts resting on
the sill. He drew back into his room where he could watch
without easily being seen.

The tall man had taken a dagger from his sock and
passed it to the boy beside him. The lad then, holding the
tree in one hand and the dagger in the other, walked firmly
forward, gazing up at the lovely, smiling Willow. The
music stopped. The youth started to cut the branches off
the sapling with the dagger, until only the slender trunk
was left, clenched firmly in his hand. Silence had fallen all
over the inn. No sound came even from the crowded room
below Willow's bedroom.

Boldly, in a gesture of clear significance, the boy planted
the tree in the soft earth under Willow's window. Down
below in the small room, the drum started throbbing. The
boy stepped back to join the tall man behind him who,
placing his hand reassuringly on the boy's shoulder, called
up to the fair girl in the window.

'Willow MacGregor,' he said in a pleasant, deep, culti-vated voice. 'I have the honour to present to you Ash Buchanan.'

'Come up, Ash Buchanan,' invited Willow.

The boy's expression was one of sober anticipation. Manhood lay ahead of him but, like every virgin lover before him, he was starting on an odyssey into the unknown. He walked to the back door holding himself straight, his pace dignified, unhurried; conscious of the many eyes upon him from the windows of the inn. Howie realized that the boy would have to cross the bar, full of the older islanders, to reach the stairs and expected to hear the lewd yells that had greeted Willow's offer to take *him* to his room. But the inn remained silent except for the steady beat of the drum. Howie could hear the boy's footsteps on the floor in the bar beneath him and then on the stairs. While he was conscious of the boy's ascent to Willow's room, his attention was taken by a curious exchange between Willow, still standing at the window, and the tall man in the yard below.

'Another sacrifice for Aphrodite, Willow,' said the man with the deep voice.

'You flatter me, Your Lordship. Surely you mean *to* Aphrodite,' responded Willow.

Howie had guessed as much, but on the phrase 'Lord-ship' he peered as hard as he could at the dark, saturnine figure in the ruffled shirt. So that was Lord Summerisle. Howie had a similar image in his mind when he tried, as a child, to imagine the corrupt Lord Byron. Only later had he learned that the wicked poet was rather short and had limped.

'I make no distinction, Willow. You are the Goddess of Love in human form, and I merely your humble acolyte.'

This sounded like the old, oily, upper-class flattery to Howie's egalitarian ears, and he hated it.

Lord Summerisle bowed before turning away and Willow blew him a kiss. But as if caught by an afterthought, he turned back to call after her.

'Willow! Enjoy yourself and him. Only make sure you're ready for tomorrow's tomorrow!'

Willow, having herself turned to meet her lover (who was tapping firmly at her door), looked back at Lord Summerisle and spoke almost breathlessly in response.

'The day of death and resurrection . . . ?'

'Yes,' agreed Lord Summerisle, 'and of a somewhat more serious offering than tonight's.'

'Death and Resurrection.' The words tolled like funeral bells in Howie's mind. Christ's Resurrection was celebrated on Easter Sunday, two days *after* the Friday on which it was customary to mark His crucifixion. What single day could possibly hold both a death and a resurrection? Unless it be some mindless religious quirkery like that of the Wee Frees at Plockton on the mainland. But suppose the death planned were that of Rowan? By what possible horrible charade could her resurrection take place the same day? Howie knew these speculations were wildly fanciful. Yet the excesses that he had seen the islanders permit themselves bred such speculation. Never in his life had Neil Howie's imagination led him to such fantasies as now crept into his mind. Rowan dead, the victim of a ritual involving a sexual assault. Why else choose a victim with the surely virginal, but probably just-mature-enough age of Rowan

Morrison? Rowan's body resurrected. But how? Here Howie's imagination boggled and the experienced Sergeant of Police's judgement took over. 'Death and Resurrection.' A phrase that could mean almost anything. It could mean Halloween! Calming himself, he knew that he must simply note what he'd heard until something else, some future evidence, should flesh it out with clearer meaning. In the meantime, the rational sergeant could not control a certain growing dread of what was happening on the island, of a future evil he might, so easily, be powerless to prevent.

Lord Summerisle had walked away and was lost in the darkness, leaving Howie unable to stop himself listening to the sounds all around him in the inn.

The door of Willow's room opened and closed and Howie clearly heard the soft gasp of the boy seeing or feeling something amazing. Howie tried to damp down his clamouring imagination. Then the inn was alive with music, with the singing of dozens of voices.

> '*I put my hand all on her knee*
> *She says to me do you want to see?*
>
> *I put my hand all on her breast*
> *She says do you want to be kissed?*
>
> *I put my hand all on her thigh*
> *She says to me do you want to try?*
>
> *I put my hand all on her belly*
> *She says to me do you want to fill'ee?*'

But before each verse, the singers sang – with a gentleness quite unlike their rambunctious rendering of the

'Landlord's Daughter' – a chorus of sweet advice to Ash and every boy who had gone that way before or since.

> 'Gently, gently, Johnny,
> Oh gently, gently, Johnny,
> Johnny, my Jingalooo!'

Howie knelt by his bed and prayed for respite from the terrible desire, the quite frightening sensuousness that was spreading through him. As he affirmed to himself that he feared God and His terrible retribution for those who defied His *Law* . . . he found himself feeling for his prayer book in the half-dark of his room. To hold it would be a reassurance. Instead, his fingers touched a tiny scroll he had previously noticed that lay upon the bedside table. Thinking with a sudden onrush of hope that it might be a note from whatever hand sent him the anonymous letter about Rowan, he took it over to the oil lamp on the table by the window.

> I think I could turn and live with animals.
> They're so placid and self-contained.
> They do not lie awake in the dark and weep for their
>       sins.
> They do not make me sick discussing their duty to
>       God.
> Not one of them kneels to another or to his own kind
>       that lived thousands of years ago.
> Not one of them is respectable or unhappy all over the
>       earth.

He read it with a growing sense of fear. Whoever had selected the text, Howie guessed, had meant *him* to read it.

He could hear the deep, cultured, umber tones of Lord Summerisle's voice. But perhaps similar homilies were placed in every guest room of the inn, as Gideon bibles might be on the mainland.

Willow's gentle laugh reached him now. It was a happy, tinkling laugh of discovery and joy. Then her voice changed subtly and she spoke in the unmistakable language of woman loving, woman loved, using no words save 'yes' and sounds that came in undulating cadences as Ash, making himself a man, drove her, at last, to her bliss.

Neil Howie longed to stop imagining her. Tried, for a terrible moment of confusion, to imagine Mary Bannock in her place. Then pulling himself together, he concentrated on the image of His Lord dying, for him, on the Cross, and he succeeded and was calm and grateful. He heard the hubbub of conversation start once more in the bar below him, was conscious that the music had stopped, and lying exhausted on his bed, slipped, at once, into a deep sleep.

## CHAPTER IV

# Monday Morning –
# the 30th of April

A DREAM, THEY SAY, LASTS ONLY SECONDS BEFORE waking. At once forgotten usually, it leaves a stain on the consciousness, like a slow-developing photograph.

Sergeant Howie awoke to the sounds of horses and wagon wheels on the cobblestones. His sleep had been so deep that it had left less impression than might have been expected from the surprises and traumas of his first day on Summerisle. But as he flipped over the pages of his notebook, all the pieces of the strange conundrum that was the quest of Rowan Morrison reappeared. Much like the first glance at a brand new jigsaw puzzle they gave him the distinct impression of being pieces from two or more puzzles and not just the one he'd come to solve.

Then, as he was shaving with the steaming hot water that Alder MacGregor had brought him, he started to remember his dream. It wasn't much that he remembered but it seemed as real as the equally extraordinary things he'd witnessed the previous night. The dream image was of Willow sitting astride him while she ran long, supple, bell-ringing toes through his 'short, back, and sides' haircut. Should he feel guilty about a mere dream?

He looked at his body as he sluiced it in the warm water, standing in the small zinc tub provided. Had she somehow come through the wall and seduced it, robbing him of his precious seed? Only the bolted door he'd had to open to admit Alder MacGregor with the can of water told him this was impossible, until, gazing at himself in the discoloured mirror, he realized the truth. Desire was moving him again at the very thought of Willow. The dream had been acted out in his subconscious, a place in which he had somehow omitted to pray for protection from what his mother had kindly called, when he was a growing boy, the 'old Adam' in him, and every man. He must beware of these people, even in his sleep. Fear of the unknown, Howie knew, had driven men to start their search for God. Yet he, who had long since found God, now seemed to be facing an unknown here on Summerisle. Gone or going were some of his own comfortable verities and in their place, dark and palpitating as a toad under a leaf, Howie sensed his own fear, waiting for him. He dismissed these thoughts for the present as the result of an overindulgence of his imagination.

After a breakfast of good, scalding strong tea and some tasty porridge (a huge improvement on dinner the night before), he stepped blinking into the bright sunlight of a clear spring day.

Willow, swathed in a practical apron, that blessedly masked her opulent charms, was scrubbing the bar tables and humming to the sound of distant music. She paused in her work to greet Neil Howie.

'Good morning, Sergeant. Isn't it glorious?'

'Very nice, Miss,' said Howie, avoiding any emotive superlatives.

'I expect you'll be going back home tonight?'

'That depends,' said Howie guardedly. 'Where's the village school, please?'

She pointed across the almost deserted green to where it rose to a kind of plateau, beyond which everything was out of sight, but from which the jaunty music seemed to be coming.

'On the far side of the green, beyond the maypole, hard by the old church. You can't miss it,' she said. 'Have a good day!'

'Thank you,' said Howie and paused. He remembered a phrase that he'd heard her say the night before. Something about which he'd resolved to question her, or Lord Summerisle, when he should meet him.

'So what's happening here on tomorrow's tomorrow?'

'That's a funny way to put it.' Willow seemed baffled by the phrase. 'Do you mean the day after tomorrow?'

'Yes, I suppose so,' said Howie. 'I thought the other was a local expression.'

'How quaint!' said Willow, as if the likes of her had never heard the likes of a phrase like that.

'Well?' insisted Howie.

'Now let me see,' said Willow, with a hint of impatience in her voice. 'The day after tomorrow will be May the second . . . nothing as far as I know!'

She smiled demurely at him as if to conclude the subject. Howie, supposing, for an instant, that she had answered him, started to walk across the green. Then realizing she hadn't, he turned.

'I mean tomorrow! What's happening here tomorrow?'

he asked. But Willow had gone, leaving the steaming, clean tables behind her.

As Howie approached the rise in the green that led to the plateau beyond, he could see just the top of the maypole in the near distance. Howie assumed it was a maypole, because of what Willow had said, but it looked, with its pale bark, like a freshly cut ash tree, its branches lopped off, leaving little stubs on the trunk, and 'topped', so that a slew of red and white ribbons could be attached. From the curious perspective of viewing the top of the pole, before he could see the rest, he was surprised to see a lad, whom he at once recognized as Ash Buchanan, climbing the trunk and placing a rounded wreath over the top so that the maypole was crowned.

A great cheer went up at this and as Ash climbed down the pole the sergeant found himself close enough to take in the whole scene. Forty or more young boys ringed the maypole holding red and white tapes, which they tied around their waists, facing inward towards the pole. The small band that had been playing in the inn on the previous night was sitting on the churchyard wall. Howie realized that it must have been here that he had walked when he had come upon the women who 'rode a cock horse'.

The beauty of the scene pleased Howie although something in the symbolism of Ash's crowning act troubled the back of his mind. It was good to see all these healthy-looking boys enjoying themselves, for they all chattered excitedly as a man who had the slightly fustian look of a schoolmaster organized them into their circle. The tune that the musicians were playing was a pretty air, which Howie half-recognized as a folk song he knew. Willow's directions had been accurate, and what was plainly a small school building stood in the background. The schoolmaster ran to the centre of the circle of boys and started to sing to the music.

Howie always felt faintly embarrassed when an adult sang out loud in public, when it wasn't either in a concert hall or in church. He knew it was a personal prejudice, probably an inhibition that came from being raised never to draw attention to himself. Then the words of this folk song filtered through to him as he walked by the now dancing boys, who shook their ribbons till they made patterns like swimming red and white fish against the blue sky.

'In the Summerisle woods there growed a tree,' sang the schoolmaster to the band's music.

> 'And a very fine tree was he.
> And on that tree there was a limb
> And on that limb there was a branch
> And on that branch there was a spray
> And on that spray there was a nest
> And in that nest there was an egg
> And from that egg there was a bird
> And on that bird there was a feather . . .'

Howie remembered the song. They had sung it in the glee club at his school, and he listened with half his attention to see if he remembered the words aright. The schoolhouse he was approaching was a similar building to the one he

had attended. Much like hundreds of others in the Highlands. Two identical wings of brick and granite. One
assigned to the boys, the other to the girls. He peered
through the window of the girls' classroom . . . to see them
all seated at their desks happily thumping their pencil
boxes in time to the boys' song. None of them noticed
him.

Howie thought how fresh and innocent they looked
with their wonderful, rosy, Highland complexions, and
listened with them to the next verse of the song.

> 'And on that feather there was a bed
> And on that bed there lay a girl
> And on that girl there was a man
> And from that man there came a seed . . .'

Howie heard *these* words with a growing sense of shock
and surprise. It was not how he remembered the song at
all. But folk songs were often earthy and he knew many
old ones such as this had been bowdlerized in Victorian
times.

He could see the back of a woman schoolteacher inside
the classroom. She sang the verse in time with her male
colleague outside, who now led the boys in interweaving
their ribbons around the maypole. The sergeant listened
closely as the song went on:

> 'And from that seed there came a baby
> And from that baby there grew a boy
> And then that boy planted an acorn
> And from that acorn grew a tree

*And the tree growed in the Summerisle wood*
*In the Summerisle wood, in the Summerisle wood*
*And the tree growed in the Summerisle wood . . .'*

The boys were now singing the chorus as they wove themselves closer and closer to the maypole. The schoolmistress had stopped singing and was calling for quiet from her pupils. Howie, who had, sensibly enough, decided that the next most logical place to gain information about a missing thirteen-year-old girl was among her schoolmates, prepared to interrupt the class. Walking from the window to the outside door to the classroom he could hear the schoolmistress saying, 'Now that's *quite* enough, girls! It's time to pay attention to me!'

Silence ensued as Howie appeared, still unseen, at the doorway, to notice their attention all centred on a handsome woman of about thirty-five, with blonde, swept-back hair, dressed more elegantly than the other women he had seen on the island. She looked as if she had bought her clothes in Edinburgh or some other fashionable place.

'Daisy,' she said, addressing a dark, plump girl who appeared to be eating something surreptitiously. 'Will you tell us, please, what the maypole represents?'

Daisy sat there, not embarrassed, but just looking blank. Around her grew a chorus of 'Please, Miss Rose . . .' 'I know,' et cetera, as some of the other girls held their hands up, and otherwise jumped up and down, in order to attract attention to themselves.

'Really, Daisy!' said Miss Rose. 'I've told you often enough. Anyone?'

'Phallic Symbol!' chorused the children. 'The Phallic Symbol!'

'Quite right,' said Miss Rose. 'It is the image of the penis that we venerate as symbolizing the generative force in nature.'

Howie's sense of shock at the schoolmistress's words was, at first blush (and he did), rooted in embarrassment. He had never heard the penis impersonally discussed by a woman in what, she must believe, not having yet noticed him, to be entirely female company. He'd heard a whore on the dockside accuse poor McTaggart of having 'a prick no bigger than a thimble', and a great deal more in that vein from women of that ilk. He thought it healthy and normal for people to speak of things straight out and not use hypocritical euphemisms. He despised the prissiness that called a woman's lavatory a 'little girl's room'. And yet to venerate the penis? Howie suddenly remembered the famous prosecution by the Attorney-General of *Lady Chatterley's Lover* as an obscene book. The prosecution had made much of the phrase in which Lady Chatterley was said to 'worship' the gamekeeper's balls. The defence had triumphed partly because an Anglican bishop, giving evidence on their behalf, had answered the prosecution's question, 'Can you imagine a decent woman worshipping a man's balls?' with the reply 'Yes, indeed.' And yet Howie knew the bishop had meant his answer in the context of what 'a wonderful thing' (as a creation of God) 'is a man'. In that context, of course, his balls, custodians of new life, were indeed wonderful. But something told Howie that when the schoolmistress said venerate the penis she meant it in the sense that he, Howie, venerated the Host when it was brought out of its seclusion in the sanctuary of the church. The implication quite simply angered him. Here, in his view, was a quirkish, obscene notion being taught to these young people in school. No wonder the adults behaved as they did, copulating in public. No wonder they sang and danced and acted as if God's precious gift of sex was a commonplace game to be acted out with familiarity, without *love*, as Howie understood and valued it. This banal and evil teaching, as he saw it, this farce of making a tree almost sacred, infuriated Neil Howie.

He threw the hall door of the classroom violently open and stood in the doorway, glaring at Miss Rose.

'Miss,' said Sergeant Howie coolly, but politely. 'May I have a word with you, please?'

Miss Rose and the children looked at him in great surprise but the teacher hurried to join him by the doorway.

'Miss,' said Howie at once, 'you can be very sure I shall report this nonsense that I've just heard here today to the proper authorities! Everywhere I go on this island I find degeneracy – brawling in the bars, indecency in public places, corruption of the young, and now I know where it all stems from – the filth taught here in this schoolroom!'

He was aware of how pompous he must sound, even as he spoke, but he didn't care. The phrases might be clichés, but they gave vent to his feelings quickly and succinctly, and he was glad he had so expressed himself.

'I was unaware that the police had any authority on matters of education,' said Miss Rose.

She had the softest of lilting accents but her mode of

speech was pedantic, superior, and ironic. She was the sort of woman who made Howie feel uncomfortable for she had a sexuality that came from a mocking, mysterious expression, from a body that moved with feline assurance and grace.

'Maybe not,' acknowledged Howie. 'But we work closely with those who do. And as I say, this will not go unreported.'

'Is that why you came here today? To snoop?' said Miss Rose, lowering her voice, hoping he would follow her example, for the girls were plainly listening.

'No, it was not, miss,' said Howie. 'And let me make it plain. I do not snoop. I investigate.'

'May one know,' asked Miss Rose, 'without too much self-important mystery-making, that is, what it is you have come here to investigate?'

'I've come to find a missing girl,' said Howie, lowering his voice now, 'a girl whom everyone says never existed.'

'How quixotic of you,' teased Miss Rose.

'Quixotic?' asked Howie, annoyed at her attitude.

'From Don Quixote – an enthusiastic visionary, a pursuer of lofty but impracticable ideals,' said Miss Rose, the schoolteacher.

'Also a man of honour, I believe,' added Howie, glad to have acquitted himself against this waspish female. Mary would have been proud of him.

'Which did not prevent him from continually making a fool of himself,' capped Miss Rose, triumphantly.

'We shall see about that!' said Howie, determined to end this colloquy and get down to business. With which he strode into the classroom and addressed the class:

'Girls, I want your attention, please,' he said, suddenly gentle as well as authoritative. 'I am a police officer.' He started smiling as they giggled at this obvious statement. 'As you can see! I am here to investigate the disappearance of a young girl. This is her photograph, which I will ask you to pass round the classroom while I am writing her name on the blackboard.'

He produced the photograph of Rowan Morrison, which he handed to the nearest girl. After two or three seconds, she shook her head and passed it to the next girl. While it was going from desk to desk around the room, Howie turned to the blackboard and prepared to write, when he saw what was already written there and read it in mild disbelief.

The Cock-Knee Stone preserves the pith of the milk.
The Snail Stone preserves the eyes from the darkness.
The Toad Stone preserves the newly born from the
      weird woman.
The Hag Stone preserves people from nightmare.

Impatiently, he rubbed this off and wrote in bold lettering the name: ROWAN MORRISON. AGE 12–13.

'That's her name,' said Howie, facing the class. 'Rowan Morrison. Do any of you recognize the name or the photograph?'

There was complete silence. The photograph was passed back to the first girl who handed it up to Howie. Still staring at the class, he put it away.

'You have your answer,' said Miss Rose, impatient now for him to leave. 'If she existed, we would know of her.'

Howie continued to stare at the class. His eye had been attracted to the one empty desk in the room. He crossed to it.

'Whose desk is this?' Howie asked Miss Rose over his shoulder.

'No one's,' she answered.

He opened the desk. Inside it was quite empty except that in the middle there was a nail driven into the wood. Attached to the nail by a thread was a black beetle. The thread, about four inches long, was already wound several times around the nail. Daisy, sitting next to the empty desk, leaned over and explained to Howie.

'The little old beetle goes round and round,' she said. 'Always the same way you see, until at the end he's tied right up tight to the nail – poor old thing.'

'Poor old thing?' said Howie furiously. 'Then why in God's name do you do it, girl?'

He slammed the desk shut and walked back up to the dais, addressing Miss Rose once again.

'I'd like to see the school register, please.'

'Do you have Lord Summerisle's authority?' asked Miss Rose querulously.

'You seem to forget, this is a police matter,' said Howie coldly.

'I'm afraid you will still need a search warrant, or permission from Lord Summerisle.' Miss Rose had a hint of desperation in her voice.

Howie ignored her, and threw open the top of the teacher's desk. Inside was the school register, which he lifted out. Now it was Miss Rose's turn to be outraged.

'Just you put that *right* back . . . and *now*, if you please,' she said, her voice cracking with anger.

'I'm sorry, miss,' said Howie calmly. 'You'll just have to bear with me.'

The book was about half-filled. That is, it appeared to record the attendance at the school for the last several years. He naturally turned to the present term's record and found it headed 'Beltane Spring Term'. Running his finger down the names: Lily, Heather, May, Marigold, Pansy, Daisy, Holly, he came to the name he had been searching for . . . Rowan. Sure enough, Rowan Morrison. Moreover, her address was c/o Mrs May Morrison, as described in the anonymous letter.

The sergeant quickly counted the names on the list and glaring at the girls, counted them too. There was, as he had expected, one girl missing in the class, which accounted for the empty desk. Now, thought Howie, his adrenaline surging with righteous anger, we can start to wrap up this case. He addressed the now scared-looking pupils with such an intensity of quiet fury that they seemed to wilt like the blooms, for which most were named, under his ire.

'You're despicable little liars!' he said. 'Rowan Morrison is a schoolmate of yours. Isn't she? She attends this class. That's her desk. Isn't it?'

The class remained silent, trying to avoid his raking gaze.

'I think you ought to know . . .' interrupted Miss Rose anxiously. But Howie cut her short.

'And you're the biggest liar of them all!' he told her. 'I

warn you, if you tell me one more lie, I'll have you "inside" for obstruction. And that's a promise, miss. Now, for the last time, where is this girl?'

Miss Rose tugged now at his sleeve.

'I will have to speak to you outside,' she said.

'All right!' agreed Howie, hoping that in private she could tell him what apparently couldn't be said before the girls. Although having heard part of their May Day lesson, he couldn't imagine what that might be.

'Children,' said Miss Rose, 'get on with your reading for the next few minutes – The Rites and Rituals of May Day, Chapter Five. I won't be long.'

Preceding Miss Rose out of the schoolroom, Howie could see that the boys were finishing tying the coloured ribbons neatly to the maypole. The band had gone from the churchyard wall. Miss Rose, looking flushed and anxious, hurried out to join him.

'Well?' Howie asked her curtly.

'You don't understand,' said Miss Rose. 'No one was lying to you. I told you plainly that if Rowan Morrison existed we would know of her.'

'You mean that she doesn't exist – that she is dead?' Howie hated the contorted way the woman spoke.

'You would say so,' said Miss Rose.

'No, hocus, miss, if you please,' insisted Howie. 'Either she's dead or she isn't.'

Miss Rose hesitated.

'We never use the word,' she said at last, mouthing the word dead, not saying it out loud. 'You see, we believe that after the human life is over, the soul lives on – in air, in

the trees, in animals, in fire, in water – so that Rowan
Morrison, for example, has simply rejoined the life force in
another form.'

The boys came running to their classroom, whooping
and shouting and followed by their schoolmaster.

'Do you honestly mean to say you teach the children
this stuff?' Howie asked incredulously, raising his voice
above the boys' din.

'Of course. I told you. It is what we believe,' said Miss
Rose.

'And you teach them nothing of Jesus Christ?' asked
Howie.

'Only as a comparative religion,' she said. 'I'm afraid
they find reincarnation far easier to picture than resurrection. Those rotting bodies have always been such a stum-
bling block to the childish imagination . . .'

'Oh, aye!' said Howie, borrowing some of her irony.
'And where, may I ask, is Rowan Morrison's rotting body?'

'Why, where you would expect it to be. In the earth,'
said she.

'In the churchyard?' Howie hated these prissy
prevarications.

'In a manner of speaking,' she agreed.

'Hell's bells, miss!' cried Howie, on the verge of saying
something worse. 'In plain speaking?'

'I mean precisely what I say,' said Miss Rose, at her most
pedantic. 'That building attached to the ground in which
the body lies is no longer used for public Christian worship,
so whether that still makes it a church, or the ground a
churchyard, is debatable. Now, if you'll forgive me, I must
get back to my girls. Good morning, Officer.'

A baffled Howie watched Miss Rose march back to the school building and disappear inside it. The sergeant walked past the now deserted maypole and stood at the lych-gate of the church, looking at the graveyard. He could see the fresh grave on which the crying girl had sat. The church itself was the usual plain flintstone building to be found on the islands, though somewhat larger and considerably more run-down. Some of the older gravestones had Celtic crosses cut into them.

Howie opened the gate and walked into the graveyard, looking carefully at the graves.

Many carried elaborate symbols and epitaphs, a couple of which he stopped to read. So strange were some of these that his mind flew to 'freemasonry'. Howie disliked cults, and while he had, of course, studied comparative religion, freemasonry was, to him, a cult. Something outlandish to do with trowels and aprons and the pyramids. Perhaps it flourished here?

One grave had the following inscription under the name and dates of life and death, which were mostly concealed by ivy: 'Deliver me from the wildly roaming, supernatural woman who took my head, mine ear, and my life's career from me.' Another grave carried the epitaph: 'Here lieth Beech Buchanan, protected by the ejaculation of serpents.' Other, more recent graves were planted in pairs with a wooden hoop joining them. Roses and other climbers had been planted on each grave and grew intertwined on the hoop. Thus he noticed that Hawthorn Campbell and Clematis Campbell lay side by side. The hawthorn shrub was embraced by the flowering clematis upon the hoop.

Walking around that side of the church he had not

previously visited, he noticed that there was a tree upon almost every grave. All had headstones, save one that had a budding sapling growing from it but which otherwise looked comparatively recent. Hanging from one of the tiny branches of the sapling was a stringy piece of material that reminded Howie of dried offal.

He was about to examine this more closely when he experienced suddenly that prickly sensation that comes from being aware, on the outer fringes of one's consciousness, that one is being watched. He looked hurriedly around. The perfectly still figure of an old man stood in the shadow of a yew tree, which seemed to have been clipped to resemble a giant phallus. He carried a pair of shears and stared unblinkingly at Howie.

'Good morning,' said Howie with uncertain cordiality.

'Morning, Sergeant,' said the old man courteously with a touch of formality. 'I'm Loam, the gravedigger here!'

'What tree is that?' asked Howie, pointing to the sapling.

Slowly the gardener detached himself from the shadow of the yew tree and approached the small grave.

'It's a rowan,' said Old Loam.

'Who lies there?' asked Howie, knowing the answer.

'Rowan Morrison,' said Old Loam, not unexpectedly.

'How long has she been dea—' Howie caught himself in time. '. . . there?'

'Seven or eight months,' said Old Loam. 'They're a mite late with the headstone.'

Howie bent down and examined the stringy bit of offal-like material.

'What's this?' asked Howie. 'It looks like . . . skin.'

'Why, so it is!' said Old Loam, apparently surprised at the question.

'But *what* is it?' insisted Howie.

'Why it's the poor wee lassie's navel string, of course. Where else should it be, but hung on her own little tree?' asked Loam kindly, but as if he were addressing a halfwit. The two men looked at each other, the older man solicitous, the younger man baffled and in a mounting state of anger.

'Who's your parish priest or minister?' Howie asked sharply.

'Priest? Minister?' Loam reacted to the question as a canon of Canterbury Cathedral might if asked the whereabouts of the Grand Inca. Then the gardener smiled gently and walked away, slowly shaking his head. Howie watched him go.

The spectre of the unknown, the fear of which he had banished from his mind as he left the inn that morning, came crowding back on him. He was in the midst of a community of several hundred souls utterly divorced from the Word of God in his very own police precinct. It was quite literally *fearful*! He made his way hurriedly into the church to pray for little Rowan's soul and for Summerisle.

The church, which Howie entered, his hat cradled under his arm, he was further shocked to find in utter ruination. A gaping roof let the sun flood down onto a floor overgrown with weeds, while the pews gave every evidence of having been hacked up for firewood. In the centre of the church was an ancient tomb with the skull and crossbones beneath a Celtic cross. The Latin legend *Memento Mori* was much worn but could still be discerned.

As Howie rounded the tomb he caught sight of the sanctuary, where a woman was sitting upon what was left of the altar rail. She sat staring at him curiously, her legs plumped wide apart, the left one in the nave, the right one in the sanctuary. In her left hand she held an egg, while a babe sucked at her right pap, which was thrust through her open blouse. Howie averted his gaze from this, to him, weird sight and faced the altar, or what remained of it.

Rotting fruit and vegetables littered the area around the altar and the shards of broken fruit boxes lay upon the Lord's table itself. Howie walked forward and reverently cleared the table, removing the debris. Then, noticing that there was no single sign of the cross in the entire sanctuary, Howie took a piece of apple box and, splitting it in two, fashioned it into the shape of a cross and placed it upon the altar and bowed his head in prayer.

Behind him the nursing mother was so surprised by what she, no doubt, saw as his curious ceremonial that she allowed her child to become detached from its eleven o'clock feed. The baby complained, a loud voice, frightening a rookery that was inhabiting a beech tree that overhung the church, filling the old ruin with a cawing and a crying that nevertheless did not disturb the sergeant's silent prayer for poor, dead little Rowan.

> *Gentle Jesus,*
> *Meek and mild,*
> *Look upon*
> *A little child*
> *And suffer her to come to Thee!*

As the sergeant left the now-echoing church, he looked back and saw something from which the sight of the nursing mother had at first distracted him. The sanctuary was quite clearly the same place in which the Thanksgiving photographs had been taken at the end of each summer. Howie remembered the piles of luscious produce in the pictures on the wall in the bar and remembered too that in each had stood a young girl dressed entirely in white, like a lass going to her First Communion back at Saint Andrew's in Portlochlie.

Could Rowan have stood in the missing photograph? He resolved to get the negative from Mr Lennox, the photographer, and check.

Indeed much would now have to be checked and double-checked. Since these folk had this strange coyness about mentioning 'death' he must revisit Mrs May Morrison and see if she changed her story in any way. Above all, he must now establish beyond doubt *how* Rowan had died. Nothing in the past twenty-four hours made Howie very sanguine about getting a straight answer on the subject. Death certificates, however, rarely lied and, at the very least, a doctor was obliged to give an opinion as to the cause of death.

Howie, as he emerged from the church, was all too conscious that his job was but half done. The anonymous letter, whose lead he had been following, was right about Rowan having disappeared from her home. Death was certainly a conclusive form of disappearance. Yet it seemed to Howie, as he stood in the graveyard watching Loam now busy deepening an already freshly dug grave, that he could tick off a whole series of questions that the discovery of Rowan's grave now raised.

Why had *no one* recognized the photograph sent him of Rowan Morrison? *Unless* the dead girl and the pretty creature in the photograph were *not* one and the same person.

If her mother was not May Morrison, why was she listed as from that address in the school register?

Why did her sister, Myrtle, insist she existed but that she was a hare? Childish gibberish, perhaps? Or containing a kernel of truth? Locked, perhaps, in some associated idea in the child's mind?

Since the anonymous letter had been postmarked Summerisle, the writer clearly either lived there or spent time there recently. Then why did he, or she (judging by the handwriting), not *know* of Rowan's death? Unless the islanders had been as reticent about the child's death with the letter writer as they had been with himself.

Who *was* the anonymous letter writer? Of course, a major fingerprinting operation would probably turn up the answer to that. But this seemed to Howie, at the moment, the lowest of his priorities.

He was leaving the graveyard when he noticed that the grave that Loam was digging was at least nine feet deep.

'That's a bit more than the traditional six feet, isn't it?' Howie asked, curious.

'Got to dig 'em deep, otherwise they'd be at 'em,' said the old gardener, shaking his head.

'Who would?' asked Howie.

'Those who need the Hand of Glory, for a start,' said the old gardener.

'What?' Howie felt he was struggling with a foreign language.

'You know!' said the old gardener. 'To make people sleep. Grave earth for a light sleep – Hand of Glory for a deep 'un. I don't mind 'em taking a bit of earth – that don't make no extra work – but the other's something else.'

'What exactly is the Hand of Glory?' asked Howie fascinated.

'Don't you ever stop asking questions?' grumbled Loam. 'I got this job to finish.'

The old man turned back to his digging.

'It's my *job* to ask questions,' said Howie emphatically. But the gardener continued to dig, unperturbed.

'Look, I'm a police officer, and when I ask questions I expect answers!'

The gardener paused briefly in his work.

'There are some answers you wouldn't understand,' he said. 'Go home. You've found what you came looking for.' He went back to work, completely ignoring the fuming Howie.

If only 'dumb insolence' were an indictable offence, he often thought, how happy it would make police officers. He contented himself with a dry retort:

'I'm not so sure *what* I've found yet,' said Howie. 'And seeing you like digging so much, old man, I think I can get you some extra employment, pretty soon.'

As Howie walked away towards the lych-gate, the old man spat expressively and went back to work.

## CHAPTER V

## *Afternoon –*
## *the 30th of April*

SERGEANT HOWIE FELT CONTENT AS HE WALKED BACK across the green towards the High Street that in spite of its frustrating and, indeed, shocking moments, the morning had been fruitful. Apart from the progress he'd made on the Rowan Morrison case, and it had been substantial, the inquiry had made it possible to discover the desperate need for some solid police work on this extraordinary island.

There was no question in his mind either but that the churches should send a minister or priest here, at once, to do the essential missionary work of bringing these poor people back to Christ. The sergeant was grateful that he, and not some atheist like McTaggart, had come to Summerisle. Not every police officer would have recognized the spiritual evil here as quickly or clearly as he. Howie allowed himself no false humility in acknowledging that.

Now that his stomach told him that it was lunchtime, he hesitated to go to the inn where the food was so disgusting. Instead, since his duty took him there anyway, he decided to lunch on a chocolate hare bought from Mrs Morrison. Well, he thought, perhaps, under the circumstances, not a hare ... For as he walked again into the shop there seemed a great deal else from which to choose. Like many people who took comparatively little alcohol and abhorred smoking, Howie had a sweet tooth. He gazed greedily at an iced marzipan sugar baby and some sherbet-filled liquorice skuttles in the window, before entering the shop. Mrs Morrison, who was in her back parlour with Myrtle, shouted through the open doorway for the sergeant to kindly await her for a 'wee moment'.

Howie was happy enough to have time to survey the other goodies on the counter but was distracted by the sound of little Myrtle whining about something. Looking up, he saw that the child was refusing to take some form of medicine that was hidden from his view by May Morrison's back.

'What a silly child you are, to be sure, making all this fuss,' Mrs Morrison was saying. 'It's just a little frog. Anyone would think you didn't want to get better. Now open wide . . . and *in* he goes.'

Myrtle reluctantly opened her mouth very wide indeed and the astonished Howie watched her mother cram a live frog into her child's mouth. Mother and child looked at each other, the former pursing her lips to show that the frog must be kept in place. The child's cheeks bulged and her eyes watered. Then Mrs Morrison took the frog out again.

'. . . And out he comes, and it's all over. There, that didn't hurt, did it? Now you can have a sweetie.'

Mrs Morrison was both solicitous and loving after the little ordeal. She put the frog in a transparent plastic biscuit box pierced with holes, and replaced the lid. Then she bustled out to attend to Sergeant Howie.

Howie decided to temper his natural anger with this woman, who, he considered, had lied to him so abominably, in favour of encouraging her to talk. It was impossible, for instance, that she could now deny her daughter's existence before death even, if, like Miss Rose, she had some hang-up about the state of being *dead* itself. Subtlety might pay dividends in this case, he thought.

'I'd like a barley sugar maypole, and a quarter pound of mint bullseyes,' said Howie.

'I made the maypoles fresh today. I put a wee spreckit of whisky in 'em to give 'em a little bite,' said Mrs Morrison as she weighed out the bullseyes. While Howie counted out some change to pay for the purchase, Myrtle spoke in a complaining voice, close to tears, from the parlour.

'You promised me a sweetie. I want a mulberry gobstopper. The froggy tasted horrid. *Horrid!*' she added with emphasis.

'Thank you,' said Howie taking his package. 'Mrs Morrison, I've just come from the graveyard!'

He was not really surprised at her reaction, although he noticed a flicker of hesitation and a slight reddening of her face as she spoke.

'Oh, dear,' said Mrs Morrison with a hint of contrition. 'And we've been so remiss about the headstone. I hope poor Rowan will forgive us, wherever she is.'

'Mrs Morrison,' said Howie quietly, 'why did you tell me that Myrtle is an only child?'

'But she is,' Mrs Morrison insisted. 'Rowan isn't my child any more!'

'I suppose you're going to tell me her soul lives on in a bush or an animal,' said Howie angrily.

'Of course it does,' cried Mrs Morrison happily. 'It's as I say, she's not my daughter any longer. She's something else. Excuse me, I've got to take this sweet to Myrtle.' Mrs Morrison, who had unscrewed a huge gobstopper jar, carried it back to a now weeping Myrtle. The child was crouched near the transparent biscuit box watching the frog.

'I hated that frog in my mouth, Mummy. Hated it! *Horrid, Horrid!*'

'I know, dear,' comforted Mrs Morrison. 'But it's all over now. Here's your sweetie for being a brave girl.'

Mrs Morrison let Myrtle select her favourite gobstopper, put her arm around her child, and pointed to the little frog.

'He's got your horrid old sore throat now, hasn't he, poor creature. Can't you hear him croaking?' she asked.

The frog croaked mournfully as Myrtle went to work on the enormous sweet in her mouth. Howie tried not to let the extraordinary idea of the frog having assumed Myrtle's sore throat distract him. He knew there was something else he'd wanted to ask Mrs Morrison. What was it?

'Is there anything I can do for you, Sergeant?' asked Mrs Morrison, anxious to be rid of him.

'I doubt it, seeing as you're all raving mad!' Howie said, but he smiled his gentle smile at the woman who had lost her daughter. He was probing his memory. Then it came to him. 'There's just one thing I'd like to know. What was the cause of . . . death?'

Mrs Morrison looked for a moment distant and sad.

'She was so hot, burning . . . poor love! I'd rather you talked to Dr Ewan about it,' she said, indicating

Myrtle. 'He only lives over the street, next to the chemist.'

Howie gazed pityingly at the three of them. The woman, the child, and the frog. From such superstition, he believed, had Our Lord delivered all Christians. Few people realized how fortunate they were in this respect. He touched his hat politely and left.

Howie found the doctor's residence at once. A shiny brass plate advertised Dr Ewan's house conveniently next door to the chemist's shop. He rang and waited. There was no answer. But the door of the chemist's shop opened and its proprietor emerged, reminding Howie of a creature that, having been stuffed, somehow became reanimated but in a limited kind of way.

'He's out on his rounds till lunchtime, I'm afraid!' the man said. 'Perhaps I could take a message or assist in some way?' Howie looked at the chemist, then up at the name above his shop, which read T. H. Lennox.

'You are Mr Lennox, the photographer?' Howie's card index mind was at work. He remembered the photographs at the inn.

'I am first a chemist, secondly a photographer, and thirdly a purveyor of Thermos flasks and hotties,' said Mr Lennox.

'Hotties?' asked Howie.

'Hot water bottles!' explained Lennox kindly. 'More efficacious than most of Dr Ewan's specifics, believe me. Do you want your photograph taken?'

'No, thank you, but I *would* like a word with you.'

'Oh, come inside then. Please!' Mr Lennox was most solicitous.

Inside the shop, the shelves and counters were full of jars containing bizarre objects like leeches and fillets of snake, omen sticks, and strips of 'witches' mummy', looking like exactly what it was, desiccated corpse flesh. On the counter nearest Howie when he entered, was a glass container of foreskins, slightly bloodstained and packed tight together. Like everything else it was clearly labelled. Howie's capacity for incredulity was again strained almost to its utmost, as he looked at the jar of foreskins.

'Foreskins? How do you *get* foreskins?' he asked.

It was Mr Lennox's turn to be incredulous.

'Circumcision. How else? I pay Ewan a reasonable price for them,' he said a touch defensively.

'But what on earth are they for?'

'If ritually burnt they bring the rain,' explained Lennox. 'But, of course, up here, there's very little call for them.'

Howie could well imagine that rainmaking might be a neglected art in the western isles of Scotland. Not for the first time he considered the possibility that he was the victim of some gigantic practical joke. That some unseen hand was trying to distract him from the truth.

'Now, how can I help you?' asked Mr Lennox, politely waiting for his visitor to come to the point.

'You take the Harvest Festival photographs every autumn, don't you? The ones I saw in the Green Man?' asked Howie.

'Yes,' agreed Mr Lennox. 'It's rather humdrum work, I'm afraid. Though mind you, I do think the one about ten years ago that's slightly fogged is just about the most literal realization of "the season of mists and mellow fruitfulness" that could be contrived. Don't you?'

Howie was not prepared to discuss Mr Lennox's *art*.

'What happened to last year's picture?' he asked pointedly.

'Isn't it there with the others?' asked Mr Lennox, sounding shocked and surprised.

'No. Apparently it got broken, or in some way destroyed,' answered Howie watching Lennox closely.

'What a pity!' sighed Mr Lennox in apparently genuine regret.

'Yes!' said Howie. 'Would you have a copy of it?'

'Oh, no. I don't keep copies!' said Mr Lennox. 'I've got the negative, of course, and I could have one printed up for you if you like,' he added helpfully.

'Thank you. Yes, I should like that,' said Howie. 'I've never seen pictures quite like them before,' he added truthfully.

'No? . . . Well, perhaps they are rather special.'

Mr Lennox was clearly flattered. Assuming the conversation ended, he went to open the door to his shop with a courtly flourish. Realizing he was being 'seen on his way', Howie paused.

'There's just one more thing,' he said.

'Yes?' said Mr Lennox courteously.

'Can you remember who the girl was in the Harvest Festival last year?' asked Howie.

Mr Lennox looked at the sergeant sadly, shaking his head.

'I've taken so many, y'know,' he said.

'Could it have been Rowan Morrison?' asked Howie.

The eyes of the two men locked for an instant, then Mr Lennox looked away.

'I'm sorry,' he said. 'I get so confused with all the different names.'

He shrugged apologetically and kept looking evasively away. Howie dragged his photograph of Rowan Morrison out of his pocket and thrust it under Lennox's nose.

'This girl,' he said. 'Was it this girl?'

'It's difficult to say,' stumbled Mr Lennox. 'Why don't we consult the picture and avoid the tricks of memory?'

'It was only eight months ago, man,' Howie insisted. 'Surely you can remember whether or not . . .'

Howie was interrupted by the sound of a 'machine' outside. The first he'd heard on the island.

'There's Dr Ewan now,' said Mr Lennox urgently. 'If I were you I'd get him before he starts his lunch. He's very particular about the time of his meals.'

Mr Lennox was pointing to a man dismounting an ancient motorcycle and making his way towards his house. He was a very typical country doctor, middle-aged and greying, with his plump figure more than adequately filling his creased tweed suit. He carried the usual black bag. Howie ran out of the chemist's shop to intercept him.

'Dr Ewan?' asked Howie.

'Yes?'

'I'm from the West Highland Police, and I'd like a word with you.'

'Before lunch?' Dr Ewan was incredulous.

'Yes!' insisted Howie. '*Now*, if you don't mind.'

'But I do. Come back at two thirty.'

He put his latchkey into his front door. Howie clutched the door knocker, keeping the door closed.

'Dr Ewan, did you sign Rowan Morrison's death certificate?'

The doctor stopped in his tracks, fidgeting nervously with his black doctor's bag, which was partly open. He took two snakes out of it and allowed the creatures to curl restlessly around his wrist. Howie noted, with horror, that they were rare (in Britain) vipers.

'They get so tetchy if they're not fed regularly,' explained Dr Ewan.

'Rowan Morrison's death certificate!' repeated Howie, impatiently, keeping his distance from the apparently irritable vipers.

'Rowan Morrison?' repeated Dr Ewan. 'Yes, I did ... Why?'

'Can I see it?' asked Howie.

'You, of all people, should know that death certificates are kept in the public records office. Now, if you'll excuse me.'

The doctor opened his front door and half-disappeared inside it.

'One more thing, Doctor. *How* did Rowan die?' asked Howie.

'Quite painlessly, I'm glad to say! A simple metamorphosis.' Having said which, the doctor entered and slammed the door of his house. Mr Lennox emerged from the chemist's shop almost at once to find a furious Sergeant Howie trying to collect himself.

'I told you he was particular about mealtimes,' said Mr Lennox.

'And I am particular about truth, Mr Lennox,' said Howie with a vehemence that made him shout, realize that he was shouting, and hope that the doctor would overhear him from inside his house. He went on, 'Not half-truth or evaded truth, but insofar as it can be achieved, unadulterated truth. Metamorphosis, indeed!'

Mr Lennox managed to look sympathetic. He was used to having to calm or soothe Dr Ewan's patients when they came to order their 'specifics'.

'I just came out,' he said, 'to tell you that I'd managed to have a quick look for the negative of that Harvest Festival picture you wanted, but I couldn't seem to find it. I'll have another look, of course, after lunch.'

Mr Lennox gave Howie a guileless stare and, skipping into his shop, closed the door and pulled down the blind. Howie turned angrily away and started to walk down the High Street. It was true, he realized, that the public records office on the mainland was an obvious source to check, but the doctor's patronizing, uncaring attitude had infuriated him.

He made his way down to the harbour to use the radio on his aircraft to call Portlochlie. A few minutes later he stood on the small quay, where he had landed the day before, clutching his bag of sweets and waiting for the harbour master to find someone to row him out to his plane.

He watched a group of children running beside a stream where it emptied into the harbour nearby. The stream was carried on its last twenty-yard journey to the ocean by a shallow, stone-paved conduit. Howie noticed that the children were following something that was being carried upon the fast flowing water towards the harbour. It looked like a doll wrapped in tattered, trailing swaddling clothes.

'We carry death out of the village!' chanted the children. 'We carry death out of the village!'

As Howie was being rowed to his plane, he could see the little doll-like figure floating in the lapping tide. Its face had been crudely painted white, obliterating the features.

The boatman waited for him by the plane while he made his radio call. The harbour master had apologized to Howie that Old Sedge, for that was the boatman's name, was stone deaf. But once his uncomplicated mission had been explained to him, he smiled a perpetual toothless, but ingratiating, smile at the sergeant. All Howie's attempts to get the old doddard to go back to the quay and return when summoned were quite fruitless. He simply cackled as if Howie were relating racy anecdotes to him, so that finally the sergeant gave up, feeling secure in his privacy.

It took the usual minute or two to get the Portlochlie police station to answer his call. Eventually, having Mc-Taggart on the line, he came straight to the point. Howie spoke slowly and distinctly.

'Check at once with the Public Records Office for the Islands, Record of Deaths department. Anyone by the name of Morrison. Christian or first name, Rowan. Age about thirteen. Female. While you're about it have the last two years checked. Put it on an "Emergency Priority".'

'Wilco!' acknowledged McTaggart. 'Will you wait?'

'Affirmative!' barked Howie crisply, looking at the gaping face of Old Sedge, sitting at his oars, and wondering if by any conceivable chance he was not actually deaf. The sputtering sound of ham radio operators came through the ether onto Howie's receiver as he sat munching his sweets.

Had it not been for the fact that the air was so *very* insecure, Howie might have been tempted to gossip about Summerisle when, a few minutes later, McTaggart came back on the air.

'The answer is negative. No record of Morrison, Rowan, dying for the last *three* years. We still have her listed in "missing persons". D'you want me to report "possible homicide" to the Chief Constable?'

Howie was looking at Old Sedge as the answer came back and, it seemed to him, although Heaven knew, Summerisle was enough to make any policeman paranoid, that Sedge was showing a glimmer of interest in McTaggart's news.

'Thanks, Hugh, but no!' said Howie suddenly informal. 'On account of you never can tell if chummy is listening in, this is a brief report. Investigation has produced so far inconclusive evidence of Rowan's death but have yet to interview local Justice of the Peace. This just could be . . .'

Howie was about to say 'an elaborate practical joke', but checked himself. If that was the case, he wanted to discover the fact for himself as soon as possible, and a strange notion had just occurred to him.

'Hugh, get onto the Public Records Office again. Ask them to check between eleven to fourteen years back for the birth of Morrison, Rowan, et cetera . . .'

A surprised 'Wilco!' came back from McTaggart. 'You'll wait?' he asked.

'Affirmative,' answered Howie, now beaming at the deaf old fisherman and offering him one of his sweets. The poor old fellow had to refuse, pointing to the two well separated fangs, which were the only teeth in his head.

'Affirmative!' came McTaggart's voice a few moments later. 'She's just over thirteen, born on April the first.'

'Thank you, Hugh,' said Howie thoughtfully. 'I will probably stay over till tomorrow. Leave Rowan in the "missing persons" category on the record. Over and out.'

It was only after he was back on the quay that the sergeant realized that he'd quite forgotten to get a report from Hugh McTaggart of the minutiae of the state of crime in Portlochlie or to send his usual 'word' to Mary. Then it was borne in on him that he was investigating a perhaps quite extraordinary crime and that he'd chosen to handle it all by himself. Quite apart from the deplorable state of the moral law on the island, which could wait, he, Sergeant Neil Howie, had gotten all to himself the kind of case for which Scotland Yard was normally asked to come up from London and 'take over'. If he had been forced, by the evidence, to announce her death, under mysterious circumstances, a report to the Chief Constable would have been inevitable. As it was, she could reasonably be left as a 'missing person' since no sane person on the mainland would accept the 'word', unsubstantiated by the death certificate of a doctor who carried live vipers around in his little black bag.

However, before he went to see Lord Summerisle to confront him, as local Justice of the Peace, with all the facts and demand an autopsy of the remains interred under the little rowan tree in the graveyard ... before that, he must just check the medical meaning of the word 'metamorphosis' in the dictionary, if indeed there was a *medical* meaning. Dr Ewan was high on the list Howie was forming in his mind of those who would be accused of 'attempting

ROBIN HARDY & ANTHONY SHAFFER   111

to obstruct a police officer in the course of his duties' when
he should have discovered exactly what had happened to
Rowan Morrison.

He was ascending the High Street, looking for someone
to ask the way to the public library, when around the
corner came the same children whom he had seen following the little dead doll down to the sea.

'We carried death out of the village. We carry summer
into the village,' they all chanted.

Their leader, who was a little girl of about seven, held
aloft a young tree from which was suspended a similar doll
to the one Howie had seen in the harbour. But this one's
face was pink and new. Its china blue eyes were unblinkingly open and its little body was clothed in a clean white
robe.

Howie stopped the children by the simple expedient of
grabbing the little tree from which the doll was suspended.
The children were shrill with indignation and almost
clawed at him to get it back.

'Where's the public library?' he asked, surprised at their
hysterical protests.

Feeling curiously as if he had done something sacrilegious, he hastily returned them their little effigy and they
continued their procession without attempting to speak to
him further. But by this time, a young man, whom Howie
recognized from the bar, where he remembered him as one
of the lewdest of the willing Willow's manhandlers, came
out of a fishmonger's shop and directed him to the public
library, which turned out to be quite close to the inn itself.

The library was deserted except for an old man reading
at one of the tables. Howie hauled a huge dictionary from

one of the shelves to a study desk in a corner and leafed through until he found:

Met'a-mor'pho-sis (met'a-mor'fo-sis; -mor.fo'sis) n; pl, -phoses (sez) L., fr Gr. metamorphōsis, fr. metamorphoun to transform, fr meta beyond, over + morphe form. 1. change of form, structure, or substance, esp. by witchcraft or magic; also, the form resulting from such a change. 2. A striking alteration in appearance, character, or circumstance. 3. Med. A form of degeneration marked by conversion of certain tissue or structures into other material.

Med. obviously meant the medical definition. It wasn't particularly helpful and he searched around for a medical dictionary for further enlightenment but could find none. If he could have found it, he assumed it would have listed the diseases that could have caused such 'a form of degeneration'. He was slightly reassured to find that metamorphosis had a medical definition but the missing death certificate remained the single most disquieting aspect of the case at this time.

He sat there at the table in the library for a moment, gazing out of the window at the back of the inn, where a small, smart little cart was being unloaded of some barrels by a figure in knee breeches and a tweed hat.

Believing Dr Ewan might have perhaps deliberately misled him, Howie made the momentous decision to leave the facts he had just gleaned out of the ordinary card index in his mind but, thinking metaphorically, to open a new file, which he tentatively headed 'Disease'. Suppose that

Rowan had died of a disease, the nature of which everyone wished to conceal? Something so unpleasant that it would affect the sale of the famous apples and so ruin the prosperous little community. Howie knew that some grain could be affected in such a way that people had been sent mad by eating the bread made from it, although he was vague as to the details. Could that happen with apples? It didn't seem at all likely. But then who would have thought, in the Scotland of his youth, that grass could be smoked or mushrooms chewed to induce hallucinations? Now these things were commonplace.

He saw that the man unloading the barrels had noticed him staring into space, and was glancing at him curiously. Howie looked away.

While he was in the library, there was one other subject on which he hoped to find enlightenment. Those Harvest Festival Thanksgiving photographs worried him; there was something out of the ordinary about them. He looked up Thanksgiving first and found that while it was listed as a kind of Harvest Festival it seemed to be principally a North American celebration dating from the first harvest vouchsafed the Puritan settlers. But on Harvest Festival, as such, there was a great deal more information. Of course, even at Saint Andrew's, back in Portlochlie, they had a service every autumn, when thanks were given by the congregation for the blessings of the harvest. Produce was displayed, in baskets, on the sanctuary steps. Unlike Summerisle, no young girl in a white dress was involved, nor could Howie think what her role might be in the island service unless it was to sing a hymn. On this point, as on others, the encyclopedia soon disabused him.

In societies as disparate as ancient Egypt and pre-Columbian Incan, the Harvest Festival was strangely enough celebrated in much the same way.

A young virgin was chosen to personify the Goddess of Fertility. She was made much of by the whole community and was dressed in the clothes and adornments sacred to the deity. The whole community attended the feast in the temple where the fruit and vegetables and grain were piled high. On a platform, above the heaped produce, the child stood, worshipped by the multitude. At a predetermined point in the ceremony, the priests would seize her, fling her down, and cut her throat, allowing the blood to saturate the produce and mark the walls of the temple. The chief priest then skinned the child and, wearing the still warm skin like a mantle, led the rejoicing crowd through the streets. The priest thus represented the Goddess reborn and guaranteed another successful harvest next year.

Sergeant Howie was so sickened by the thought, however fleeting, that such a thing might have happened to Rowan, that he exclaimed out loud, 'Dear God! Even these people can't be that mad!'

The old man who had been reading at his table looked up and said, 'Sh!'

Howie was irritated to recognize him as one of those who, like the fishmonger, had danced obscenely with Willow the night before. He was incensed at the man having the nerve to shush him, a police sergeant who, in the course of his duty, was boggling out loud and justifiably so! Howie gave him a sour look and returned to his reading.

In Europe, on the other hand, the young virgin was usually burned, together with the abundant produce, in a huge sacrificial bonfire.

'*Burned!*' exclaimed Howie, remembering vividly May Morrison's momentary pain as she recalled her daughter's death 'so hot, burning . . . poor love!' Howie'd thought she was talking of a fever, and so perhaps she was, but a great deal suggested otherwise. Few things Howie could imagine would degenerate tissue faster than being burned to death. The old man had shushed him again and this time Howie banged his encyclopedia shut, but then tiptoed out, feeling a little ashamed of his gesture.

In the yard behind the Green Man, he found Alder MacGregor sharing a drink, in the sunshine, with the person Howie had watched unloading the cart.

'Afternoon, Sergeant!' twinkled Alder. 'You've had a busy day by all accounts. This is Sorrel MacKenzie, Lord Summerisle's gillie.'

The sergeant nodded politely to the gillie whom he could see, close to, was a muscular-looking female.

'Aye,' he said, 'it's been a busy day. I'd like to make an appointment to see Lord Summerisle as soon as possible . . .' He looked questioningly at the two islanders.

'The best thing,' said the gillie, 'is to just go to the castle. If he's not "mating the strains", and this is the season for that, I'm afraid, he'll see you at once!'

'Och, he's ver'approachable,' said Alder MacGregor. 'Not a bit the feudal tyrant some folks from the mainland imagine. Sorrel can take you, I'm sure. She's just been delivering the week's grog.'

'Thank you,' said Howie pleasantly. 'Was it cider in those barrels?'

'Bless you! Not just cider. His Lordship makes the best malt whisky in the islands. His sloe gin, we call it "Sorrel's Ruin"' – the gillie laughed heartily in this teasing – 'is as smooth as a lassie's thigh!'

'An illicit still, eh?' Howie couldn't help exclaiming, although he'd promised himself to let all these matters pass until the Rowan Morrison case should have been concluded.

'Did you see any money change hands last night at the bar?' asked Alder gently.

'No, why?' Howie was perplexed.

'A private still making whisky is illicit only if you sell the drink. We never do. Lord S. calls it "our rations"! Not that they've ever run out, mind you!' explained Alder.

The gillie had readied the cart for departure. Howie got up on the cushioned box beside her, shaking his head in a genial way, determined not to make any unnecessary enemies among these people.

Then she cracked the whip, and the smart grey cob in the harness took them on their way at a high-stepping trot.

'How long will it take us?' asked Howie, as they skirted the green.

'It's just up through the Mistletoe Woods. It won't take half an hour.'

But before they reached the woods they passed through miles of orchards whose different coloured blossoms denoted a variety of apples and other fruit. Howie noticed a piper wandering along the side of the road playing a tune and then, above the sound of the iron-trimmed wheels of the cart on the gravel road and the rhythm of the hooves, he could hear the mature voices of a number of women singing:

> *'Take the flame inside you, burn and burn below*
> *Fire seed and fire feed and make a baby grow.*
> *Take the flame inside you, burn and burn belay*
> *Fire seed and fire feed make the baby stay.'*

Howie strained to see the singers.

'Can't you see them?' asked the gillie, amused. 'They're big enough in all conscience.'

And then he *could* see them. Five of them, walking steadily between the rows of trees, touching every tree in their allotted row. All of them pregnant.

'Why on earth are they doing *that?*' asked Howie, who knew that agriculture was not his long suit, but had never been so aware of this deficiency before.

'Because they're in pod, of course, poor old things!' laughed the gillie expansively. 'Must be damned hot carrying all that weight around and having to touch up all those trees. I know I wouldn't care for it. Still, it's worth it at harvest time for the rest of us . . . and, of course, Lord S. absolutely showers those girls with extra beer, milk, and eggs . . .'

'You mean their touching the trees like that helps the apples grow?' Howie was incredulous.

'Well, of course it does. Well known. That and plenty of good, fresh, natural manure!'

Howie was literally speechless in the face of the gillie's irrational certainty. It reminded him of other familiar 'certainties' one heard on the mainland: 'Of course their brains are smaller than ours, that's a scientific fact.' So went the rationale of a fascist organization's anti-black man crusade. There was a flat-earth society thriving in Britain, a group impervious to the evidence of space photography or any logic. Few competed, in Howie's view, for sheer nuttiness, with the lunatic convictions of the Seventh-Day Adventists who sent hordes of American missionaries to Scotland each year to explain, door to door, that Christ was due on a certain date (worked out carefully, he'd heard, by a semiliterate in Boston). In a way he would have found all this rather endearing in its eccentricity (and Howie genuinely liked eccentrics) if it weren't so irrelevant, if it didn't, in his view, so get in the way of people having full lives in the sure knowledge of Christ's message.

The gillie had, up until this conversation, reminded Howie of one of those horsey ladies on the mainland who rented out ponies from livery stables. He'd never thought of them as a notably imaginative group but on Summerisle few of the convenient categories into which he was used to putting people seemed quite adequate.

They had entered a wood of giant oak trees whose upper branches were festooned with mistletoe. The gillie fell silent as they moved through the wood and every attempt to engage her in conversation received only monosyllables in reply. It was almost as if she was in awe of her surroundings and Howie, who could understand a communicated sense of reverence better than most, responded to her mood. He contented himself with gazing up at the great Gothic arches the trees made above them and imagined himself in some vast cathedral in a golden age, some time before the 'fall' from Eden. The thought made him smile. He could hardly think that he and the gillie made an ideal Adam and Eve, standing there by the *tree* not realizing that they were the only people on earth who would never have navels, and waiting for the serpent. His poor Sorrel–Eve wouldn't even have an apple, 'seeing they'd all been exported'. He laughed out loud at his fantasy and she shushed him sharply. It was ironic, he thought, that he, one of the few people hereabout who didn't sing and carry on half the night, was always being shushed by the islanders.

As they emerged from the wood into open ground, Howie could see that the trees made a semicircle around a bare hilltop on which stood two structures. The first was a huge circle of giant stones, which reminded Howie of pictures he'd seen of Stonehenge. Some of these rocks were capped by other, equally large, pedimental rocks. The second structure, standing further away, on an isthmus jutting out into the sea, was the castle Howie had seen from the air on his arrival. It became clear, as they got nearer the stones, that some kind of activity was taking place there. A whirling, eddying coil of smoke seemed to indicate a fire at their centre. Figures appeared to be moving in the smoke that drifted towards them on a wind that also bore fragments of music and singing. Gradually, the path led them around the great mound of stones and Howie could see quite plainly what was happening.

A blonde woman stood under the main pedimental rock in a diaphanous white robe, the sun, behind her, etching the silhouette of her body through the material. Her long hair blew gently in the wind. With a start of surprise

Howie recognized Miss Rose. But the surprise was as nothing in comparison to what he felt when he saw her girls, palely, unself-consciously naked, as they stood in a circle, within, and concentric to, the stones. In the very centre of their circle a bonfire blazed and the fire itself seemed the focus of Miss Rose's and the girls' attention. Lying languidly on the grass nearby, three musicians played a tune and watched Miss Rose's pupils sing and dance, in an attempted unison that was endearingly ragged and spontaneous. The tune, oddly enough, was *exactly* the same as the lone piper had played for the women 'in pod', back in the orchards.

> '*Take the flame inside you, burn and burn belong*
> *Fire seed and fire feed and make the baby strong.*
>
> *Take the flame inside you, burn and burn belie*
> *Fire seed and fire feed make the baby cry.*
>
> *Take the flame inside you, burn and burn begin*
> *Fire seed and fire feed and make the baby King.*'

The rhythm of their dance was by now frenetic, and each girl, in turn, detached herself and leapt over the bonfire. Howie craned his neck to watch them, for the cart, by now, was past the stones and heading for the castle.

Howie knew that here was a sight that would have got to the 'old Adam' in most men, and he was no exception. The sweet, soft rhythm of the girls' childish breasts as they danced, the tantalizing glimpses of the little fleecy fruit between their legs as they leaped the fire – these were the most sexually arousing images he'd ever seen. But with the stiffening of his flesh there came out into the open that old toad, fear. It was as if in seeing the girls as he saw them now, he had, at last, seen enough of the Summerisle jigsaw puzzle put together to glimpse the entire picture. Here, he realized, was not simply an island where an unusual number of inbred, dotty Scots were going eccentrically to seed in their own sweet way. Here, if you started to put the disparate experiences he had undergone together – the quasi-religious nonsense in the school, the sexual excesses at the inn and on the green, the ruined church – put all these things together with the scene he now witnessed, and he could sense the cohesive pattern of a totally alien society. The canvas that was emerging showed him a Summerisle as foreign to him as India. 'The fearful hand or eye' that could have wrought such a strange community from the familiar blood and bone of his fellow Scots frightened Howie and turned the girls' wild dance into a strange signal of foreboding. It also occurred to Howie, as he tried to drag his gaze away from the lovely dancing children, that the scene seemed to make one of his theories about Rowan's disappearance slightly less likely. Why should a people so totally free in things sexual produce a kidnapper with a purely *sexual* motive? Of course, he realized that there might exist some perverted sex-oriented ceremony beyond his imagining. Almost anything started to seem possible on Summerisle. But he now doubted that this was the cause of her disappearance. The idea that she might have died from some cause the islanders did not wish to be known, such as an epidemic or fruit poisoning, seemed a more tenable theory. Reluctantly he looked to the route ahead of him. He was pleased that his reluctance was due now more to a sadness at leaving the extraordinary beauty and innocence of the scene, than to unrequited lust.

'So you're another that prefers young lamb to mutton,' said the gillie salaciously. Noticing Howie's angry glance, she added, 'Oh, I don't blame you. Feel exactly the same way myself. Bless their little, dimpled butts.'

Howie was anxious to avoid either acrimony or lewd conversation with the gillie but determined to brief himself, as well as he could, for the upcoming interview with Lord Summerisle, which he knew could be vital to the solution of the Rowan Morrison case. He therefore tried to use the time left them, as they approached the impressive Scottish baronial pile ahead, to draw the gillie out in amiable conversation.

'What's it like working for Lord Summerisle?' he asked.

'Well, he's moody, like most men. But a wonderful leader for the community. No detail too small for him to take an interest. Communicates well with everyone, unlike that Rose, the schoolteacher.' She hesitated. 'Don't know if you've met her, but she's a preachy bitch!'

'Oh, but I have. That was exactly my expression!' laughed Howie guilefully. The gillie seemed pleased to have a fellow critic of Miss Rose.

'Of course it doesn't do to *say* so. She and Lord S. . . . are very close. Or she wouldn't have got the job she has. I mean *I* prefer the outdoor life but *I'm* quite as qualified as Rose.'

Howie felt at home with this kind of conversation. In talk like this an astute policeman could usually discover far more than in formal interrogation. The trouble was that you needed enough time and the right circumstances, and he'd had little of either since he'd been on the island.

'It's obvious to me that you're an educated woman. Where did you "school" on the mainland?' he asked.

'Funny thing! I've no desire to go there. In fact, I've never been. But, of course, like Rose, I took a correspondence course with Saint Andrew's University. Lord Summerisle's late father paid for everything,' said Sorrel, not without a certain pride.

'Really, what subjects did you take?' asked Howie politely.

'Forestry, and I have a veterinary diploma of course. While I'm Lord S.'s official gillie, the stalking on Summerisle has never been very good. Too much agriculture. Not saying, mind you, that Lord S. isn't keen as mustard on the sport. When he can find time. You'll see a good few splendid stags he bagged on the walls in the castle.'

The stalking and killing of stags had, Howie knew, an arcane language all its own.

'What did Miss Rose study?' asked Howie, digging a little further.

'Comparative theology. And, I believe, pre-medieval music! It's a bit artsy-craftsy for my taste,' said the gillie complacently.

They had passed through an enormous stone gateway with a raised portcullis. Above the pediment was a coat of arms topped by Lord Summerisle's baronial coronet. A huge courtyard followed, flanked by battlements that looked out to sea. The sun was slowly sinking towards the horizon.

'Well, here you are,' said the gillie, stopping by a fine

studded oak door flanked on either side by two rampant, stone staghounds and set into the clifflike side of the towering castle.

'I have to go back in about forty minutes. How's that for you?'

'I'll be ready,' said Howie quite gratefully, feeling that she, alone of the people he'd met, so far, was genuinely friendly towards him.

## CHAPTER VI

# Evening –
# the 30th of April

HE ASCENDED THE STONE STAIRS BETWEEN THE RAMP-
ant beasts and pulled the large, wrought-iron bell ringer. A
muffled clanging came to him from faraway inside the
castle. While he waited, he braced himself for the encounter with Lord Summerisle. He sorted through the things he
knew about the man.

Symbolic leader of the community by virtue of social
class and wealth.

Owner of the island, which, of course, didn't mean he,
in any sense, owned Her Britannic Majesty's subjects who
lived there under her Scottish law. However, he employed
everyone on the island and as far as their land or houses
were concerned they held these as his tenants.

He was Justice of the Peace, an office he held from the
Crown, although, in practice, the appointment was made
by the office of the Secretary of State for Scotland, in
Edinburgh. Although the secretary was a cabinet member
of the elected government in London, Lord Summerisle
had remained their appointee on the island under alternate
socialist and conservative administrations. He must have
some solid influence somewhere on the mainland.

He had had the right to be elected from among the Scottish peers to sit in the House of Lords in the British Parliament but Howie, a convinced socialist, who followed these things, knew that he had never been so elected. Perhaps the giving of his vote to secure some *other* Scottish peer a seat had ensured his continuing in his post as local magistrate.

Howie rang the bell again, twice. Not that he was getting impatient, for it was a relief to have time to prepare himself. It was just that, in so huge a pile, he couldn't be sure anyone had heard him. He wondered if there was a 'Mistress of the House'.

Lord Summerisle's name had been linked with Miss Rose but there was, as far as Howie knew, no Lady Summerisle. The womenfolk spoke of him with a friendly respect tinged with awe. The worst that had been said of him was that he was sometimes moody. Howie was ready for a testing encounter when the door was flung open by a rather breathless, kilted young man.

'I'm so sorry to have kept you waiting, sir,' he said, 'but we've had mice in the steam organ and the piano tuner and I were down in the boiler room. It's almost a quarter of a mile away. Lord Summerisle is expecting you.'

'Expecting me?' Howie was surprised.

'That's what His Lordship said, sir,' confirmed the man.

Interviewing the servants was a frequent necessity in crimes involving the aristocracy, Howie knew. Always get their names right from the start. The Police College had been most specific on the subject.

'I'm Broom, sir. Lord Summerisle's piper. It's the butler's

day off,' said Broom helpfully, as if he read Howie's thoughts.

As he followed Broom down a labyrinthine passage, Howie reflected bitterly what an unfair advantage Lord Summerisle had over any ordinary citizen who was due to be interviewed by the police. A man who could only be approached via his personal gillie and his very own bag-piper, living in a castle large enough to rehouse half a Glasgow slum. It was right, he thought, that people like Lord Summerisle should be taxed 'till the pips squeaked'. Howie didn't really feel vindictive towards the rich but he had, in his work, seen too much grinding poverty not to resent the social injustice of too much inherited wealth.

They had now reached the great hall of the castle and Broom left him at this point, quietly closing the doors behind him.

The hall was hung with the tattered banners of long forgotten regiments, and magnificent stacks of antlers. Its floor was flagged with stone and largely covered with deerskin and sealskin rugs. At one end of the hall stood a huge organ whose silvered pipes climbed some twenty feet, halfway to the vaulted ceiling. Howie presumed it to be that steam organ that was said to be suffering from a plague of mice.

A carved stone fireplace into which a carthorse could have walked, without bending its head, was surrounded by an assortment of ear-warming armchairs and the back half of an enclosed carriage-sleigh. Across the quarter-acre area of the rest of the room were set a number of tables, a grand piano, and a large gilded harp.

Howie walked around the silent, empty room, acutely aware that his shoes were squeaking. A merciful clock chimed the quarter hour as he gazed up at the stern, equine features of Lord Summerisle's ancestors and then, finding himself at a latticed window, saw again in the distance the stones, where the young girls of Miss Rose's class were still leaping the bonfire and dancing around.

'Good afternoon, Sergeant Howie. I trust the sight of the young people refreshes you,' said Lord Summerisle's voice. Howie was happy to be in a position to recognize it and so turned calmly and challengingly to say, 'No, My Lord, it does not refresh me.'

'I'm sorry,' said Lord Summerisle, as if genuinely saddened. 'One should always be open to the regenerative influences.' He had been sitting concealed in the sleigh and now stood.

Howie studied Lord Summerisle closely. Here was the 'hand and eye' that had shaped the personal fiefdom of Summerisle. He was dressed in a suit so tweedy that it looked as if moss might have taken to growing on it. Howie recalled his handsome, somewhat swarthy features and his shock of carelessly groomed hair. But now, close to the man, he was impressed by his eyes. They were a deep brown and had an adamantine directness of gaze that slightly disconcerted Howie. He looked down at the floor for an instant and found himself staring at Lord Summerisle's shoes. They were American sneakers of exactly the same make as those worn by the 'peeping jogger' back on the mainland. There was nothing so extraordinary in that, Howie realized, for the shoe shops were full of them.

'Your piper said you were expecting me. How was that?'

asked Howie warily, looking back at Lord Summerisle and measuring his height against the remembered tallness of the jogger in Portlochlie.

'It had to be only a matter of time before you came here,' answered Lord Summerisle gently. 'I hear you're looking for a missing child.'

'I've found her!' said Howie sharply, and he put the sneakers out of his mind as being quite ridiculously irrelevant.

'Good!' said Lord Summerisle as if that was that.

'In her grave!' said Howie watching Summerisle's face carefully. 'I want your permission, as a Justice of the Peace, to exhume her body and have it removed to the mainland for a pathologist's report.'

'You suspect "foul play"?' Lord Summerisle seemed slightly amused.

'Yes. Murder and conspiracy to murder,' retorted Howie.

'In that case, you must go ahead,' said His Lordship matter-of-factly.

'Your Lordship doesn't seem very concerned.' Howie was both annoyed and curious about this.

'I'm confident your suspicions are wrong,' said Lord Summerisle. 'We don't commit murder here. We're a deeply religious people.'

'Religious!' expostulated Howie. 'With ruined churches and no priests?'

Lord Summerisle went to the piano and picked out, with two fingers, the air that the girls had been singing.

'They do so enjoy their divinity lessons,' he said, gazing out the window with an affectionate smile.

'But they're naked!' cried Howie.

'Naturally!' said Lord Summerisle reasonably. 'It's much too dangerous to leap through a fire with your clothes on.'

'What kind of religion can they possibly be learning, jumping over bonfires naked?' demanded Howie.

'Parthenogenesis!' said Lord Summerisle ringing the word out in his beautiful voice. 'Literally, as Miss Rose would doubtless explain, in her assiduous way – reproduction without sexual union.'

'What nonsense is this?' shouted Howie, maddened by this smug Lord of the Manor telling *him*, Neil Howie, about religion, of all things. 'You've got fake biology, fake religion! Sir, have these children never heard of Jesus?'

'Himself the son of a virgin impregnated, I believe, by a ghost,' said Lord Summerisle very quietly, but distinctly.

Howie not only looked outraged, but was, in fact dumbfounded. Lord Summerisle motioned him to a chair.

'Do sit down!' he said to the sergeant. 'Shocks are so much better absorbed with the knees bent,' and he smiled at Howie's bewildered face. 'Oh yes, Sergeant,' said Lord Summerisle. 'Even Christians believe in parthenogenesis. As for those children out there – they're leaping through the flames in the hope that the god of the fire may make them fruitful. And really, you know, you can hardly blame them. After all, what girl would not prefer the child of a god to that of some acne-scarred artisan?'

'And you encourage all this . . . this rubbish, My Lord?' asked Howie in half a mind not to listen any further. But his training was slowly reasserting itself. 'To listen is to learn' is one of the first rules of detection. Let a man talk enough, if he has a will to, and he may well end up by hanging himself!

'It's most important,' Lord Summerisle was saying, 'that each new generation born on Summerisle be made aware that here the old gods aren't dead.'

'But what of the true God to whose glory monasteries and churches have been built on these islands over the centuries? What of Him?' Howie could not help asking.

'Oh, He's dead all right.' Lord Summerisle said it thoughtfully, but with conviction. 'And He can't complain. He had his chance and, in modern parlance, blew it!'

'What!!!' Howie got to his feet scandalized. He knew, however, that he must not let his personal feelings about God interfere with this vital interview. He strongly suspected the laird of deliberately baiting him.

'How?' Lord Summerisle was saying. 'That's the question you should be asking me, Sergeant. "How?" not "What?"'

Mutely the sergeant told himself, 'Set him talking. Don't get angry! And sort it all out in your own mind later.' He knew (all the evidence pointed to it) that he faced, in Lord Summerisle, an evil of the subtlest kind. Evil that was camouflaged in the plausible personality of a man of education and intellect, of imagination and flair. Howie disliked Lord Summerisle instinctively but he was pleased to feel that his detachment was returning.

'All right, My Lord,' he said aloud, 'how?'

'The people,' said Lord Summerisle, 'were persuaded that your God, the God of the Christians, the Jews, and the Moslems, had become less powerful than the old gods who still lived on in the woods and the water and the fire and the stone. That's *how*!'

'After sixteen hundred years? You're joking!' laughed Howie.

For the first time in their interview Lord Summerisle looked angry. Howie decided to humour him.

'Who did it then? Who persuaded them?' he asked dutifully.

'My great-grandfather, actually,' said Lord Summerisle. 'It wasn't all that difficult. The tradition of the arcane and the mysterious cleaves to the people of this island with a tenacity that makes it seem an inherent and inalienable possession. They're Celts after all!'

'So they are!' said Howie ironically. 'But I'm still waiting for you to tell me *how*!'

'It's very simple,' said Lord Summerisle soothingly. 'In the last century the islanders were starving. Many were emigrating to Canada and Australia. Fishing and sheep brought in a marginal income, much as it does today on our neighbouring islands, but mullet and mutton, so to speak, are hardly the counters of prosperity. Dutifully, every Sunday, the people – Baptist and Catholic, Presbyterian and Free Kirk – bowed as low as their respective religions permitted to the Christian God and prayed for prosperity. But inevitably none appeared. In due course they came to realize that their reward was to be either in the colonies or, as the various priests indicated in a rare moment of agreement, in heaven. Then in 1868 my great-grandfather bought this barren island and set about changing things. He was a distinguished Victorian scientist, agronomist, and free thinker – look at his face. How formidably benevolent he seems, essentially the face of a man incredulous of all human good!'

Lord Summerisle indicated a large oil painting hanging, in the place of honour, above the fireplace. Howie rose and looked at the picture with distaste. It showed a haughty Victorian figure of Lord Summerisle's stature, but with a face almost entirely obscured by moustache, eyebrows, and whiskers.

'You are very cynical, My Lord!' was all Howie could find to say.

'I simply know my family, Sergeant!' said Lord Summerisle. 'But let me *show* you what he did.'

He steered the sergeant away from the picture and towards a door at the far end of the room. Together they marched through a huge dining room and out onto a terraced garden facing the sea.

'What had attracted my great-grandfather to the island, apart from the profuse source of wiry labour that it promised, was the unique combination of volcanic soil and the warm Gulf Stream that surrounded it.' He paused for Howie to take in the fecund scene. Palm trees nodded in the breeze, and a magnolia was in full bloom.

Twenty feet away, enclosing the garden, was the castle's crenellated, defensive wall above which Howie could see skuas flying, hovering over the unseen ocean beyond. Howie paused, out of habit, to identify the birds. He could see three different kinds of skua: a pomerine, an arctic, and a great, and while none of them was rare in the Hebrides, he had seldom seen them all together before.

'The only *Stercorariidae* that would seem to be missing from our ramparts today is a Buffon's skua. But you hardly ever get them here in the spring. I think they nest up in Spitsbergen, off Norway,' said Lord Summerisle.

Howie looked, now, at the laird with interest and respect. He knew that the island was a bird sanctuary, like Saint Kilda to the east, but His Lordship clearly 'knew his birds', although it was typically pompous of him to refer to skua by their Latin family name.

'Am I wasting your time talking for a moment about birds?' Lord Summerisle asked Howie, who smiled, certain it would make little difference if he were.

'No, My Lord. Birds are my main hobby. Watching them, you know.'

Lord Summerisle looked at the sergeant speculatively, as if trying to make his mind up about something.

'Sergeant Howie. Can you keep a secret?' he asked.

'If it's not against the law, I'm quite certain I can,' said Howie, smiling at the schoolboyish mysteriousness of the peer.

'Then come and have a look over the parapet.'

Lord Summerisle led the way to the crenellated wall and together they looked down the sheer cliff-face at the pounding sea below. Half a dozen different families of seabirds were present nesting, feeding, preening, and flying in huge numbers from the gigantic cliffs that were the natural foundations of the castle.

Howie could see scoter ducks, gulls, puffins, storm petrels, and gannets, and then his keen eye saw something that made him, for the first time in many years, feel tears coming to his eyes. Diving from a rocky promontory at sea level were some large flightless birds. Howie had seen this bird before – stuffed, never alive, its back a greeny black, its bill not dissimilar to that of a puffin only longer and

black, a white patch near the eye and white breast plum-
age. It used its smallish, prehensile wings as paddles in the
water. Howie knew he was looking at a little colony of
great auks, a species that, it was believed, man had made
extinct in the mid-nineteenth century because the great
auks, unable to fly, were so easy to club to death from a
boat.

'Your secret will be safe with me, My Lord,' Howie said
in a voice made a little taut with emotion. God sometimes
chose the most mysterious vessels for His Divine will, he
thought. Any family that could have guarded such a secret
for four generations received at least some of Howie's
respect. But he could not help the somewhat ungenerous
reflection that the Lord Summerisles and the great auks of
this world had a certain amount in common. Evolution
was against them.

'My great-grandfather *forbade* any mention that we still
had 'em here, knowing the last one anywhere else was
killed on Eldey Island off Iceland on June 4th, 1844,' said
Lord Summerisle. 'Nowadays we'd call him a conservation-
ist. But that wasn't at all his view of himself. He saw
himself as a scientist first and foremost. It was a crime
against science for any creature, part of the earth's great
inheritance, to be made extinct. It was equally a crime for
this island to remain unfruitful when the scientific means
to cultivate it were to hand.'

Lord Summerisle led the way across the terraced garden
to a conservatory, equipped as a laboratory might be in a
horticultural research station.

'You see, Sergeant,' continued Lord Summerisle, 'his

experiments had led him to believe that it was possible to induce here the successful growth of certain new strains of fruit that he had developed.'

Howie gazed around at a row of glass cases containing here a growing graft, there a shrunken apple, apricot, or pear, with its history plainly marked beside it. Clearly this was a kind of museum dedicated to Lord Summerisle's family's achievement.

'. . . And so you see,' Lord Summerisle was saying, 'with typical mid-Victorian zeal, my great-grandfather set to work. But of course, almost immediately, he met opposition from the fundamentalist ministers, who threw tons of his artificial fertilizer into the habour on the grounds that if God had meant us to use it, He'd have provided it. My great-grandfather took exactly the same view of ministers, and realized he had to find a way to be rid of them. The best method of accomplishing this, it seemed to him, was to rouse the people, by giving them back their joyous old deities; so he encouraged, as it were, a retreat down memory lane; backwards from Christianity, through the Ages of Reason and Belief to the Age of Mysticism.'

'And didn't the joyous old deities used to require people to be burnt to death with piles of vegetables and fruit?' asked Howie.

'The Celtic imagination has much to answer for. Heard of that dreadful old preacher Knox inveighing against "the monstrous regiment of women"? Quite unchristian I'd have thought!' said Lord Summerisle.

'I've read my country's history and my bible, thank you, Lord Summerisle,' said Howie a little haughtily. 'Even the *simple* folks like me get a proper education on the mainland these days. I would have thought that a healthy dose of the socialism that helped educate me would have done these islanders better than all the mumbo-jumbo your great-grandfather gave them . . .'

'Really?' rejoined Lord Summerisle. 'It's done damn little for our neighbouring islands . . . Or hadn't you noticed?'

'You're right there, Lord Summerisle,' Howie acknowledged bitterly. 'The landlord system is far too tenacious. Anyway, I oughtn't to be talking politics, in uniform, as you know. I just can't imagine a sane body of men and women believing in a whole ridiculous family of gods . . .'

'What about the whole subcontinent of India?' asked Lord Summerisle. 'The Hindus – that's what they believe. Dismiss them all as insane, would you?'

Howie, who was basically as chauvinistic as any other Scot, was not a bit surprised at anything the Indians might believe.

'Your great-grandfather's tenants were *Scots*, My Lord!' he said, as if there ought to be nothing further to say on the matter.

'And I refer you again, sir, to the spiritual vision of the Celts,' said Lord Summerisle. 'No, these islanders needed little urging. My great-grandfather simply told them about the stones – how they, in fact, formed an ancient temple, and that he, the Lord of the Manor, would make a sacrifice there every day to their old gods and goddesses, particularly those of Fertility and Fruitfulness, and that as a result of this worship . . .'

Lord Summerisle sounded more and more as if he were talking from a pulpit. His gestures were sweeping as if he were addressing his islanders en masse as Howie had no doubt he often did.

'. . . The barren island would burgeon and bring forth fruit in great abundance. For an atheist, Great-grandfather had a singularly biblical turn of phrase, don't you think?'

'Again, if you say so, sir,' said Sergeant Howie, in a chilly voice, tired of all this patronizing talk about this toffee-nosed lord's exploiting, robber-baron family. But he realized that he had spoken insolently and knew that he shouldn't allow his feelings of 'class-anger' to get the better of him. But if Lord Summerisle had noticed Howie's rudeness he didn't show it, but went right on explaining how the islanders had come under his family's sway.

'Well, of course, at first, people worked for him because he fed and clothed them. Then naturally, when all the trees started fruiting, it became a different story. The ministers told the people to withdraw their labour as they were "trucking with the devil". My great-grandfather told the people that if they did so, he would leave, and the island would become as barren again as all the others. In this way, the old gods appear to have defeated the Christian God, and the ministers fled the island never to return,' Summerisle concluded triumphantly.

'But how did the trees come to fruit, when so many other attempts to grow things on these islands have failed? Don't tell me your great-grandfather really worshipped the Gods of Fertility?' Howie almost spat out the phrase.

'Come, come, Sergeant,' said Lord Summerisle patiently. 'As I've already told you, he worshipped science. What he did, of course, was to develop new cultivars of hardy fruits to suit local conditions. Out here we have his original experimental orchard. Much developed, of course. Come and have a look.'

Lord Summerisle led Sergeant Howie out of the conservatory into what was clearly an experimental orchard, for there were tags and labels on all the trees.

Lord Summerisle was about to pontificate further upon the wonders of his family's achievements in the field of horticulture when at last he really seemed to notice, and take in, Sergeant Howie's mutinous, offended expression.

'My dear Sergeant Howie,' said Lord Summerisle, 'I am afraid I have been guilty of preaching again. I can see it in your face. Guilty of going on about my favourite hobby-horse, if you'll forgive the allusion?'

Howie was almost as put out by a contrite Lord Summerisle as he had been by the peer in the full flood of his proselytizing fervour. He was annoyed that Lord Summerisle had told him only exactly what he *wished* to impart! Howie had, so far, had little chance to steer the conversation in any of the other directions that might help his investigation. Now was his chance, and he realized it could only help if he took it tactfully.

'It is I, My Lord, who should, perhaps, apologize for being rather prickly on the subject of religion,' said Howie gracefully, and he intended to go on and probe the possibility of a fruit-related disease being involved in Rowan's death, but Lord Summerisle interrupted him.

'You know *why*, of course?' he asked suddenly.

'Why what, My Lord?' Howie was confused.

'Why I was so anxious to have the pleasure of a friendly chat with you about religion, Sergeant?'

'*No.*'

'Because Pinky Stuart-MacEwan had told me something about you. About your background.'

'Pinky . . .? You mean General Sir Pauncefoot Stuart-McEwan?'

'Exactly, Sergeant. Our Chief Constable, your boss as well as mine, in my capacity of Justice of the Peace, y'know!' Lord Summerisle gave a matey laugh, as if this made the sergeant and him just a couple of colleagues under the skin.

'I can tell you, in the strictest confidence, he thinks the world of you,' said Lord Summerisle. '"A man of total integrity and devotion. Helped by the fact that the chap's a devout Christian. An officer who should go straight to the top!" I'm paraphrasing what he said, of course, but that was the gist of it.'

Howie had been, naturally, quite overcome by this relayed accolade from his superior. His face reddened.

'Good to see ourselves as others see us!' said Lord Summerisle kindly. 'So you can well understand that, when I heard you were on the island, I was looking forward to this little "ecumenical confab" of ours. No fun talking about religion to an agnostic, which is what all too many mainlanders are today. An American, Richard Nixon, once said, "I don't care what religion a man has, as long as he's got a religion."'

'About the apples!' blurted out Howie, desperate to change the subject.

'The apples?' It was Lord Summerisle's turn to be confused.

'I am most interested in your apples. I'd be so grateful if you could . . .' he managed a conspiratorial laugh of his own '. . . let me in on a few of the secrets. We keep a small garden back at . . .' His sentence was once again cut short by his host's eagerness to take up this welcome subject.

'Sergeant Howie, nothing could give me greater pleasure. How very *kind* of you to take such an interest. It'll mean visiting the ice house, I'm afraid, so be prepared to shiver a bit after this nice warm day . . .'

So, chattering ceaselessly on, Lord Summerisle took Sergeant Howie through the experimental orchard to a sunken ice house which was set incongruously in the middle of a lavish subtropical garden. They descended some steps and Lord Summerisle unlocked the heavy door and swung it open.

Inside the chill was considerable, but there was a marked absence of damp. Howie had to wait in the dark till Lord Summerisle had lit some pressure oil lamps, and then he could see that the whole place was lined with neat stacks of racks containing apples and other fruits.

'How do you keep it at this temperature, My Lord?' he asked, wondering how this could be achieved without electricity.

'In winter, we get plenty of ice from the pools high on the hills in the eastern part of the island. We gather it, as our ancestors did, wrap it in straw, and stack it behind those metal panels against the summer months. My great-grandfather built this place before there was any electricity in the Highlands at all. People used their ingenuity in those days. They will again. Look how the sun has been rediscovered and brought back into fashion as a source of energy . . .'

Sergeant Howie was already eyeing a tray of brownish

apples and wondering how, if one of these breeds of fruit was proving to be poisonous, he would ever be able to tell which it was, let alone get hold of it and test it. On what, for instance? The gillie's horse? Somebody's tame rabbit? Ridiculous, of course. Once identified, he must get it back to the mainland for expert analysis. Always supposing there was anything at all in this rather wild theory of his. But it was a theory about Rowan's death and lack of a death certificate that, at least, provided a motive. The fruit of this island was clearly a matter of life and death to the entire community.

Lord Summerisle had finished lighting a number of lamps and joined the sergeant by the brownish apples, fingering one and speaking of it with affection.

'You are looking, Sergeant, at the great-grandparents of the Summerisle Famous apple. Ashmead's Kernel here on my left was originally raised by a Dr Ashmead of Gloucester in the year 1710. As you can see, it is a grey-brown russet, which is not particularly attractive in appearance but was originally selected on account of its age and excellent flavour, superior, many have judged, to the famous Cox's Orange pippin. Here, see for yourself.'

Taking a curiously shaped (long handled, short, stubby bladed) knife from his pocket, Lord Summerisle split the apple deftly into two segments, handing one to Howie who suddenly, ridiculously, he realized, hesitated to eat it. But Lord Summerisle bit into the segment left in his own hand, and Howie immediately followed suit.

'Very sweet!' was Howie's considered comment.

'As I say,' agreed Lord Summerisle, 'it has a fine flavour but its appearance is somewhat against it and it has a regrettable tendency to shrink in refrigeration. Now let's look over here . . .'

Lord Summerisle was a professional in his element and Howie found a liking for him, in this capacity, that he could never accord him in his role as semifeudal aristocrat, forever justifying his bountifulness to the people of Summerisle. Meanwhile, the apple expert was holding forth:

'In order to combat the refrigeration problem Great-grandfather crossed it with Saint Athelstan's pippin, an orange, flushed russet of great sturdiness and quite phenomenal shelf life, discovered about 1830 by a Mr Talmadge of Saint Ives in Cornwall. Receptivity to the beneficial effects of the Gulf Stream, combined with a high resistance to saltwater air currents, was bred in at this stage.'

As Lord Summerisle pointed out the contours of this apple and explained its manifest uniqueness, Howie experienced that pleasant shock that comes from suddenly seeing in nature new horizons, undreamed-of patterns, that, like the world of atoms and particles, are all around us, but which we are all too seldom privileged to see because we know not either *where* or *how* to look.

'Note,' Lord Summerisle was saying, as if he were Lord Clark surveying a Botticelli for a television audience, 'the large, partly open eye with convergent to erect sepals set in a wide, shallow, unusually even basin. Extraordinary, isn't it?'

All this to describe just the *top* of an apple. Lord Summerisle went on talking about the family trees of his apples as if he were discussing a genealogy from the *Almanach de Gotha* or *Debrett's Peerage and Baronetage*. Howie, who would have been bored or resentful had the dynasty been of dukes or earls, found the fact that it was the pedigree of an apple quite fascinating.

'I suppose the introduction of all these new *strains* is done by grafting?' he asked.

'It's one method but when a notable marriage is to be consummated between two recognized apples we preside over the mating ourselves. We call it "mating the strains". It is like the "bedding" of a young couple after a wedding. Great fun but also a moving, tender moment. I have a special glasshouse for it. Two absolutely faultless trees of each species are housed in the glasshouse. We see that there is no insect whatever enclosed with the bridal pair. Those sexy old bees can be fatal, covered with illegitimate pollen as they are. Because it is one of the few little privileges that I like to preserve, I, myself, take a very fine camel-hair paintbrush, scoop up the pollen from a single, perfect blossom of one tree, and deposit it on the virgin stamen of a single perfect blossom of the other tree. Then we pray.'

'That reminds me of a little poem we used to learn in school,' said Howie, quite lost for a moment in the minu-tiae of God's creation:

> 'Who hammered,
> Who wrought you?
> From iron silver vapour
> God was my maker.'

'Exactly!' agreed Lord Summerisle. 'As the snowflake, so the apple. *Which* god is little more than *semantics*! That obstacle to ecumenism.'

While he had been talking, Lord Summerisle split the Saint Athelstan's pippin in his hand with his special knife. Howie was on the point of taking a segment and tasting it, when Lord Summerisle simply took it back from the sergeant's hand and threw both segments into a shallow box of sawdust on the floor.

This action yanked Sergeant Howie back into a state of extreme alertness. There must be something wrong with Saint Athelstan's pippin, just conceivably something serious.

'Don't bother to taste it,' he'd said, 'it's quite unremarkable. Unlike those splendid Pauncefoot Pearmains, which you can see in that tray over there, and which were brought in at the last mating in order to correct appearance. My father called the apple for old, or rather young Pinky, as he was then. It was bred when he and I were at school together . . .'

A sudden disturbing thought occurred to Sergeant Howie. Could the Chief Constable know this incredible island intimately and have never interfered because of 'the old school tie'?

'Has the Chief Constable ever been here, My Lord?' asked Howie, almost sharply.

'To my great sorrow, no. You may not have heard, but he suffers most dreadfully from hay fever. The pollen count, as you can well imagine, is quite astronomical here. My father had to advise against it. And he's been wise enough never to risk it. Now I mustn't keep you in suspense any longer. I threw that Saint Athelstan's pippin away because I wanted you to keep your palate clear for this fella!' Lord Summerisle flourished an apple he had just taken from a tray. 'The renowned Summerisle Famous.'

As Lord Summerisle split the apple and passed him a segment, Howie was half-convinced that the Saint Athelstan's pippin was the problem apple, the one he must retrieve from the sawdust bin, and he felt fairly confident as he bit into the Summerisle Famous. It was quite literally the most delicious apple he'd tasted . . . since the last time his mother had bought some of the same at the local fruiterer in Portlochlie and complained about their outrageous price.

'Extraordinary, My Lord! Naturally, I've tasted them before,' said Howie.

'Yes, of course you have,' said Lord Summerisle, caressing the famous apple like a lover. 'Creamy white flesh, firm, full-flushed, blood-red, bloomed skin with a truly noble, sweet, vinous flavour. The lifework of three generations of my forebears, but it's been worth it for on this we base our prosperity.'

'Your father's too?' interjected Howie, embarrassed by the extravagance of Lord Summerisle's language.

'Oh, indeed. This beauty was only perfected just before his death. He produced some other marvellous fruit as well. Expanding our base, as it were. There's Star of Summerisle, a remarkably heady pear. You can make a smoothly potent pear brandy from it. He produced the Flame of Summerisle, an extremely juicy, slightly subacid apricot of superb colour . . . but you must be getting very chilly, Sergeant.'

Lord Summerisle was turning down the lamps in preparation for leaving the ice house.

'Perhaps you'll open the door for me, Howie,' he said as darkness was descending on them.

'Gladly,' responded Howie, surreptitiously dipping into the sawdust box and retrieving the sliced Saint Athelstan's pippin on his way to the door. He made sure that Lord Summerisle, as he turned down the last of the lamps, had his back to him and certainly didn't notice.

By the time they found themselves outside in the subtropical garden again, Howie had pocketed the Saint Athelstan's pippin segment and was guiding Lord Summerisle back onto the subject of religion, satisfied that he probably had the evidence he required to prove, one way or the other, his theory about the poisonous apple. Conclusive proof would probably have to come from a postmortem, if that were not already too late, due to the length of time Rowan's body appeared to have been in the ground.

'Your grandfather and your father, did they continue to encourage the religious ... er ... charades ... of your great-grandfather, sir?' asked Howie, wondering at what point, if ever, this curious family had begun to believe in their own myths.

'My grandfather became fascinated by the old ways, if that's what you mean,' said Lord Summerisle. 'But my father went further. What my great-grandfather had started out of expedience, he continued because he truly believed it was far more spiritually nourishing than the life-denying God-terror of the kirk. And I might say, Sergeant, he brought me up the same way – to love the music and the drama and the rituals of the old pantheism, and to love nature, and to fear it, and rely on it, and appease it where necessary. He brought me up to . . .'

'To be a pagan!' interrupted Howie, wishing to cut short this little orgy of self-dramatization.

There was a silence at last, a measurable silence, between the two men as they surveyed each other. Each sizing up where the advantage now might lie in continuing the interview and both deciding that it was probably time to retire from the 'field' and take stock. In reply to Howie's accusation that Lord Summerisle was a pagan, the latter smiled ironically and corrected the sergeant gently enough.

'A heathen, conceivably,' he said, 'but not, I hope, an unenlightened one.'

'I'm only interested in the law, Lord Summerisle, and I must remind you, sir, that you are still the subject of a Christian country. Now may I have permission to exhume the body of Rowan Morrison?'

'I was under the impression I had already given it to you,' said Lord Summerisle, his noble smile a little tighter and steelier than usual.

Howie found himself back in the courtyard where the gillie and the cart awaited him in the huge shadow thrown by the castle.

Lord Summerisle extended his hand to Howie once the sergeant was up beside the gillie and the latter had gathered her whip and her reins, somewhat impatient to leave. The surprised Howie shook the peer's hand a little awkwardly, but couldn't help smiling at his farewell words:

'It's been a great pleasure meeting a Christian copper,' said Lord Summerisle.

## CHAPTER VII

# Night –
# of April 30th

As the horse and cart pursued its monstrous shadow back along the path towards the distant township, its brass oil lamps already lit against the falling night, the gillie and Howie were, for a moment or so, silent, each wrapped in private thoughts.

'I wonder if I could ask you a favour, Sergeant?' said the gillie, coming out of her reverie first.

'Of course,' said Howie, 'if I can.'

'I have an errand I want to do before it's too dark. It'll mean taking a slightly longer route back. D'you mind?'

Howie was anxious to go and find Old Loam, the gardener-cum-gravedigger, as fast as he could, but he recognized that the friendliness of the gillie could prove essential in the work that was to follow. (An exhumed body had to be transported!)

'Please carry on,' he said. 'I'm most grateful that you waited for me.'

'I have to make a detour and leave some food off for my brother,' she said patting a basket, covered with a brightly chequered napkin, that sat snugly beside her.

The path had forked, Howie noticed, just after they

passed the stones, deserted now by the divinity class and standing like monoliths of pink coral in the sunset. The new road seemed to lead to another part of the woods where the oaks were older and more gnarled than the ones they'd passed earlier, and the mistletoe more profuse. A stream trickled down the side of their ascending pathway and then diverged, winding its way from the wood where the path continued.

Suddenly, they came abreast of a grove of well-spaced, huge trees that seemed to open to a small lake beyond. Darkness had so far fallen, by now, that Howie could only tell that the distant body of water was there because of the reflections of the dimly lit trunks of the trees in its slightly ruffled surface. The gillie had been as hushed for the last several minutes as she had earlier in the afternoon driving through the wood. But now there was a tension about her, an alertness, that communicated itself to Howie, making him watchful.

The gillie drew the horse to a halt, smiled reassuringly at Howie, indicating by the pressure of her hand on his arm, but no words, that he should stay exactly where he was. Howie watched her walk slowly, the basket upon her arm, towards the lake. But because she was taking a diagonal path away from his line of vision she disappeared from view, from time to time, behind the intervening trees. Suddenly another figure, that of a huge kilted man, detached itself from behind one of the trees and seemed to stalk her. To Howie's horror (he had already leapt from the cart), the man following the gillie seemed to carry an enormous basket-hilted sword, whose steel glinted in the dying sunlight.

'Sorrel!' shouted Sergeant Howie. 'Look out!'

Hearing the shout, the man turned to face Howie, who wondered, not for the first time in his police career, if the people who decreed that the British police should remain unarmed ought not occasionally to be exposed to this kind of emergency.

'I'll have at ye, if ye take as much as another step for'ard,' said the stranger advancing, his sword pointed straight at Howie's throat. Howie continued to walk forward, staring the man straight in the eye, not daring to look to see where the gillie had gone.

'You thought to catch me in my sleep. Don't you know I never close my eyes? I've learned to sleep like the beasts upon my feet and with one eye open. Get back, man, before I fillet you. I'll take the other one after,' said the kilted man, quietly, as if he were giving Howie an honourable cause for retreat before turning to deal with the poor gillie. And, indeed, Howie thought as he stood still, only feet from the threatening blade, that he had never in his life seen a face so strangely, but exaltedly, tired as that of this man. Then he heard the gillie's voice.

'Beech, love, lower your claymore, man. He hasn't come to attack you! Sergeant, please go back to the cart. This is my brother, Beech. He hates any man to approach this place. I usually come in daylight and he must have mistaken me for an attacker in the gloaming.'

Something in the man's wild but grateful glance at his sister, and the way his claymore now wavered, convinced Howie that the gillie knew what she was doing. He returned to the cart as slowly as he could, and looking over his shoulder, prepared to rush to the gillie's aid, if this clearly insane brother should try to attack her. But instead of attacking her he stood quite still, thrusting his claymore into the turf beside him so that it was well within reach, and folding his arms in a gesture of simple, almost royal dignity.

She knelt at his feet, with her basket beside her, and, taking the napkin, spread it on the turf and laid some bread, cheese, and ham upon it.

'Since we have company, do you wish me to anoint you?' Beech asked her kindly.

Howie, who was leaning against the cart now, could just see her nod her head in the half-light. Her brother took a water flask from his hip and uncorked it.

'I like it better when we can do it at the Source,' he said, 'but this too is the water of life and I anoint you with it.'

Gravely, he poured some water into his hand and, cupping his palm, gently poured a little onto his kneeling sister's brow. She kissed his hands and after smiling her reassuring smile at him, hurried to the cart, taking her empty basket with her. Seconds later she and Howie were on the move again, the sergeant looking back at the shadowy figure in the gathering darkness, under the gnarled oaks. He had gathered the food in one hand and, taking his claymore in the other, hurried back into the wood, as if he had been kept from something.

The gillie did not speak again for a while and something told the sergeant not to be the first to break the silence with questions, but to await her explanation when she should be ready to make it. As they emerged from the far side of the wood and the cart's oil lamps illuminated the ordered orchards that, once again, lined the road, the gillie gave a little sob. Howie could tell that she was swallowing back tears and tactfully pretended not to notice.

'He would never have hurt you unless you attacked him. It's just that I've never been so late before. Beech must have mistaken me for a man. He does doze off, you know. It wouldn't be human not to,' she said.

'What is your brother doing in that wood?' asked Howie gently. He realized that Beech was certainly unhinged, but probably not really dangerous. Why, he wondered, hadn't he been put in an institution? Even as he asked himself the question the answer was clear to him. There was no institution on Summerisle. It would have meant sending him to the mainland.

'He believes that he is the king that guards a sacred grove. He's quite harmless. Lord Summerisle thinks he can be cured of the delusion eventually. Meanwhile, I'm really the only person allowed to visit him,' she said.

'Why is he afraid of falling asleep?' asked Howie.

'Why, in case a man should come and kill him and take his place,' said the gillie. 'He keeps on expecting a challenger and, of course, one never comes!'

Howie had a terrible moment of identification with the mad guardian of the grove. He too spent every waking hour more conscious of his uniqueness among these people, more fearful of what unimaginable thing they might confront him with next. From inside the asylum of his own skin, he looked around a world that he peopled suddenly, in his imagination, with strangers whose motives

or intentions he could in no way predict. He knew he, like
Beech, would remain wakeful, wary till the answer to the
riddle of Rowan's death should have been revealed to him.

But in his everyday policeman's mind the everyday
questions kept posing themselves, and he asked them with
as much nonchalance as he could muster, disallowing and
qualifying much of what he heard in the answers.

'Lord Summerisle and the rest of you don't believe that
there is anything for Beech to guard, is that right? Maypoles
are *in* and sacred groves, as it were, are *out*?'

Howie realized that this had come out as a flippant
question but the gillie took it at its face value.

'Well, of course there are always *Protestants* . . .' she said.
'That's what we call people here who don't understand the
truth. They protest that the sacred grove is at the heart of
our religion. Lord Summerisle is very patient with them.
He uses reasoned argument and logic and they *always* see
the light. But, of course, Beech has been very strange since
he was a little boy. Mother was a bit odd too. Convinced
she'd conceived Beech bathing in the Source. For a time,
Beech thought he was the rightful Lord Summerisle. It was
so *sad* and embarrassing for the rest of us in the family . . .'

The poor gillie was close to tears again.

'Of course, I should have taken him his food at midday
but I was having a little booze-up with Alder MacGregor
instead. Then the pleasure of meeting you quite put it out
of my mind till late this afternoon. Lord Summerisle
wouldn't be at all pleased to hear I'd taken you there, so
you won't tell him, will you?' Her voice was genuinely
anxious.

Howie felt he could promise what she asked with a clear

conscience. Someone from the County Department of Health would have to be told about Beech as soon as he got back to the mainland. But to discuss him with Lord Summerisle was quite pointless, might even be dangerous.

'I promise I won't mention it to His Lordship,' he said, noticing they were on the outskirts of the village, not far from the church and the green.

'Where does the old gravedigger live?'

'Old Loam?' she asked. 'Why d'you want to see him? Grouchy old thing he is. I was hoping we could go straight to the Green Man. There'll be a great "knees-up" there tonight. You wouldn't want to miss that surely?'

'I don't care for dancing,' said Howie firmly. 'I'm afraid I have to find Loam right away. But perhaps he'll be at the inn too?'

'Not he,' said the gillie. 'Drinks alone in his cottage. People are afraid of him because of his job. It's a shame really, but he's not very welcome at the inn. Particularly at this season of the year, of course.'

The gillie obligingly left Howie off at Old Loam's cottage and hurried on to the 'knees-up' at the inn. The music from it could be heard wafting its way across the green. She promised Howie, before she left him, that he only had to walk across the green to fetch her, and she would be glad to be of service to him in providing her cart.

Howie expected Old Loam would be sour and angry at being asked to come out and dig up a grave, on such short notice, at night. On the contrary, he could hardly have been more pleased at the request. His first question, after the sergeant had aroused him from a semi-stupor at his fireside and explained the need to exhume Rowan, was:

'Did Lord S. say I could keep the earth what was over the grave?'

'We didn't discuss it, I'm afraid,' said Howie, puzzled and impatient. 'But I can't imagine why you shouldn't. What'll you do with it?'

'Sell it, of course,' said Old Loam. 'Lord Summerisle strictly forbids taking the earth off the top of graves. Course he's right. We'd have the place plundered right and left if it was allowed. But at an "exhuming", as you call it, I reckon the earth off the top of the coffin'd be mine by rights.'

Loam was collecting his spade and some rope from the tiny hallway of his cottage as he chattered. He also took a wooden box from a cupboard. It was marked 'finest grave dirt', under which was written, in smaller letters, 'for deeper sleep'.

Howie patiently watched the old man light a hurricane lamp and put on a pair of rubber waders, babbling with excitement about the 'grave dirt'.

'There are that many people who sleep poorly these days. Always going to Dr Ewan or Mr Lennox for rubbishy specifics made from poppies and the like. When grave dirt on the floor of the room above your bed makes you sleep like a baby and no after-effects in the morning . . . and not a great long sleep like the Hand of Glory, y'understand. You can't beat grave dirt for giving you a lovely, deep, deep, sleep . . .'

Their arrival in the graveyard was heralded for all the living creatures, in the dark yew trees and on the ruined walls of the church, by a loquacious owl. It hooted incessantly, unnerving even the bats that had been happily hunting somnolent fruit flies that lurked in the meadows of the adjacent orchards. Howie wondered if the animal kindgom shared man's instinctive taboo and dread about digging up the dead.

The digging process was not quite as lengthy as Howie had feared because Rowan appeared to have been buried at the normal six feet level and not at Loam's precautionary nine.

Howie saw, in the lantern light, a sprinkling of soft pellets beside the grave. He picked them up and examined them in the palm of his hand.

'Spoor,' said the old man glancing at the pellets, wiping the sweat out of his eyes.

'No,' said Howie. 'Are there rabbits around here?'

'That's never rabbit spoor,' said the old man scornfully.

'I know that,' said Howie impatiently. 'It's the regurgitated bone and fur from an owl's dinner! The dinner could have been a rabbit by the look of it.'

The gravedigger looked at Howie with a glimmer of respect.

'So he's quite the detective,' he said, adding, 'that's right. But no owl could eat a rabbit, 'fore makin' that pellet of its bones and fur. Mouse or rat maybe. Plenty of rats hereabouts. Wait till we open the coffin!'

'These are the pellets of a snowy owl. I heard its voice when we came into the graveyard. It could eat a rabbit I should think,' said Howie.

'Aye, I've heard of snowy owls taking hares at night right out of their 'forms. Like a bairn being taken out of its cradle by a wolf in the old days,' said the old man, addressing himself again to his task. 'But I've never seen one here myself,' he went on. 'I'm too busy guarding this graveyard from humans to worry much about birds.'

Howie warded off Loam's further whispered discussion of the dangers of people robbing graves of the corpse's hands or arms for the Hand of Glory. The old man was just drunk enough to be repetitious and Howie had already determined to recommend a guard for the graveyard, while police and priest or minister would go about their urgent work of cleansing the whole island of its insistent heresies. Meanwhile, he held the hurricane lamp and helped get the ropes around the coffin when it was finally reached and the clinging clay was scraped away from it by Old Loam's spade.

When the coffin had been hauled out and placed on the grass in the graveyard, Howie ordered Old Loam to lever open the top of the coffin with his spade. In the event the wood splintered, they both would have to heave the several separate planks that formed the lid away from the coffin. Howie had, in the course of his police duties, seen a good many stomach-turning sights, mostly as the result of road accidents. Here, he was prepared for the corpse of a girl who had been burned or poisoned and who might already have suffered six months' decomposition.

Instead, he found only the rather smelly remains of a hare!

Not a 'silly old rabbit', he felt sure, but a 'lovely March hare', remembering Rowan's mother's words.

Staggered by this discovery, Sergeant Howie stared and stared at the dead animal while Old Loam first broke into giggles, then laughed out loud. It was a very unpleasant sound.

But a nastier sound by far interrupted Loam's laugh so that he strangled it with a kind of screech. Coming at them from the ruined belfry of the church was a white shape that seemed to hoot and howl as it came. Howie looked up at its yellow eyes in the lamplight and threw himself down across the open coffin. Loam did not look twice at the creature that descended upon them like a blast of cold wind moving through the night. He just turned and ran, tripping and tumbling and screaming, from the graveyard. The snowy owl Howie had heard was after the little dead hare in the coffin, but faced with the protecting figure in thick blue serge, it flapped its great white wings furiously and wheeled up into the air, striking out over the orchards in search of voles or moles or any other succulent little rodent that might be abroad that night.

Howie watched the snowy owl depart and then grabbed the little hare by its ears and walked away from the graveyard without a further word to Old Loam, who cowered trembling at the lych-gate. As he strode across the green and was still thirty or forty yards away from the inn, he saw the gillie driving her cart around from the courtyard and onto the road that led back to the castle. She was whipping up her horse into a fast trot, and when Howie shouted at her, asking her to take him with her, she didn't appear to hear him.

That Lord Summerisle was at the bottom of almost everything that happened on the island was clear enough to Howie. The sergeant knew that he couldn't sleep until he'd confronted the laird with the sacrilegious evidence of the desecrated graveyard. For it was plain that either Rowan's body had been burned so that nothing but ashes remained, or her person, alive or dead, was still being kept elsewhere on Summerisle.

Searching his mind desperately for some form of transport that he could commandeer, Howie was forced to dismiss horses and carts, for he couldn't drive them himself. Some people had a way with horses. Howie knew *he* hadn't!

Now that even the friendly gillie had obviously been avoiding him, what chance of real cooperation would he have from any of those drunken jokers in the inn whose carts and traps or carriages and broughams were parked in the courtyard? He went on to thinking of where he could find a bicycle when he remembered the single piece of mechanized locomotion he'd seen on the island: Dr Ewan's motorcycle.

Thanks to his careful, early reconnaissance of the township on the day he'd landed (how long ago that now seemed), Howie was easily able to find his way back to the doctor's house. He rang the bell, but there was no answer. Howie went around to a wooden gate that stood between the Ewan house and the Lennox chemist shop next door. He unlatched this gate and went through to a small yard behind. To his relief the sergeant found the doctor had not taken the motorcycle with him, wherever he'd gone, but left it in a little shed. Howie wheeled the machine out into the street and wrote a note to Dr Ewan explaining that he'd commandeered his property temporarily, in the name of the law. As he put the dead hare in one of the copious saddlebags, he worried about taking a doctor's *transport*, although, strictly speaking, he was within his rights in an emergency. An apparent murder case was certainly *that*, he reassured himself, as he kicked the aging B.S.A. motor into life.

Unlike horses, motorcycles were very familiar to Howie, who'd excelled in riding and maintaining the machines while at the police college. He roared through the empty streets of the township, skidding slightly on the cobbles that had recently received their daily ration of fine, warm rain from the Atlantic. Avoiding the environs of the crowded inn, he rode straight across the green, scattering the evening's complement of lovers as he went, and found the road past the schoolhouse that he'd taken with the gillie that morning. He was surprised not to overtake the gillie's cart, but supposed she'd taken the other route, perhaps again to visit the poor, deranged Beech.

The great castle, fringed by its moonlit, silvery palm trees, was almost entirely dark when Howie arrived in the courtyard outside the front door, except for some light peeping through chinks in the curtains at the huge window of the great hall. He could hear singing from inside, distant but distinct, coming from the great hall and accompanied on an organ. The singing was not disturbed by his ringing of the bell and he listened while he waited, sure that it was Lord Summerisle's voice he could hear, accompanied by that of a woman.

'A maiden did this tinker meet and to him boldly say
Oh sure my kettle hath much need, if you will pass my way
She took the tinker by the hand and led him to her door.
Says she, my kettle I will show and you can clout it sure.'

The refrain was at least as strange and lewd as any of the songs he'd already heard on the island.

> *'For patching and plugging is his delight*
> *He hammers away both by day and by night.'*

When Broom opened the door the sound that greeted Howie from the great hall boomed louder still.

'I hope you're not going to tell me Lord Summerisle is expecting me again, *with this?*' said the sergeant angrily, before Broom could speak, waving the dead hare in his face. The piper only smiled and led the way, once again, to the great hall, whose door was open. He left Howie to enter, unannounced.

The sergeant stamped into the huge room and then stopped breathlessly to take in the new scene. Lord Summerisle sat, in his dress kilt, at the vast steam organ, playing it with virtuoso skill, and singing in his basso profundo. He had just pulled the stop marked 'flute d'amour, 4 feet', adding a most mellifluous sound to the song. It took Howie fifteen seconds more to find the owner of the female voice, who was, as he had expected, Miss Rose.

The schoolmistress lay stretched upon the skins, by the roaring fire, leaning against a huge deerhound and dressed in something clinging that looked like gossamer cheesecloth. She sang with Lord Summerisle, keeping time with a great silver goblet, that looked as if it had been left behind on Summerisle after the last bout of Norse rapine. Their salacious glee at the words of the song nauseated Howie, but he was a singer himself and listened for a moment or so and marvelled at the beauty of their voices and the rich tones of the steam organ. Lord Summerisle's bass voice was alone with the flute d'amour as he sang:

> 'Fair maid says he, your kettle's cracked.
> The cause is plainly told.
> There hath so many nails been drove,
> That mine own could not take hold.'

Listening to them and watching them, resentment and fury mounted in the sergeant so that he could feel the bile rising in his throat. A child, a *child* was at stake. Murdered or missing. Lost and unhappy, in pain or, thanks to God's mercy, perhaps in heaven. Whatever had happened to little Rowan – whether by a sin of this dreadful couple's omission, or of their truly frightful commission – they quite clearly didn't care a damn.

He marched noisily into the great hall and hurled the hare across the room so that it landed on the flat stones between Lord Summerisle and Miss Rose. They both looked up at Howie, startled and bewildered. The organ's sound died away with a great hissing groan.

'I found this,' shouted Howie, 'in Rowan Morrison's grave.'

'Little Rowan loved the March hares,' murmured Lord Summerisle wistfully.

'It's sacrilege. A crime still, My Lord, on the statute book of the kingdom of Scotland,' shouted Howie.

Miss Rose, who looked at the dead hare with a blandness and complacency that astonished Howie, now explained the matter in her maddeningly assiduous way.

'T'would only be sacrilege if the graveyard were conse-crated to the Christian belief. Personally I think it's a very lovely transmutation. I'm sure Rowan is most happy with it, aren't you, Tease?' she said, calling Lord Summerisle by this odd nickname. But the sergeant was standing for no more of this.

'Look here, miss,' he said furiously. 'I hope you don't think that I can be made a fool of indefinitely.' Whereupon he shouted at them both. 'Where is Rowan Morrison?'

'Why there she is,' said Miss Rose, quite unruffled, 'what remains of her physically. Her soul, of course, may even now be . . .'

The sergeant interrupted her by standing with his back to her and addressing Lord Summerisle.

'Lord Summerisle, for the last time, where is Rowan Morrison?' he asked in a thunderous voice.

Lord Summerisle rose to his full six and a half feet and stood looking grimly down at the sergeant.

'I believe, Sergeant Howie, that *you* are supposed to be the detective here,' he said coldly.

'My Lord, a child is reported missing on your island,' Howie explained with a kind of desperate patience. 'I come here and, at first, I'm told there is no such child. I find there is and that she is dead. Has succumbed to a meta-morphosis, according to Dr Ewan! I subsequently discover there is no death certificate, and now I find that though there is a grave, there is no body.'

'Very perplexing for you,' said Lord Summerisle not unsympathetically. 'What do you think could have happened?'

'Though I have absolutely no hard evidence for this,

*yet*, it is my theory that Rowan Morrison may have been murdered under circumstances of pagan barbarity, which I can scarcely bring myself to believe as taking place in the twentieth century. It is my intention to return to the mainland tomorrow and report my suspicions to the Chief Constable of the West Highland Constabulary, and demand a full investigation into all the affairs of this heathen island!' Howie spoke grimly, curtly.

'You must, of course, do as you see fit, Sergeant!' said Lord Summerisle, apparently unconcerned by the threat. 'It is perhaps just as well that you won't be here tomorrow to be offended by the sight of our May Day celebrations.'

On the word 'tomorrow', something came back to the sergeant from the card index of the case he had organized in his mind.

'Tomorrow's tomorrow,' he repeated aloud. 'Of course. My Lord, I may even return from the mainland in time to prevent your *celebrations* taking place!'

Lord Summerisle lifted a silver bell from a sofa table, smiling ironically at Howie as he rang for Broom.

'I think it will take stronger powers than yours to stop them, Sergeant,' said Lord Summerisle of the threat. 'Over the centuries they have proved very durable.'

Broom was there in response to the bell, with his bagpipe under his arm.

'Ah, Broom! Will you kindly show the sergeant out? Then we'll be ready for your pibroch. Miss Rose is in perfect voice this evening!' said Lord Summerisle.

Broom smiled and bowed discreetly. He ushered Howie towards the door.

'This way, sir,' he said.

Howie hesitated and then marched from the room.

As he started Dr Ewan's motorcycle for the return journey to the township, Howie could hear the lively sound of organ and bagpipe and Miss Rose's rich, clear voice, most unScottish in its gaiety and its earthy promise, soaring into an 'air'. More a rude old saraband, he thought, than a proper pibroch.

Howie rode back by the short route, terrifying hundreds of rabbits and a few deer, one of which was so startled that it nearly collided with his borrowed machine. He supposed that, to the population of Summerisle, these creatures must represent transmuted souls as he'd heard the Indians regarded their sacred cows, which were allowed to wander everywhere. What an absurd religion, thought Howie, although privately he had to admit to himself that Miss Rose had been right about the childish imagination finding 'resurrection' hard to grasp. Sergeant Howie had been troubled, himself, as a child, at the idea of everybody clambering out of their graves or being reassembled if they'd been blown to bits in a war, so that there could be a vast parade of all the people who'd ever lived, on Judgement Day. Eventually, he'd come to accept, as an article of faith, that God would organize it all in His own miraculous way.

He stopped the motorcycle on the green and wheeled the machine quickly down the High Street to Dr Ewan's house. Everybody appeared to be in bed and the doctor's house was quite dark and still when he replaced the motorcycle in its shed.

Howie felt a twinge of guilt for what he meant to do next. His plan included an immediate 'breaking and entering' of the chemist's shop and the subsequent 'searching without a magistrate's warrant' of the premises. It was not long past midnight and he hoped to do it all quietly enough not to get caught. His excuse if he were apprehended would be that Lord Summerisle, as Justice of the Peace or local Magistrate, was too implicated in the case of Rowan Morrison to be a proper or reliable person to approach for a search warrant.

## CHAPTER VIII

# The Wee Small Hours –
## of the 1st of May

THAT EX-POLICEMEN MAKE EXCELLENT CROOKS IS inevitable. They have to make a study of chummy's methods. They are nearly always summoned to the scene of the crime to see just how chummy got away with it and why. Of course, Sergeant Howie was the last police officer in the whole West Highland force who would have been in the least likely to actually become a criminal of any description. But he had always prided himself on being a thinking cop, whose own moral sense, being so much more highly developed than that of his colleagues, could allow him to bend regulations intended for less worthy police officers.

As he approached the chemist's shop, he took the normal precaution of making sure there was no one about. Seeing he was the only person abroad, except for a pair of amorous cats, he slipped, from his pocket, a piece of mica that he always carried. Burglar alarms were forever being set off accidentally behind the doors of locked stores in a town the size of Portlochlie. The only way to quiet them, if the owners were absent, was for the police to be able to gain entry, exactly as a burglar would. It was the work of about twenty seconds for Howie to insert the mica at the right point, next to the Yale lock, and to be inside the shop with the door closed behind him.

Howie lit a match to get his bearings. The bottles of appalling specifics were in their ordered rows. 'Fillets of fenny snakes' were in a jar quite close to him, leading Howie to wonder, with horror, if somewhere there could actually be a bottle of 'little fingers of babes, ditch-delivered by drabs'. Not for nothing had he helped Mary Bannock and her class stage Scotland's favourite Shakespeare play, *Macbeth*.

His immediate destination was at the very far side of the room, where a heavy black felt curtain indicated Mr Lennox's darkroom. Just before he had to blow out the match, to avoid burning his fingers, he spotted a staircase behind the end of the counter, which clearly led to the floor above. Having committed all this to memory the sergeant crept to the foot of the stairs and listened. The racking snores of, he presumed, Mr Lennox seemed to almost shake the timbers of the upper storey of the old building. If there were a Mrs Lennox, Howie hoped, for her sake, that Lennox provided adequate earplugs.

Once inside the darkroom, he struck another match and lit the oil lamp that hung from the ceiling.

Howie started to search through negatives filed away on shelves in yellow boxes. They were labelled 'weddings, sports days, portraits, etc.' Finally, he came to a box marked 'Harvest Festival'. He opened it and found inside a number of negatives, each marked with its date. The negative for the previous year, which Mr Lennox had claimed he was unable to find, lay at the bottom of the pile. Howie held it up briefly to the light to make sure that there had been an exposure, then quickly prepared the developing trays, measuring in the chemicals, and carefully checking the temperatures. The printing box was an ancient affair but it seemed to work well enough.

While the photograph was developing, Howie tiptoed back to the foot of the stairs to check on the sleeping, snoring Mr Lennox. Satisfied that all was well, he started to examine other boxes of photographs. He selected one labelled 'Divination' and opened it. Inside was a number of photographs in folders. The first was labelled 'The Blade-Bone of the Black Pig (Slinneineachd)' and contained a photograph of a crowd of islanders standing in a circle round Lord Summerisle, who was minutely scrutinizing the bone of an animal. The second was labelled 'Omen Stones (Col Coetn)' and showed half a dozen people throwing white round stones into the embers of a fire. The third was labelled 'The Seer in the Bull (Taghairm)' and had a colourful picture of a man wrapped in the hide of a bull being rocked by others on the bank of a pool. The fourth was labelled 'The Elucidator (Peithyrnen)' and contained a number of photographs that showed Lord Summerisle manipulating a machine consisting of several staves on which judicial maxims had been cut. (When turned, the staves apparently spelled out messages of three or four lines.) The fifth was labelled 'The Living and the Dead Graves' and showed a woman wrapped in a blanket and lying on the ground between two holes. One had a sign by it reading 'Living Grave'; the other read 'Dead Grave'. A small circle of people looked on with concern.

Sickened, Howie thrust the photographs back into the

yellow boxes and returned to the developing bath. A photograph of the familiar scene of the Harvest Festival emerged before his eyes. He took it out and laid it on a table to dry. Searching around, he found a magnifying glass and held it to the picture. In spite of a lot of distortion, due to magnification, he could see that the girl standing among the fruit and vegetables was *not* Rowan Morrison but Daisy, the girl who had explained about the beetle. Howie's face showed his perplexity. He applied himself to examining the photograph in detail and noted the surprising fact that there was markedly less produce than usual. A few pears, tomatoes, and cauliflowers . . . and a number of diminutive apples. Howie was suddenly very excited at his discovery. It was a clue that helped explain a great deal. The crop had *failed* the previous year, he was sure that was it! The crop had failed . . . No wonder he got canned soup and vegetables the night before . . . No wonder there were none of the famous Summerisle apples. The few good ones were, no doubt, those he'd seen in Lord Summerisle's cold store. The poisoned apple theory remained, for that might have been part of the crop disaster. But it seemed less and less likely.

He wondered, at once, what the old religion did about crop failure. And then he remembered something Lord Summerisle had said in the subtropical garden.

'He brought me up the same way – to love the music and drama and rituals of the old pantheism, and to love nature, and to fear it and rely on it and appease it where necessary . . .' that or something very like it was what Lord Summerisle had said.

'Appease it where necessary!'

Appeasing, Howie realized, was the key to all pagan religions. He'd sometimes thought that the Papists' confession and absolution was a form of pagan appeasement. But these people would feel the need to appease in quite a different way. He found himself staring at a wall calendar with May Day ringed heavily in red. Tomorrow, he thought for a moment, and then glancing at his watch realized it was already *today*.

'Only make sure you're ready for tomorrow's tomorrow!' Lord Summerisle had said to Willow and she had responded, 'The day of death and resurrection?'

'Whose death?'

Of course, he'd half-suspected it then. Now it seemed quite clear, Rowan's death, which had still to take place. Today on May Day.

'My God! I've got to find Rowan!' he said out loud.

His exclamation had interrupted the even flow of the snores upstairs. There was a sudden noise.

Hastily he replaced the negative in the box and, putting the wet photograph as fast as he could through the stop bath and the fixing bath, lifted it out gingerly, and turned out the lamp. He moved through the shop as quietly as he could. There was dead silence for an appreciable time while Howie waited to open the door and leave. Then the snores resumed, at first softly but growing to a crescendo. Howie made his exit and walked fast up the hill towards the Green Man.

Inside the bar of the inn everything was unusually quiet. Willow stood behind the counter drying some glasses. Howie came in looking and feeling very weary. She turned and smiled with pleasure when she saw him.

'Hullo,' said Willow. 'You look tired. Can I get you a drink?'

'I'll have a pint, please!' said Howie gratefully.

Willow turned to draw the beer while Howie contemplated the empty space on the wall where last year's Harvest Festival photograph was missing. He surreptitiously brought out his own recently developed, and still tacky, small photograph, and made a comparison with the most recent (and enlarged) version of the Festival on the wall. The difference between plenitude and famine was obvious. He put his photograph quickly back in his pocket and walked over to the bar where his beer stood waiting. He lifted it and drank deeply. Slowly he was solving the puzzle. But he was a long way, he realized, from rescuing Rowan, wherever she might be.

'Willow,' asked Howie, 'what did you mean by the phrase "the day of death and resurrection"?'

'I don't remember saying that!' said Willow.

'You said it last night to Lord Summerisle when he was sending that lad up to you.'

'Oh, so you overheard that, did you, Sergeant Sleuth?' giggled Willow.

'I'm right next door, you know,' said Howie.

'I know where you are!' said Willow. 'I only hope Ash Buchanan didn't keep you awake. He's a lively boy and very anxious to learn – I expect I could teach you a thing or two, Sergeant, love . . . if you're not too tired.'

She did something so sexy with her luscious lower lip that Howie had to frantically reprove his all-too-responsive flesh. He was sitting by now and Willow put her hands gently on his shoulders – massaging them softly. Howie half-flinched but, thinking better of it, let her slowly caress his neck, allowing himself the pain that the illicit pleasure gave him.

'I'm only interested in the meaning of the phrase "the day of death and resurrection",' said Howie trying to control his breathing.

'It's just a saying,' said Willow softly. 'It's something to do with fertility, Sergeant . . . and May Day, and all that.'

'Willow, what happens here on May Day?' asked Howie lightly. 'Does anyone . . . well, I mean, is anyone specially chosen for a . . .'

'You must think of it as a day of rebirth, Sergeant. That's the best way,' said Willow seriously.

'Do you know where they're keeping Rowan Morrison?' asked Howie boldly, waiting for her reaction. He was disgusted to find himself wondering in the long silence that followed, how, if he were alone with her, he might contrive to make her talk. She would be impervious to sexual threats even if he were the sort of man to make them. Then the possibility of inflicting pain on her, to gain the information he so desperately needed, crossed his mind. To his horror he found that the idea excited him. Was almost every male, he wondered, afflicted with this atavistic desire to master a woman – to bend her if need be? It was the 'received wisdom' that this was so.

If he had ever been tempted to succumb to Willow's repeated invitations (and he had), the fear that he might break his own code of gentleness and honour, once he was alone with her, made him the more determined to resist her. Disturbed at this unsavoury morsel of self-discovery, he wondered whether there was an innate violence in him for any and every woman, even for Mary. But fortunately for his peace of mind, he could not imagine wishing to inflict any hurt on 'his Mary'. It did not occur to him, in his innocence, that Willow's rampant, taunting sexuality was the magnet that would draw every basic urge from her lovers, whoever they might be; that to rejoice, with Willow, in walloping Willow would probably be the merest footnote to any night that Howie might conceivably spend with her, and hardly qualified him to be listed as a sadist (which is what he greatly feared).

'You're so nosy, aren't you? And anyway who cares about all that?' asked Willow, breaking her silence. 'But why don't you come to my room later tonight? I'm sure I can show you *something* to your advantage. The door won't be locked.'

With which she went off to help her father close the inn for the night. Only the musicians, who appeared to be residents, remained drinking.

Howie sat for a moment with his beer. What she had said was a clear admission of what he had already deduced: Rowan was, so far, almost certainly not dead.

Of one thing he had made up his mind. At first light, he would fly off to fetch reinforcements who would probably have to be armed. To radio for them might precipitate Rowan's death, for Howie couldn't be quite sure there was no radio receiver/transmitter on the island. The thing to do, he determined, was to get the reinforcements back to Summerisle before the islanders had time to get up to whatever horrible ceremony they planned, and for which, Howie felt sure, Rowan was being made ready.

Willow had meanwhile gone up the stairs to bed,

cheekily pinching the lobe of his ear as she passed him. He followed shortly afterward (leaving his beer unfinished, finding it rather too bitter for his taste). Heading for his own room, across the landing, he was appalled to see Willow standing at her door inviting him in. She was quite bare, and lovelier naked than even Howie's aroused imagination had allowed him to dream.

He permitted himself one long glance at her extravagant person. The aureoles around her nipples had the swollen bloomed look of fresh plums ripe for the nibbling. Howie felt his jaw clench and then he allowed himself to look at her tapering, golden fleece. The sight of it made him slow his gait so that he actually almost came to a halt opposite her. The lighting of her body reminded him of a religious postcard that he had always held dear since the day 'his Mary' had sent it to him, after their first date. It was called *The Education of the Virgin*, by a French painter, and it showed the Blessed Virgin Mary as a child, holding her hand close to a candle, to stop it guttering, so that the light of the flame showed through the very flesh of the little girl who would become the Mother of God. In Willow's room, behind her boldly opened legs, burnt the flame of an oil lamp, set on the floor, by the distant bed. Etched into Howie's mind and eye was the heart-shaped gap where her long legs met the coral line that split her fleece. Her flanks, her thighs, had the same quality of transparency as the painting, mocking this sacred image in his mind. Upon the inside of her satined thighs Howie thought he saw the spreading glaze of her desire, and the delicious musky smell of woman was intense.

Her face he ignored for he did not care to meet her

gaze now, when she could see how much the promise of her body moved him. Instead he watched, fascinated, the movement of her fingers. In one hand she held a long corn-dolly. (While Howie knew what it was called, he wondered why, for its phallic shape was all too evident.) The outrageous Willow caressed the oblong, ribbed corn-dolly with her other hand and sang in a low voice that was hardly more than a whisper.

> 'I saw a maid milk a bull,
> Well done liar.
> I saw a maid milk a bull
> Every stroke a bucketful
> Isn't that a comical thing to be true?'

Oh, how easily he could have whipped this Jezebel, this mocking public whore, thought Howie. The thought itself was desire. He recognized it and saw the new trap. In the instant before he was about to grab her wrist and haul her into her room and flay her with his belt he saw it. She expected to reach him on one level, if she failed on another. She knew men from the weight of their balls in the hand to the most complex trigger mechanisms in their minds. But she had never met the likes of Sergeant Neil Howie before, of that he would be certain. Simulating a coolness he didn't feel, for his body was soaking with a sudden, heavy sweat, Howie walked determinedly to his door. Entering, he closed the door and turned the key, ostentatiously, in the lock.

His room had its oil lamp already lit, and freshly cut flowers were arranged in jam jars of various sizes. Muslin

bags full of sweet smelling lavender were tucked into his
sheets. Beside his washstand was a china jug of steaming
hot water, and bottles of oil and unguent, hand labelled,
'oil of sunflower seed' and 'essence of heather'. Why, Howie
wondered, was he suddenly being honoured in this extravagant way unless it was merely part of Willow's plan to
seduce him? Or, to put it another, likelier way, part of the
wider conspiracy of Lord Summerisle, MacGregor, and
others to have Willow seduce him in her role as Aphrodite.

Howie had found a jug of chilled cider by his bedside.
He poured himself a little in a glass. It was sweet and chill
and perfectly to his taste, unlike the rather bitter beer
served in the bar. He shivered, as the sweat cooled on his
body, certain that he was one of the very few cops who
would have resisted the bait that they had offered him.
Their single-minded resourcefulness when it came to his
seduction was very frightening. McTaggart, he was sure,
would not have hesitated to go in there with Willow and
rut himself blind. As Howie knew him to have done with
the whores on the quayside at Portlochlie. Of course,
Howie had to admit that Willow was as far superior to any
whore he had ever seen as Aphrodite, the Goddess of Love,
was to an ordinary woman. Aphrodite! He turned the word
over in his mind. It had a pretty ring to it and it was only
as Howie had drained the glass of cider that he made a
disturbing connection . . . aphrodisiac.

Panic was not an emotion that Sergeant Howie had
suffered much before. But now the thought that there
might, just possibly, be coursing through his veins an
agent that could twist or bend his will, turn what he
regarded as the base desires that he shared with every

other man, but with God's grace had learned to control, into a lust that he would be powerless to deny ... that thought was the stuff of panic for Howie. For a moment he so far forgot himself that he assumed that this might be an extreme in which even God could not help him. Worse, he was tempted by the notion that the aphrodisiac, if one had indeed been administered, with the cider, freed him, at last, from moral responsibility. This idea came to him at about the time the music started again. It wafted up from the bar, starting with an extraordinarily seductive beat.

Howie, who had once read a sex manual called *The Young Christian's Guide to Sanctified Bliss in Marriage*, remembered that there was a great deal of discussion of the body's rhythms.

This insistent beat awakened a rhythm in Howie's own body that soon bewildered and enthralled him. He could detect, now, that it was not only the drum in the bar below that gave the agonizing pulse, but a knock upon the wall that divided Willow's room from his; the supple fingers that had stroked the corn-dolly so provocatively were summoning him again. The other instruments wound the beginnings of a lovely melody and Willow started to sing:

> 'Heigh ho! Who is there?
> No one but me, my dear.
> Please come say, How do?
> The things I'll give to you.'

Howie's window was open and he could tell by the clarity with which her voice came to him that her window too was open. Yet he didn't dare lean out and look at her as he had the night before.

> 'By stroke as gentle as a feather
> I'll catch a rainbow from the sky
> And tie the ends together.
> Heigh Ho! I am here
> Am I not young and fair?
> Please come say, How do?
> The things I'll show to you.'

Her song was a simple enough invitation to him. As if the invitation her body had already made to him needed only to be underlined – enchantment to be added to the power of raw desire. Indeed, it was the sweetest, most *enchanting* song (how many overused words, he thought, took on their real meaning on this island) that a woman could sing to a man she was offering every pleasure it was in her undoubted power to bestow. That they were *unimaginable* pleasures for Howie, who had only the *Christian's Guide* to go by, made them somehow more tempting.

He longed for Willow's initiation. And while he longed, she sang:

> 'Would you have a wond'rous sight
> The midday sun at midnight?'

To open *his door* and walk the few steps it would take to open *her door* and find himself in those voluptuous arms would be a journey, Howie thought, slipping steadily further into temptation, like that of Marco Polo entering

fabled Cathay, the China of our ancestors' quests. More
marvellous in the telling, perhaps, but quite extraordinary
enough to be the recurring dream, the incomparable memory of the man that made the journey. Howie wished
desperately that he had not glimpsed the palpable reality
of Willow. If only succulent, ripe Willow had not, but
minutes before, been within his grasp and could in ten
paces be so again. Howie stood, literally trembling with
uncertainty, washing his body in the warm water, pouring
just a drop or two of the essence of heather into the palm
of his hand and spreading it across his chest before taking
the cold water and rinsing it quickly off again. His thoughts
never once went to the nightly report he should be writing,
let alone to his prayers. It was Willow's sweet prayer that
besieged his senses:

> 'Fair maid, white and red,
> Comb you smooth and stroke your head
> How a maid can milk a bull!
> And every stroke a bucketful.'

Now she was just the other side of the wall. In counterpoint to the rhythm of the drum below, he could hear her
slapping her own flesh in a tantalizing tattoo as she sang
on. He put his ear to the wall and he could hear her deep
breaths between the words of the song she still sang. He
knew that he must go to her, for she was now in a kind of
pain that only he could assuage. He knew that and was on
the way to the door when it came to him, *how* he knew
that. God, he felt suddenly, was with him and all at once
he was able to shut out the song and fell to kneeling by his

bedside as he had done every night since he was a child. He knew of the pain Willow felt because he remembered that Mary Bannock had felt it too.

Mary was the antidote he was sure he must use for the tempting poison that flowed from Willow or the cider or both. Mary had breathed like that when, on a walk along the cliff-top fields outside Portlochlie one night, he'd held her very tight and 'kissed her', as the old song had it, 'o'er and o'er again among the sheaves of barley'. Again in the car, before he'd asked her 'to name the day', she'd breathed like that. He'd sensed her pain when he had taken his hand from inside her thigh. The look in her eyes and the warmth of her kiss had told him what he had not yet been prepared to accept, that she'd waited long enough – that it had been unnatural of him not to marry her far sooner and take away the pain of waiting.

He was appalled to think he might have given to a pagan slut what he'd saved for Mary; worse, he was about to take from Willow what he'd made Mary save for him! Now that, at last, he had exorcized Willow's image from his mind, he longed to get back to Mary, to marry her so that they could explore each other spiritually and physically, guiltlessly and in joy. He was sure the *Christian's Guide* would be a well-thumbed relic soon forgotten as he and Mary discovered their own 'wond'rous sight'. In the sanctification of marriage and with procreation as their higher purpose, that, of course, would be well understood between him and Mary. He said 'Amen' to that out loud.

In the surge of triumph that followed Sergeant Howie's victory over Willow's temptation of him, he noticed that the music had stopped and the whole inn had fallen quiet.

He thanked God that, in His mercy, He had saved him from both sin and humiliation.

Calmly then did he dutifully sit and write up his notes for the day, concentrating on the Rowan Morrison case rather than the many other little irregularities he had noticed. He had a new set of facts to record at the end of his notes:

1. It seems plain that Rowan is not dead. No body, no death certificate, no convincing description of *how* she has died.

2. This points to the anonymous letter writer being an islander. Someone with real concern for Rowan's life. But may not have wanted to write about religious/sacrificial aspects of the child's disappearance. Could that person be the gillie? No one else I have met so far seems a likely writer of the letter. The only possible reason (apart from sheer humanity) that the gillie might wish to write to us is her obvious rivalry with Miss Rose. A comparison of her handwriting could be useful.

3. Otherwise, there is every evidence that almost all of the islanders are in on the conspiracy to hide the whereabouts of Rowan Morrison. With the possible exception of her mother, who might, along with a few other simple-minded people, believe in the metamorphosis story that Rowan runs in the fields as a hare. Her resurrection later today will be awkward for Lord Summerisle and Miss Rose to explain to the mother, but I suppose some mumbo-jumbo will be produced. After the sacrifice. Hey, presto! Rowan will be provided with some

convenient transmutation, which will be invented as a sop to the poor mother.

4. The horrifying possibility that this intended sacrifice of Rowan may be part of a pattern will have to be considered. Can Daisy, the girl in the broken photograph, be an intended victim? Or is the photographic evidence being hidden simply to obscure the fact that last year's harvest failed? Aren't victims usually chosen from the brightest or the beautiful? Poor Daisy hardly qualifies on either count. So she's probably safe enough.

5. I cannot entirely discount the possibility that Rowan was made sick by eating a Saint Athelstan's pippin. In which case it is just possible that she *still* lies sick or is already dead. Others may have become sick and/or died too. This hypothesis could explain:
   A. The lack of a death certificate.
   B. The absence of a body.
   C. The conspiracy of silence on the part of the community, because the fruit is their livelihood.
   D. The hidden Festival photograph, if more than the apples were affected.
   The only way of elucidating facts on this hypothesis are the same as if she were an intended sacrifice. Except, of course, that the sample apple in my possession will have to undergo immediate analysis on the mainland. I think the 'sickness' theory less likely than the 'sacrifice' theory due to the other circumstantial evidence.

6. Since it must now be known all over the island that Rowan is being sought, but no one has come forward, and since May Day is upon us and there are only twenty-two more hours of it as I sit and write this, I intend to take the following action:

0700 hours.    Fly straight to Portlochlie.

0800 hours.    Report to the Chief Constable and request immediate police task force be formed under my command consisting of at least twelve constables.

0900 hours.    Attend opening of County Court with application for issue of firearms to officers of special task force. Also ask Judge to authorize an application of military aid to the civil power in the form of Royal Air Force helicopter to airlift the police out to the island. (Our seaplane would have to make five trips.)

1000 hours.    Call relevant ministry in Edinburgh, through the Chief Constable's permission and ask for Order-in-Council to impose a complete curfew on the island, while a 'search and question' operation is carried out.

Before 1200 hours, hopefully, task force arrives at Summerisle Township leaving nine constables to impose the immediate curfew confining everyone to their homes. Three other officers to be landed near Lord Summerisle's castle. Lord Summerisle to be kept under strict surveillance till Rowan is found. Six motorcycles to be brought in with police officers.

Howie smiled to himself ruefully as he scribbled a final note:

No police officer will ever have had as much egg on his face as I, if this whole thing turns out to be a joke and Rowan is simply hiding for fun. But on the facts before me I can do no less than is proposed above, if I am to ensure the child's safety.

Howie closed his book and climbed into bed preparing to turn down the oil lamp and set the alarm on his wristwatch, when he saw the still unfinished jug of cider. What nonsense, he thought, to think it had been an aphrodisiac. Willow had stirred his senses with that glimpse of her body and her inviting song, but that was all. The cider itself was clearly innocuous, and very refreshing. Howie drank the remainder and, turning down his lamp, fell almost at once into a deep sleep.

It might be imagined that of all the images that had impinged on Sergeant Neil Howie on the thirtieth of April and in the early hours of the first of May, Willow, luscious Willow, would have won pride of place in his subconscious – Willow or perhaps an erotically imagined Mary Bannock, since his love for her had won the battle for his soul, not to mention his body.

Yet Howie dreamed of no woman at all unless you counted Rowan and *she* did figure in his dream. But as a little virgin dressed in white like the children in the Harvest Festival photographs. Of all odd places to find her, she sat in a huge oak tree that grew on a tiny peninsula in the lake by the sacred grove, her hands bound to a branch. She seemed to cry out regularly for help like a little cat caught in a similar predicament.

Howie was there looking up into the tree wondering what was the fastest way to climb up and rescue her when Beech, the kilted madman with the claymore, appeared and rushed at Howie, slashing at him with his sword. The sergeant ducked and tripped Beech, who fell heavily to the ground. Before the guardian of the sacred grove could rise, Howie stamped hard on the wrist of his sword hand, making him lose his grip on the claymore. The sergeant grabbed the weapon and, looking down at the big man, saw only the withered trunk of a fallen beech tree, where before the man had lain.

While it was now his intention to climb the great oak tree to rescue Rowan, Howie realized that he was not alone in the grove of trees. People seemed to him to be coming towards him in the distance. Behind a clump of ferns, near the lake, he could make out the figure of a man moving, or perhaps it was the fern clump itself that was advancing like the 'woods at Dunsinane'. Hoping to forestall his attacker's assault, Howie rushed forward and lunged at the ferns with his claymore, but the man who rose to ward off his blow was Broom, the piper, and the only weapon he had was his bagpipe, which Howie split like a pig's bladder. It made a sighing sound as the air went out of it. The piper had gone and a broom shrub stood in his place.

Then it seemed as if an entire army were marching towards him through the wood to the tuck-a-tuck of drums. Lord Summerisle was at their head dressed in his full regalia as a chief of the clan Morrison and all the other men he'd seen in the bar and elsewhere, young and old, Dr Ewan, Alder MacGregor, young Ash Buchanan, even the stringy figure of old Lennox, marched behind their laird.

The strange thing was that none of them dressed in the neat showy kilts that tourists and Scottish nationalists from Glasgow affected but rather in the great shambling old kilts that men tucked into their sword belts when going into battle in the last great rebellion in 1745. Their shirts were undyed homespun, mostly worn under leather jerkins, and the band from the inn started to skirl their pipes to add menace to the drums. They wore long feathers in their bonnets and woad smeared upon their cheeks. They were, Howie thought, like an army of ghosts marching out of several obscure pages of Scotland's history all at once.

It had always been the lot of Scotland's military and police to fight the prophets and the madmen, the romantics and the seers of their own race. On behalf of the Scottish Crown. On behalf of law and order. On behalf, as often as not, of Christ the King.

He took the claymore and stood beneath the tree, his weapon raised to ward them off. But they did not even look at him as they advanced. Instead they gazed up at the girl in the tree. Sergeant Howie stood on the small peninsula that led to the oak, trying desperately to think of some adequate way of stopping the mob from snatching from the upper branch the poor wee cower'n' virgin girlie, who was his charge. This, he knew, was his testing ground and he must not fail. He would fight them off till he fell, or reinforcements came. But there must be something he could say that would deter them. In Britain a mere word from a policeman should be enough. A piece of doggerel from his childhood came out of his mouth before he could stop it.

Yet surprisingly, it stopped Lord Summerisle dead in his tracks, although his troops remained anxious to grab the child.

'Lars Porsena of Clusium,' quoth Howie, wondering why as he said it. 'By the Nine Gods He swore . . .' Nine Gods! That was it. These people must have at least nine gods!

> '*That the great House of Tarquin*
> *Should suffer wrong no more.*'

But at this point Lord Summerisle couldn't resist interrupting, in his deep umbrous voice.

> '*By the Nine Gods he swore it!*
> *And named a trysting day.*
> *And bade his messengers ride forth*
> *East and west, and south and north,*
> *To summon his array.*'

The ragged array behind Lord Summerisle had come to a halt and was listening intently to their laird's words. Although they had lost the thread of his meaning, they looked like men who felt sure all would soon be explained.

'The sergeant will tell us how it goes on, won't you, Sergeant? Otherwise we'll have to scale the tree and capture little Rowan, won't we, lads?'

'Aye!' they all shouted in unison. Howie was not at all sure how it went on but knew he must bluff it out if he could.

> '*Then up spake brave Horatio . . .*
> *Of . . . of Tuscan blood was he . . .*
> *Oh, I will stand at thy right hand . . .*
> *And hold the Bridge with thee . . .*'

'Wrong, ridiculous, pathetic!' shouted Lord Summerisle, and the whole army surged forward, engulfing Howie. A dozen sword blows were striking Howie's claymore from his hand. He felt himself falling from the small peninsula towards the cold water of the lake . . .

When Sergeant Howie woke he was lying on his stomach, his sheets quite damp from his sweat. While his dream was full of the nonsense of typical dreams, he could see, at once, that it might contain a kernel of truth. Suppose Rowan were being guarded in the sacred grove? Suppose Beech was her real (possibly sane) guard? Suppose that the gillie and Beech were the real captors of Rowan and that she was a pawn in a battle between the 'Protestants' (as the gillie had called her brother Beech's pagan schism) and the followers of Lord Summerisle's catholic version of the old religion?

Then again suppose Beech might simply be Lord Summerisle's hired jailer, with his role dressed up for Howie's benefit with the story of his *strangeness* and the myth of the 'sacred grove'.

Howie could see from his window that the sun was not yet up, although the lightning of the sky had begun and it was still not five a.m. by his watch. God, he believed, had shown him, in his vivid dream, the one quite obvious clue of the previous day, which he had ignored. Now he must act on the hint God had given him. It was a reward, perhaps for his resistance of last night's temptation that he'd been granted this grace.

The dawn song had started. Howie could hear a black-cap and, appropriately enough, a willow warbler. Soon a chiffchaff and a sedge warbler and some starlings joined in with their song. The sun's pale rays had reached Howie's window when the nightingale, perhaps knowing it, at last, to be May, added his incomparable voice to the chorus.

## CHAPTER IX

# Dawn –
## on May Day

WITHOUT A MOMENT'S HESITATION, WITHOUT PAUSING to shave or clean his teeth, suppressing even an urgent need to relieve a bladder awash with cider, Howie donned his uniform and crept from the still-darkened inn, carrying his shoes.

He did not put his shoes on his feet until he had crossed the gravel path outside the inn. Once on the green he ran all the way across it till he reached the start of the High Street. Here, once again, he took off his shoes and, braving the dew, in his stockinged feet, he made his way directly to Dr Ewan's house.

Moments later he was wheeling the ancient B.S.A. motorcycle back up the hill towards the green. Only when he had gotten it onto the grass, having seen no one, not so much as an alley cat, on his entire expedition, did he don his shoes once again and start the machine. He rode along the route that the gillie had used to bring him back from the castle via the sacred grove.

Behind Howie the sun was rising, lighting the tops of the fruit trees. Tree pipits, swallows, and chaffinches were busy breakfasting among the blossoms. Beyond, the distant wood, with its huge oaks, was coming into view.

Howie was afraid that he would not easily be able to recognize the place on the outskirts of the wood that they had called the 'sacred grove'. Then he remembered that a stream ran downhill from it, emerging presumably from the 'source' that they had mentioned, probably some spring, by that lake he'd seen through the trees.

When he finally spotted the stream, he realized that he was within sight of both the circle of stones and the castle. This proximity to Lord Summerisle's lair added to Howie's natural nervousness at the possibility of having to do battle with the mad Beech. He remembered the ploy he'd used for disarming Beech in his dream and hoped it would work in real life. It was, after all, only one of the simpler manoeuvres of unarmed combat that he'd learned at Police College.

Dismounting at a spot where he could once again glimpse the lake through the trees he hid Dr Ewan's machine in a clump of bushes. As he was walking, as quietly yet alertly as possible, among the huge oaks he heard the distant trickling of a spring (perhaps itself the Source?) that gave him an almost unbearable urge to relieve himself.

Yet behind any of the huge, gnarled tree trunks, their bark sometimes twisted into curiously menacing, half-human expressions . . . Beech, the guardian and self-styled king of the scared grove, might be lurking. This was no time to unzip himself, when, at any instant, a sharp claymore might be aimed at any part of his person.

He looked all around him continuously, searching, as

he had been taught to do – the distance, the middle distance, and the near-about-him – always listening, trying to sort out in his mind's ear the sounds that were manifestly birds or rabbits or the maddeningly trickling water so that he would recognize the sound of a man moving, if and when it came.

After travelling in this way for about forty yards the old oaks thinned out, and he could see the lower part of a tree that could only be described as a giant oak, its trunk being four times larger than the average tree around it. About it there seemed to be lying on the ground an extraordinary collection of rubble. From the twenty yards' distance that Howie now saw it, his first thought was that it might simply be at the centre of a garbage dump. While it was not on a peninsula as he'd imagined the 'special' tree in his dream, it did stand in a large clearing and its huge roots seemed to border the lake itself. Its branches were obscured from him by the overgrowth of nearer trees. Ominous to Howie were the voices of dozens of ravens coming from the direction of the oak.

Then he heard a sound that he had not expected in the grove. Some people were riding horses nearby. Howie crouched behind a thornbush to watch. Such was the camouflage of the many intervening branches that he saw first a handsome black stallion, prancing and frisky in the cool morning air. Then he could make out its rider as being the gillie dressed in a smart stag-hunting coat of dark green. Behind her she led a riderless, bay mare on a leading rein.

'Beech,' she called, 'you must come now!'

The tall figure of Beech materialized from behind a stunted tree trunk only twelve yards from the point the sergeant had reached.

'Sorrel, how can I leave when someone may desecrate the tree, the Source? All that it is my high duty to guard and preserve? Suppose I return to find someone has taken my place?' Beech seemed to try to sound reasonable.

'On this one day each year Lord Summerisle has promised no one will challenge you to take your place. No one! As for desecration . . . Beech, you know that no one would dare! Your place is with the rest of us today. Please, Beech, for my sake,' she pleaded.

'What about the policeman?' Beech seemed half-persuaded.

'He'll be looking for the Queen of the May,' she answered, and went on: 'He's dead ignorant, poor thing, but even he could hardly expect to find the Queen of the May in the sacred grove.'

Reluctantly, Beech looked around him and then climbed on the back of the mare, taking the reins from his sister.

'Ride on, Sorrel,' he said quietly to the gillie. Then, wheeling his horse, he shouted down the echoing corridors of primeval oaks:

'If someone lies waiting to take my place out there, let him remember that only by killing *me* in battle can he truly be King here. Or if he dare to desecrate this holy place, he must remember the awful penalty: that when I return I will cut his navel from his belly and nail it to the tree. By his intestine unwinding from within him, shall I bind him to the trunk. Only by sacrificing him in this way can the goddess be appeased. He has been warned.' With which he put his mare to a canter, and followed his sister out of the wood.

Howie's mind reeled at all that he had just heard. What he could not wait to see was the whole of the great tree. Feeling quite safe now he ran forward until all of it was revealed to him, and even before that, when he had only glimpsed part of it, he already felt an urge to vomit. For hanging from every branch there were the mangled bodies of animals. Hens, pigs, deer, dogs, cats, kittens, puppies, ducks, geese, swans, and several horses large and small had been hanged from the tree – had clearly died by *hanging* from the tree!

Cawing cacophonously, the ravens left the grisly breaking of their fast and fluttered up into the topmost branches of the oak.

For Howie, gazing around him in fear and dread, this ghastly manifestation of the excesses to which the islanders had been driven by their frightful cult brought down further 'horror upon horror's head'.

That fear had crept more frequently about his flesh these last twenty-four hours, than ever before in his life, was certain. Now, for a measurable minute, he thought of running, actually running to the motorcycle and riding straight for the safety of his seaplane and the familiar voice of McTaggart on the radio. Then he controlled himself and somehow forced himself to note, not dispassionately (that would have been asking too much), the dreadful details of his surroundings.

Hard though he looked, Howie spotted no evidence of human sacrifice either on the tree or upon the ground.

Among the thick tentacled roots he examined what he had thought was garbage, at a distance, and so, in a way, it was. The bones of long since decomposed 'victim' sacrificial animals lay everywhere, but among them was something more unexpected. Close to the tree, upon the side that faced the lake, were hundreds of crudely carved hands and feet, hearts and ears, et cetera. Some were made of wood and others of clay. Scratched upon them were names like Jonquil, Maize, Peony, Yew, Poplar, and Sycamore. People's names, as Howie had learned now to recognize them.

Howie had read somewhere that the Roman Catholics went in for something like this at shrines where saints were supposed to preside over miracles. But where *they* simply paid for candles to burn – exactly as he made offerings as a sideman at Saint Andrew's to support the church – these Summerisle people, if you could grace them with that human name, clearly offered up the suffering of animals so that the goddess would grant their requests. And their various ills would be cured. There could be no other explanation for the unspeakable scene above him on the tree.

In a rage now that made him feel as if his very heart would explode with the pace of his own quickened, pulsing blood, he determined to desecrate that tree. When he had finished, he felt both physical and symbolic relief at being able to defile the thing he hated; the sacred pool too had been gratifyingly polluted by his Christian effluent.

It was only as he was walking back to the motorcycle that it occurred to him to wonder whether sacrilege could possibly also be the offence of desecrating someone *else's* shrine. But their involving *animals* surely made the difference? The Jews had them ritually bled to death, but he'd been assured by a Jewish acquaintance that it was quite painless. Would he arrest a man who deliberately pissed on a vivisectionist? Howie supposed he would, and was suddenly somewhat conscience-stricken by what he had done to the mad Beech's sacred tree.

That Rowan was who they meant, when they talked of the Queen of the May, was quite evident. Equally certain was he that she was not in or around the sacred grove. He therefore rode straight back to the township. In doing so he passed Lord Summerisle with Broom, the piper, and another hearty figure in a kilt. They were as unnerved to see him riding by at this early hour on Dr Ewan's machine as he was surprised to see them in the curious activity in which they were involved.

Lord Summerisle appeared to be abroad in a white smock, and hard at work. Up a ladder that was leaning against one of the oaks he was using a golden sickle with which he was carefully cutting large sprigs of mistletoe from the tree. Standing immediately below, with a look of intense concentration on their faces, were Broom and the other man, holding a large muslin net outstretched between them. It seemed to Howie, as he sped by, that it was as if they were playing some game, in which there was some dire penalty if the mistletoe fell onto the ground. Lord Summerisle carefully let fall a piece of mistletoe that was carried by the wind, so that the two below very nearly miscalculated and almost dropped it. All three shouted at each other like a group of bad-tempered tennis players who have forgotten that what they were playing was *only* a game.

Howie was back in his room at the inn by six thirty, having returned the motorcycle, with Dr Ewan still apparently none the wiser. He found hot water waiting for him again, in a jug outside the door, and he set about shaving and washing himself with the self-satisfaction of a man who has got a good start on the day.

Rowan was to be Queen of the May, whatever that involved, and with twelve cops coming to the island it shouldn't take long to find her.

## CHAPTER X

# May Day –
# Morning

WILLOW KNOCKED AND ENTERED WITH A TRAY OF TEA and toast and whistled to see the slightly hirsute, muscular sergeant stripped to the waist.

'Morning, Sergeant Sleuth,' she said admiringly. 'Wish you'd given me the favour of a little of that brawn of yours last night.'

The sergeant looked up at her and grunted.

'G'morning!'

'Och! Well, it's May Day. No time for hard feelings. But I did ask you. Never had a refusal before. I must be getting old and haggard before my time.'

She pulled the still-closed curtains in the room open with a smug smile on her face, knowing all too well that she was utterly gorgeous.

'I thought you were going to come and interrogate me between the sheets last night. I was looking forward to it.'

'I never said I would,' protested Howie, putting on his shirt. 'Would you have told me where the Queen of the May was kept, if I'd visited you?' he asked.

'D'you think they tell me things like that? It'd be much too easy for the likes of you to worm it out of me, don't you see? But I was still sad you didn't come . . . and say a special "how do!"'

'I'm sorry,' said Howie gently. 'I'm engaged to be married.'

'And *that* stops you?' She giggled at the outrageousness of such a notion.

'It's just that I don't believe in it before marriage,' said Howie.

'I must say you *are* a gallant fellow, Sergeant,' said Willow making for the door, a little piqued. 'Still, suit yourself. I expect you'll be going back today, won't you? You wouldn't want to be around here on May Day . . . not the way you feel.'

'Aye, I'll be flying back within the hour to Portlochlie. But I'll be back later with some more police officers.'

'Tell me, Sergeant, do they all think like you?' asked Willow teasingly, lingering at the doorway while he finished dressing. 'Or can I count on you bringing me back some husky mainlander to show me a real good time? They say the men over there are starved of it.'

'By your standards, Willow,' said Howie disappearing down the stairs, munching some toast as he went, 'they certainly are!'

As Sergeant Howie walked down the High Street towards the harbour he noticed that the township seemed entirely deserted. He looked down the side streets and up towards the green but there was no sign of a human being anywhere. Except for the solitary figure of Miss Rose bicycling towards him on the other side of the street, as if she hoped to escape notice, perhaps because her fair hair was wound tight with old-fashioned curlers.

Unfortunately for her, she was at the place where the hill was at its steepest.

'Where is everyone this morning, Miss Rose?' asked Howie, crossing the road at a run and managing to stand in front of her, blocking her progress.

'They're all inside preparing,' said Miss Rose, breathless, and dismounting.

'For May Day?' asked Howie.

'Of course!' she answered.

'Miss Rose, you're the teacher of comparative religion. Tell me, a Christian, about what May Day means to you?'

Miss Rose looked rather flattered, as Howie expected she would.

'It is a feast of fecundity, Sergeant,' she explained, 'celebrated in the form of an ancient dance-drama, which has, as you may well expect, a complete cast of characters.

'Firstly, there is the Hobbyhorse, or man-animal, who leads the ceremony chasing the girls with his tarred skirts.

'Secondly, there is a man-woman, what we call the Betsy, or Teaser, always played by the community leader, in this case, Lord Summerisle.

'Thirdly, there are six sword dancers who throughout the dance continuously make a lock of their swords – a clear symbol of the sun.

'And fourthly, there is the sacrifice whose death and resurrection, of course, is the climax of the dance . . .'

Sergeant Howie had taken out his notebook and a pencil.

'Would you care to make a statement on where the victim is being kept?'

'The victim is as symbolic or not as the Christian's

bread and wine, my dear Sergeant. What does that represent?' asked the schoolteacher.

'The body and blood of our Lord Jesus Christ,' said Howie.

'You eat it at Communion, do you not? And the Roman Catholic Christians believe it is turned miraculously to the real thing in their mouths. Others believe it is symbolic. A matter of taste, I suppose, if you'll forgive the pun.'

'I can't forgive it,' said Howie furiously. 'Now perhaps you'll tell me where your sacrifice is being kept.'

'Like your bread and wine or Host, as I believe you quaintly call it, our sacrifice is reserved. We haven't even told the sacrifice of their honourable, indeed, sacred, fate. It is doubtful that the sacrifice would understand if the truth were suddenly made plain.'

'Are you suggesting some kind of fatted calf?'

'Symbolically that is exactly what I'm suggesting. I'm sure I've said enough now to one who is on his way to report all this to the Chief Constable of the West Highlands. I must say the mainland must be becoming more like a police state every day. When you're not interfering in education, you're poking your nose into religion. Sad that it has to be such an ignorant nose at that! Good day, Sergeant!'

With which Miss Rose climbed unsteadily aboard her bicycle and wobbled laboriously up the High Street hill.

Howie, now seriously concerned about the time, hurried on down to the harbour.

The harbour master was sitting on a bollard, painting an eye on the front of a beached fishing boat when Howie reached the quay.

'Morning, Sergeant,' said the harbour master, cheerfully enough.

'Morning,' responded Howie. 'I need to get to my plane.'

'You won't find a cat stirring this morning. I'd best take you out myself,' said the harbour master obligingly. He rose and the two men made their way down the steps of the quayside to a small dinghy, which they boarded.

As the harbour master was rowing Howie across the water to the seaplane, a crowd of fishermen came out of the building where the nets were manufactured and mended. They stared silently out to sea at the retreating rowboat. All wore elaborate animal masks – otters, badgers, foxes, eagles, rats, et cetera.

In the curious attention to detail of their masks lay a bucolic seriousness of purpose that denied these figures any air of simple revelry. These were not the trivial pretendings of people who were simply throwing off identity to be freer in their enjoyment of a masked ball. Rather, each figure that watched Howie seemed to wear the mask sympathetic to his or her own soul, rather as transvestites wear the clothes of the sex with which they wish to identify.

The masked figures watched in Howie a stranger, so strange to them, that he alone of the people abroad that May morning on Summerisle nursed no alter ego.

The rowboat arrived at the seaplane, and Howie scrambled up into the cockpit. The harbour master waved a friendly goodbye.

'Have a good flight, now!' he called.

Howie began to start the engine, but found the whole electrical system dead. He tried again and again with similar results. He checked the radio, but it too was quite dead. He looked for the emergency batteries but they had gone. Perhaps, it was just possible, they'd disappeared on the mainland. Howie hadn't looked for the last few days.

With a grim face he climbed out onto the wing and tried to swing the propeller. The ignition was on, but no juice seemed to be getting to the starter mechanism. He swung the prop twice, but there was no murmur from the engine.

That was it. He knew now that the plane was going nowhere that day and he was without any radio. At least McTaggart knew where he was.

The figures near the fishing net factory had now melted away. Standing on the float, Howie bleakly regarded the retreating harbour master.

'Hey, you! Come back!' he ordered.

The harbour master continued rowing. Howie waved. The harbour master waved back and continued rowing. Howie remembered his loud hailer and took it out of the cockpit.

'Come back!' shouted Howie through the loud hailer. The gift of hearing seemed suddenly to have returned to the harbour master. He turned his rowboat round and headed back to the seaplane.

'What's the matter?' asked the harbour master anxiously. 'Won't she go?'

'No. Has anyone been near here?' He asked this in the almost sure knowledge that someone had. He put from his mind the implication that *if* someone had deliberately sabotaged the plane, then it was likely that they were desperate enough to risk using violence on him. Their real purpose, he felt sure, was simply to stop him from getting help.

'No one would touch your plane, Sergeant,' said the harbour master.

'Are you sure? Bit of a coincidence that neither the engine *nor* the radio is working. Even the emergency power is gone!'

'If any of the kids had been interfering with it I think I'd have seen 'em,' said the harbour master with apparent certainty.

'I'll want a boat!' said Howie. 'Something fast.'

'It's not possible, friend!' said the harbour master. 'Nothing puts out from here today.'

'This is police business,' said Howie raising his voice. 'I've *got* to have a boat.'

'I'll give it to you straight, Sergeant,' said the harbour master, suddenly rough and abrasive. 'No one is going to give up their May Day to take *you* to the mainland. Now I can either leave you here on this seaplane or take you back to the island. Which is it to be?'

'Don't think you won't hear more of this,' said Howie furiously. 'Obstructing a police officer . . .'

'No one's obstructing you!' said the harbour master firmly. 'Use your plane – if you can!'

Ill-humouredly, Howie stepped into the boat. The harbour master dug in his oars and Howie sprawled on his back. The old salt looked apologetically at Howie as he helped him pull himself out of the swirling bilge. But Howie's mind had passed on from the affront and the indignity of the situation. He was already trying to solve the huge police problem that faced him. If he *really* were to be marooned here without help for a whole twenty-four hours without access to a radio, where would he begin? But perhaps he was giving up on getting help too easily?

For in leaping ashore a glimmer of hope came to Howie as he caught sight of the rows of sailboats and rowboats pulled up on a shingled beach near the quay. They were designed for inshore fishing, not for pleasure sailing, certainly not for speed. None appeared to have engines.

'Have none of the island craft got engines?' asked Howie.

'What for?' asked the harbour master. 'The lads catch all the fish we need under sail, and with the "eye" to ward off any danger.'

'So what about *those*?' Howie said to the harbour master, pointing to the sailing boats. 'Get a lad to help me, and I can sail to Stornoway.'

He mentioned the nearest island of the Outer Hebrides group.

'Aye, you could do that. Thirty-seven miles. Can you sail at all?' the harbour master asked doubtingly.

'Damned right I can. Have you a chart? For the Stornoway water, I mean?' asked Howie.

'Aye, I've got a chart. The east side of Stornoway's a mite dangerous without one,' mused the harbour master. 'Specially as you could hardly make it before sunset!'

'Sunset?' the sergeant was trying to work it out. The man might be right. He was too much of a realist to think he knew more of these waters than the locals. Although he was, he knew, a competent sailor of dragon-class fourteen-footers in the archipelago-sheltered waters off Portlochlie.

But only competent, nothing more. Yet with a local seaman he might have a chance.

'If you could only get me a man to take his boat out . . .' said Howie.

'Tell me, would a Portlochlie man dare go out on the Sabbath?' asked the harbour master, trying to get through to the sergeant.

'It's like that, is it?' asked Howie fully, genuinely comprehending the problem for the first time.

'On May Day here, it's like that!' confirmed the harbour master.

Howie knew when he was beaten. He'd seen English and American tourists standing baffled and angry on the quayside in Portlochlie, with a fistful of money in their hands, trying in vain to persuade a local fisherman to take them out on the Sabbath. The same fisherman, Howie knew, might sneak out alone and unobserved, to fish, if he thought he could get away with it. Getting away with it meant literally *not one* of his friends noticing his transgression. These people here might have a different religion but they were of the same blood. His own blood. Stubborn, a bit hypocritical, and very proud. 'Bloody Scots!' said Neil Howie, to himself, under his breath.

Howie turned and looked into the harbour master's face. It was almost luminously red with the constant stream of malt whisky that must have flown past the yellowing teeth that grinned at him now in a regretful smile. The bloodshot blue eyes laughed their crinkly laugh that seemed uncorrupted by any real guile, only by time and that ocean of liquor.

'Then I'll have to find Rowan Morrison myself,' he said

to the harbour master, confident that whatever passed for
tom-toms on this outrageous island would circulate that
news fast enough. Having uttered this announcement, the
sergeant started to walk back up the hill into the township.
From now on he glanced over his shoulder at regular
intervals and made sure at all times who or what was
behind him. From now on Sergeant Howie walked warily.

The High Street was empty save for a few young
children making their way down from May Morrison's
sweetshop, sucking and slurping at huge yellow and orange
lollipops. An old couple toiled upward on the same side as
Howie.

Then, unnoticed by either children or the old couple,
the most extraordinary apparition appeared out of a side
road farther up the hill. At first it reminded Howie faintly
of a picture he'd seen of a jousting knight. But as it
progressed, all alone, straight across the High Street and
into another side road, he was able to make out more
exactly what it was.

He saw a single, bearded man of considerable height
who was wearing an oblong hooped skirt, from the front of
which obtruded a horse-sized head, which had the rolling
eyes and flared nostrils of a pantomime dragon. From the
back of the skirt trailed a long jointed tail that clattered
on the cobblestones in the man's wake. The skirt itself
looked as if it had been made, like a patchwork quilt, from
a dozen different spare pieces of material. It was, Howie
supposed, the Hobbyhorse that Miss Rose had so recently
described: a figure from the dance-drama in which she'd
explained Lord Summerisle played the Teaser, or Betsy;
'Tease', Miss Rose had nicknamed him at the castle. Howie

remembered that now. He'd thought it referred to something intimate between them – something personal, even sexy. Now he suspected the meaning might easily be more sinister.

Even as he was thinking this he had broken into a run so as to discover where the Hobbyhorse had gone. But on reaching the side road it had entered, he could see no sign of it. Once again he was glad he'd studied the geography of the township on his first evening. He knew that the lane he faced eventually led around to the green, emerging near the back courtyard to the inn. He looked up the High Street and could see a crowd of people gathered near the top of the hill, moving in the general direction of the Green Man.

Howie decided the inn was probably the focus of whatever was going on.

If there was so general a movement of people, he reasoned, it must be because a meeting, a rally, or a ceremony had been called for a specific hour. He watched some hurried stragglers go up the High Street and decided to wait until he could approach the meeting obliquely and have a chance to eavesdrop.

He strolled slowly up the street and paused outside a courtyard where some undertakers, stonemasons, carpenters, and coopers had their several signs, advertising their place of business.

A cart, wreathed with flowers, served as a catafalque for a coffin. It looked like a float for a civic carnival. The phrase 'May Day parade' was in Howie's mind as he watched a number of laughing, excited men hurrying to put a huge Suffolk Punch horse into the cart's traces. But the atmosphere seemed a far cry from that of the cloth-capped beery worthies who marched raggedly behind their trade union banners on a mainland May Day. Howie had always regarded those parades as simply a sentimental celebration of their 'right' to march, by the 'left'.

Why these islanders needed such a large animal to pull the small, lugubrious burden of the coffin became plain when Howie saw the now-sweating men roll a couple of twenty-gallon wood barrels up a ramp and wrestle them onto the flat bed of the cart, beside the coffin.

Howie walked wordlessly into the courtyard just as they were urging the carthorse out into the High Street. The animal had faltered for an instant, his big, white-spatted hooves slipping a bit on the cobblestones. The men stared, without hostility, at Howie as he lifted the lid of the coffin and peered in. It was empty and he waved them on with that economy of gesture that he might have used to speed traffic back in Portlochlie.

Here, at last, he believed, was Rowan's real coffin. All it awaited was her death and not, he assumed, by burning.

As the sergeant followed them up the High Street, he tried to induce in himself a feeling of detachment. Apart from actually finding Rowan he had solved the riddle of her disappearance and the reason for it. A sacrifice of some kind was going to take place and he, Howie, was as irrelevant to what was going on as an animistic aborigine attending the Easter Sunday celebration at Saint Peter's Square in Rome. The people of Summerisle were about as likely to hand over Rowan Morrison to him as the faithful at Saint Peter's would be likely to hand over the Pope. But it was certain that if he tried to stop them from doing what they planned he would be in as much danger as Rowan.

He had faced too many evasions and prevarications in the interviews he had conducted so far – he had been told too many lies to expect that suddenly in answer to the question, 'Can you tell me where they're holding Rowan Morrison?' someone would answer simply 'Sundial Street, number four, the house with the blue shutters!' He knew it wasn't going to happen like that. He would have to exploit all his wit and energy to finding clues as to where they were keeping her. That, in the absence of any help from outside, had to be his priority.

What, he wondered, would he do to protect her, once he found her? Forming that plan, in any detail, would have to wait for at least an hour or so. But two things might work in his favour. First, even McTaggart would regard his failure to report in, on the radio, as a matter to be communicated, at once, to the Chief Constable. The police officer on Stornoway would probably be telephoned and sent, at the very least, in a coastguard launch, which could be at Summerisle in not too many hours. McTaggart knew that he was still on the island because he would never have taken off in the plane without making a prior radio contact to 'air control'.

Secondly, any defiance of the law by the islanders, once he'd found Rowan, might be averted if he were able to explain to them that they were *all* in danger of being charged with conspiracy to commit murder and that should they carry out their sacrifice, every one of them would be accessories to the capital crime. Conviction on the first count alone would carry a stiff prison sentence for all concerned. If they actually sacrificed the girl they would *all* be liable to get life imprisonment on conviction. Such was their isolation, under the tutelage of Lord Summerisle, that very few of the islanders probably realized these grim facts. It would be his duty to point out to them that 'ignorance of the law is no defence'. He would also have to use his persuasive powers to show them that *he*, Howie, could influence what charges, if any, were brought, provided the girl was, at once, freed and allowed to accompany him to the mainland.

'If' was the operative word. *If* they gave him the chance to say any of this.

Sergeant Howie had reached the edge of the green now and could see the cart, with the barrels, being welcomed into the courtyard of the Green Man by a crowd of people. They stood staring in the direction of the distant orchards, as if waiting. Then a ragged cheer went up for they could all see that Lord Summerisle was arriving in a smart trap, driven by the gillie. The laird was clothed in the kind of 'uniform' that Scots gentlemen affect to race meetings and other sporting events. Bareheaded, he wore a tweed jacket and his Morrison workaday kilt of mossy green. In his hand he held his deerstalker hat, which he raised and waved in polite acknowledgement of his tenants' greetings.

On his feet he wore his American-style sneakers.

Watching the distant arrival of the island's laird, Howie recognized that the game he must play out this day was primarily between himself and Lord Summerisle. If one were to liken the problem to a chess game, then Lord Summerisle was the opposing Queen, who still had all his/

her players on the board. Rowan represented the ever-
protected King, virtually powerless and symbolic. On
Howie's side there was only himself, who nevertheless had
all the power of a Queen who had, however temporarily,
been deprived of all his/her other chessmen. Summerisle's
game would be to keep him as far from Rowan as possible.
Translated into real terms, that meant to Howie that Lord
Summerisle, who would clearly prefer him to be elsewhere
while the sacrificial ceremony took place (provided he was
not on the mainland summoning police reinforcements),
had probably already devised a means of keeping him out
of the way. Howie must watch vigilantly for the diversion-
ary move that would surely come. That it was *likely* to be a
diversion rather than any actual physical restraint was,
Howie thought, more Lord Summerisle's style.

Seeing that, so far, no one was taking the slightest
notice of him, the sergeant walked in a semicircle till he
reached some woodland on the edge of the green, not far
from the inn. He now threaded his way among the scrubby
trees until he came to the patch of giant rhubarb that grew
behind the inn's courtyard. From there he could survey the
whole gathering and, in the deeply shadowed cover of the
leaves, remain unseen.

If the Merrie Scotland of Auld had ever really existed,
and Howie knew enough history to be aware that the
plague-ridden poverty of most simple folk in the good auld
days was far from merry, then this scene was what the
sentimental might have preferred to imagine. A long trestle
table bore a feast of cakes and pies, soups and puddings.
Not unexpectedly there was no fruit, but glasses of amber
beer and golden cider came by the trayload from the back

of the inn. The cheerful folk glowed with a pleasant goodwill towards each other, like people at a Christmas party.

Lord Summerisle was practising a complicated dance step with the band. It seemed like a processional version of a Highland reel. Howie couldn't help smiling at His Lordship's garish but serviceable American sneakers, which seemed incongruously out of place with his otherwise impeccable country-gentleman garb.

In the centre of everybody stood the Hobbyhorse, and Willow was pouring beer down the man's throat for him, while the 'horse' itself rolled its eyes. Able to study this bizarre figure more closely now, Howie realized that the tall bearded man didn't have the use of his arms, which were enclosed in the quilted material. It was left to the 'horse's head', whose jaw could snap, to bite playfully at Willow's charming rump as she moved away with the empty glass.

'Everything seems to be in working order, Oak?' shouted Lord Summerisle to the Hobbyhorse man over the din of the gathering.

'Aye, My Lord!' answered Oak, practising little charges at some squealing, excited girls nearby.

Lord Summerisle turned to Alder MacGregor, who was climbing out of a Punch costume flanked by six kilted men who were practising the making of a knot with their swords. The swords were thrust simultaneously into an interwoven star pattern by the six men. Howie was fascinated to see that the pattern the knot made was exactly like the famous Star of David of the Jews.

'Mr MacGregor, I trust we aren't going to have to let your costume out again this year?' asked Lord Summerisle jovially. There was a general burst of laughter around the innkeeper, who scratched his belly with relief at being released from the tight costume.

'I'll manage, My Lord!' smiled Alder MacGregor. 'Thought it does seem to shrink a bit every year!'

Lord Summerisle crossed to the swordsmen and watched as they locked and withdrew the swords a couple of times.

'Are you men all right?' asked Lord Summerisle; his tone was that of a benevolent colonel inspecting his troops.

'We *will* be, My Lord!' said one of the swordsmen.

Lord Summerisle smiled and then moved over to supervise some men who were heating up a barrel of tar. All around him people milled about eating and drinking and greeting latecomers with most unScottish kisses and hugs.

Lord Summerisle signalled to the band and climbed onto a platform nearby. Above him, mounted on the side of the inn, was a great, smiling, sly rendering of the face of the sun. The drummer was giving a roll on his kettledrum to command silence, and the crowd fell quiet, looking up towards Lord Summerisle.

'My friends,' said Lord Summerisle, 'enough now! We will all reassemble on the green at three o'clock sharp, and proceed through the village and countryside to the beach under the stones by the route that has become sacred to our rite. This year, at the procession's end, as has been proclaimed, a holy sacrifice will be offered up jointly to Nuada, our most sacred God of the Sun, and to Avellunau, the beloved Goddess of our orchards, in order that we may furnish them with renewed power to quicken the growth of our crops. Hail the Queen of the May!' he shouted, in conclusion.

'Hail the Queen of the May!' everybody echoed.

Sergeant Howie, standing in the shade of the giant rhubarb leaf, wondered if he ought to go straight to the beach. But which beach? Somewhere close to the stones, which were themselves just inland from a peninsula five miles long, so that the area he might have to search would be ten miles or more in length. As he'd seen from the air, there were dozens of beaches and coves below the towering cliffs. With a helicopter, a fast motorboat, or his seaplane such a search might be practical. Alone on foot, even with the motorcycle, there just wouldn't be time.

The gathering was slowly dispersing. Howie started to make a mental note of anyone he'd met who might be missing and therefore perhaps watching over Rowan, the Queen of the May, poor wee girl, in her last hours. Miss Rose had been there and so had everyone who'd been at the inn on the first night as far as he could remember: the sailors, the shopkeepers, Dr Ewan, Mr Lennox, young Buchanan, Broom, even the old gardener. Some one, obvious person was absent and it was only when Howie realized that no young children under the age of puberty were present that it struck him who was missing.

May Morrison and her daughter Myrtle.

Five minutes later, Sergeant Howie was coming through the door of the sweetshop to find May Morrison placidly carving a slice out of the belly of one of her exquisitely bloated sugar babies and serving it to Myrtle to eat. She seemed genuinely surprised to see the sergeant.

'Why, Sergeant,' she said, 'I thought you'd gone back to the mainland.'

'Mrs Morrison,' said Howie panting slightly, 'whether you know it or not, Rowan's not dead. They've got her hidden somewhere!'

'They?' Mrs Morrison was totally disbelieving.

'The village . . . the whole island. Everyone's in on it,' he told her.

He was expecting some spark of anguish or hope. Yes, shouldn't she *hope* that her child, even against the evidence of everything they'd taught her or told her, might still be alive? But there was nothing from May Morrison but a blank, courteous stare. Was it disbelief or complicity?

'I suppose you're in on it too. Dear God,' asked Howie savagely, 'what kind of a woman are you to stand by and watch them slaughter your own child?'

'I've already told you, Sergeant, this is my child,' said May cuddling little Myrtle, whose mouth was sticky with marzipan and strawberry jam from her slice of the sugar baby.

'What about you, Myrtle?' shouted Howie, hoping to get a quick, honest reaction from the child. 'Isn't it time to tell the truth about Rowan? Is she here perhaps? In the house? Upstairs? When did you last see her, child?'

Myrtle gazed at him for thirty seconds in silence and slowly started to cry, burying her head in her mother's large, cushiony bosom.

'Now see what you've done,' said Mrs Morrison. 'If I were you I'd go back to the mainland, Sergeant, and stop meddling in affairs that are no concern of yours.'

'But they are my concern,' retorted Howie hotly. 'I warn

you, Mrs Morrison, I'm going to try to search every house in this place and anyone, including you, who stands in my way, I'll charge as an accomplice to murder.'

He made to go into the back parlour of the shop. Mrs Morrison obligingly opened the door for him.

'You'll simply never understand the true nature of sacrifice! Hunt all you like,' she said. She went back to helping herself to a piece of cake and calming the tearful Myrtle, taking no further notice of the sergeant. Howie, whose sense of frustration became momentarily intolerable, shouted at her as he poked in the cupboards and stamped up the stairs:

'Heathens. Bloody heathens!'

But by the time he left the house, not having seen a trace of Rowan ever even having lived there, Howie had mastered himself and prepared to carry out a dogged search of every likely place he could think of until the time should come for the islanders' procession.

The sergeant had determined to leave the township well before three o'clock, the hour of their procession's departure. His plan was to try to shadow the islanders. Not a conventional tactic for the West Highland Police but something he'd always wanted to try. Moreover, now that nagging fear was his constant companion, action and plans of action kept his adrenaline pumping.

Inspiration for his plan had first come to him from the cowboy films he'd seen as a child in the cinema theatre at Portlochlie. He'd never enjoyed the American cops and gangster films, disapproving of the flashy way the police drove around making a lot of unnecessary noise in their automobiles and nearly always shooting the gangsters instead of bringing them to a proper trial. His hero figure was a character played by an actor called Van Heflin (although there must have been many others), who had retired honourably from the confederate cavalry, married a squaw, and worked part time for the US Army (the none-too-bright ones in dark blue uniforms and braces). It was *he* who always knew that the sound, at night, of the greater-crested tawny owl was actually a Nez Percé brave sending a warning to his ally, the Sioux. Of course, the US Army colonel never believed him and they were all forced to slaughter hundreds of Indians before Mr Van Heflin could ride off into the sunset. He usually became a widower in the process, since squaw wives appeared to be completely expendable in these motion pictures. What Mr Van Heflin was particularly good at was shadowing Indian war parties. Sometimes the Indian war parties would make him prisoner and, bound and gagged, he'd been taken along while *they* shadowed the US Cavalry. Howie indulged in this fantasy of how he would keep abreast, but just out of sight of the procession.

He did so as he fruitlessly searched house after house all up and down the High Street with meticulous care.

The owners seemed to half-expect him but they were far too busy getting dressed and putting on their masks to pay much attention. Howie's only problem with the island-ers, as he entered their houses uninvited, was his occasional insistence that some young woman or other take off the mask she had already carefully put on and around which she had already painstakingly arranged her hair. He looked constantly for the unusual colour of Rowan's hair, knowing it was always possible that it might since have been dyed.

The masks were elaborately made of real fur or feathers or painted canvas. They represented birds and animals of all kinds but were restricted to breeds of creatures that actually survived in the West Highlands. Thus there were eagles, gannets, puffins and stoats, foxes and deer and many more of the like, but no exotic fowl like parakeets or emus, no alien mammals like lions or bears.

In the women's hairdresser's shop he met a total refusal to remove their masks by a half-dozen women whose hair was being carefully dressed to go with their characters as animals or birds. The hairdressers stood mutinously in front of their customers.

'I don't wish to teach a policeman his job,' said one of the hairdressers whose own peacock mask stood on a stand in the corner of the shop. 'But if you just want to make sure they're none of them a wee girl of thirteen, however well developed . . . just look at their hands, why don't you, Sergeant?'

Sergeant Howie looked and had to agree none could have been Rowan's hands. But before he left the collection of clearly middle-aged women he decided to make a plea to them.

'Ladies, I need your help. As you all must know, by now, Rowan Morrison is missing, and I believe she is being held somewhere on this island for a hideous purpose. A purpose you must, by now, know. Whatever your beliefs may be, you must see you cannot, as decent women and mothers, allow yourselves to become accomplices to murder. Tell me where can I find this child?'

The women remained silent, staring at him through their masks.

He wondered for a moment if he and they weren't separated by a very wall of incomprehension. Did not the word 'mother', connoting tenderness, compassion, and gentleness, mean the same thing to them as it did to him? Women, he knew, were the traditional torturers among primitive people, bringing an imaginative flair to their torturing that seemed denied to them in other less visceral arts like painting or musical composition. Perhaps the she-wolf cared only for her very own whelp. But if his theory about Mrs Morrison was true, even that basic instinct might be absent from these extraordinary women. He longed to shout at them about their unnaturalness but knew it would be useless. The ordinariness, the very banality of their responses, maddened him, but continually disarmed him. Their voices were exactly like his own, like the voice of Mary Bannock, and superficially they seemed as like the people of Portlochlie as any near cousins do in a family. Their language was the same too but somewhere along the line the meaning of the most basic words and phrases seemed to have subtly changed for them. Nor had he any dictionary to help him. So that he knew he might as well rave against Hottentots, as against these, his own people.

After a moment he left the hairdresser's, slamming the door behind him.

Howie started to work outward from the High Street, picking every third house, in a random search that he thought might have more success, because people could not know, for sure, that he was coming.

In one house he found all the doors locked so that he had to break the catch on the back door. Once inside, he

heard someone humming on an upper floor in a childlike
voice:

> 'Baa, Baa, Black Sheep,
> Have you any wool?
> Yes, sir, yes, sir,
> Three bags full . . .'

Creeping up the stairs he traced the voice to a room,
the door of which was closed. The high little voice
continued to croon to itself as Howie flung the door
violently open. Seconds later he was retreating as a huge
fat lady sitting naked in a hip bath threw a sponge at him,
but then seeing the identity of her supposed ravisher,
rushed after him like a great, gleaming, white leviathan,
sloshing bath water about her as she grabbed at the panic-
stricken Howie's coat-tails.

'Och, you're that lovely. I thought you were Old Rue,
the rapist, and that's a fact. Com'n back, man!' she cried,
as if it were the best offer she'd had in a decade.

In another house he was admitted by a man wearing the
mask of a codfish and who exuded a breath so infectiously
whisky-laden that Howie winced away from it and ran
upstairs to search the bedrooms. He was opening a double-
doored cupboard only to find nothing in it, except some
old overalls and a raincoat, when the door to the other
half of the cupboard started to creak inexorably open of its
own accord. Startled, Howie stood back to watch, in
horror, as the absolutely stiffened body of a fully clothed,
young girl fell headlong to the floor. He could see at once
that it was *not* Rowan but another child with curly,

chestnut brown hair and freckles. What looked like dried blood seemed to have flowed (and was now congealed) from the corner of her mouth to her chin.

He bent to feel her pulse when she opened a wicked, laughing brown eye and leapt to her feet, to run giggling from the room. Howie could also hear the liquorish laugh of the cod-faced man downstairs, who had obviously been in on the game. In a revenge that made him feel both exhausted and mean-spirited he was determined, by turning this particular home upside down, to make sure that the brown-haired girl's game was not really a blind to distract him from the actual presence of Rowan somewhere else in the house. Rowan was not there.

The next household was aflutter with three extremely elderly ladies and their cats.

The old lady who admitted Howie treated him exactly like a guest who had been expected, instead of ignoring him as people elsewhere had done.

'We had so hoped you'd come!' she said, and introduced the other ladies. 'This is Swallow and this, Lark. I'm Cuckoo . . . and you're not to laugh at my name. We were all *wild* birds in our youth, you see. We're Willow Mac-Gregor's aunts. Have you met Willow yet?'

'Of course he has, Cuckoo,' said Swallow. 'He's staying at the inn.'

'I'm sure Willow overdoes it,' said Lark. 'That girl's not strong. I keep telling Alder. Beautifully put together, of course. But a weak chest. Always had, ever since she was a little girl. You *will* take a little parsnip wine, Sergeant?'

They had pushed Howie gently into the parlour and produced a trolley on which a number of bottles of quite nauseous-looking drinks were assembled. He found a glass put into his hand by lace-mittened fingers and Swallow was pouring a viscous, saffron-coloured liquid into it. He sipped it very cautiously and held the contents in his mouth.

'I'm looking for a young girl called Rowan,' said Howie trying to seem stern and businesslike. 'I have reason to think she is going to be a sacrifice today.'

'Lucky girl. How well I remember when I first sacrificed myself. It was with the young lord's grandfather. What a magnificent figure of a man he was,' said Swallow most nostalgically.

'He named us all, you know. Lark because she sang so prettily,' said Cuckoo inconsequentially. 'Will you try some of my tipsy cake?'

Howie was determined to find out something worth knowing from these old biddies or escape at once, leaving them with their memories.

'Ladies, has there ever been a human sacrifice on this island "to . . ." what is the phrase Lord Summerisle uses? "to quicken the growth of your crops"?'

'What a poetic way of putting it. Such a dear boy he is!' said Cuckoo. 'Yes, of course, when we were young we all "came out" together. The Old Lord gave a priapic ball. He used to call it our "mass sacrifice". He had a great sense of humour. But that, of course, has quite gone out. Heaven knows what the young get up to these days!'

'No one *died* of it?' asked Howie impatiently.

'Good gracious, no!' said Cuckoo with a giggle that couldn't quite help turning into a cackle. 'I never heard of anyone dying of it.'

'Lord Summerisle's father once told us that he thought

he might die *without* it,' said Swallow. 'It was when he was getting on a bit. We nicknamed him the "old bee". He had all the young girls called after delicious honey flavours like Thyme, Heather, Lavender, and so on . . .'

'Where the bee sucks, there suck I,' sang Lark, and Howie could hear that she must have had a very pretty voice in her time.

'He used to say that an old man who couldn't learn to like sipping honey would have a very lonely old age,' added Cuckoo wistfully.

'I expect you'd like to come up to the bedrooms?' asked Swallow suddenly quite brisk. 'I can see, you impetuous boy, that you're in no mood for drinking! But are anxious to get down to business!'

She took his still almost untouched glass of parsnip wine from him.

Howie was following the three ladies to the staircase, his mind reeling from the preceding conversation. He'd seen the Safeway Supermarket (Cooked Meat and Fats Department) amateur production of *Arsenic and Old Lace*. Were these old ladies exactly what they seemed and proclaimed themselves to be, or were they purveyors of doctored parsnip wine? Could this be Lord Summerisle's trap and diversion? That, from the first moment he'd entered the house, and the old women had launched into their effusive welcome, had been his suspicion. Behind their backs, he spat the small quantity of liquor he'd sipped, and so far held in his mouth, neatly into a potted philodendron, at the foot of the stairs. Then he spoke to them in a firm, loud voice that quite startled them and sent the various roving cats scurrying.

'I'll thank you ladies to stay downstairs while I search the premises!'

'He wants to be masterful,' said Lark with a tremor of excitement in her voice.

'Nonsense!' said Cuckoo. 'It's a form of extreme shyness. Anyone can see that!'

But they all stayed downstairs while he rummaged around the bedrooms with what sounded to them like increasing fury.

'I hope you saw the picture of us as the "three Graces",' called Swallow, as he was starting to make his way down the stairs again.

He stood on the landing looking down at them in extreme distaste.

'Graces?' he roared at them. 'You filthy old women. Never in my life have I seen such obscenities as you have up there. But to hell with that. What, may I ask, is *this*? And how did *it* get here?'

Howie held up a lock of hair bound with a thin gold cord. It was exactly the shade of Rowan's hair, as seen in the photograph, which the sergeant now held in his other hand for comparison.

'The old lord had it as a keepsake!' said Cuckoo. 'His son gave it back to me after his father died.'

'It's *your* hair?' questioned the sergeant disbelievingly, looking at the grey-haired, ravaged old woman's face with the still-fine bone structure and the violet-blue eyes, in which, to the sergeant's great discomfort, tears now gathered, spilling down her wrinkled cheeks and making the rather excessive kohl she wore run. He took out his handkerchief and wrapped the hair in it before slipping it into his pocket.

'Don't worry. If you're telling the truth, it'll be returned to you after analysis. And if I were you, I'd take ... that ... obscene rocking chair you have up there and burn it. Good day, ladies!'

He spat the last word out sarcastically as he slammed the door behind him.

'He wants us to burn our lovely priapic chair?' he heard Lark twitter in amazement, as he made his way to their garden gate.

What he neither heard, nor saw, was the strange sight of the three old women racing upstairs as fast as touches of arthritis and the burden of old age would allow. Elbowing each other aside in their attempt to get ahead in the race, the three of them finally reached the room in which the priapic rocker stood alone in the window. The excitement of Howie's visit had aroused a kind of cackling hysteria in them and only the rollicking pleasures of the chair could now fulfil and relieve them. Each grimly fought for the chance to be the first to, up with her clouts and closing her eyes, sink thankfully onto her hardening vision of the essential Howie.

The sergeant stood in the street thinking over the lock of hair in his pocket and trying to put the evidence at his disposal into a new pattern to see if it would fit. Suppose the hair was Rowan's? Any *old* lady could make up a story about her hair once being the same colour. The old harridans had been teasing him, of course, in pretending to misunderstand his questions about sacrifice, but something

Miss Rose had said earlier came back to him now. She had hinted that she viewed the Christian taking of the sacrament, particularly in the Roman Catholic rite, as a form of symbolic cannibalism, at best.

He took stock anew. Suppose that Rowan was dead and not buried but that she was 'reserved' in a frightful pagan parody of the Christian eating of flesh and drinking of blood, to be literally *consumed* by the community? Nothing, now, would surprise him. Her hair could then have been divided up as a keepsake, which might be thought, by the credulous, to have some magic power. Perhaps to the three frightful old birds, it might be hoped to bring rejuvenation. The cannibal theory, as he privately dubbed it, was not one that the sergeant was yet ready to entirely embrace. For it still seemed less likely than that she was alive and being prepared for sacrifice. But the impossibility of searching the whole island was already discouragingly clear to him. What he *could* do was go to the places where a dead body might be prepared for human consumption. The butcher, the baker, and so on. He remembered that these shops were clustered together at the foot of the High Street. He walked straight there.

Howie recognized the baker as he entered his bakery and shop. The two were all part of one large room with a plain counter, for serving, to one side. The baker Howie remembered as one of the swordsmen he'd seen at the rehearsal. As the sergeant entered, the man was raking out the charcoal from the open space under the large iron door, which enclosed his oven, on the back wall.

'What's in here?' asked Howie, pointing to the iron door.

'That's bread in my oven,' explained the baker. 'Would you be thinking I've toasted the little girl up in it?' he asked laughing.

'Open it!' thundered Howie.

The baker looked incredulous.

'I don't like opening my oven when she's cooling,' he said and moved to bar the way to the oven door. But Howie thrust him aside with a forceful push that sent the man sprawling. Before the now angry baker had time to recover, Howie had opened the door. Inside, Howie saw a long coffin-shaped baking tin about seven feet in length. He stared at it for a long moment before reaching to remove it, then he burned his hands and was forced to look around for, find, and put on a pair of oven gloves. The baker stood watching him in mute and angry puzzlement, but he made no move to interfere with Howie, to help him or hinder him. Howie managed to slide out the huge baking tin and lay it on a table. He removed the top to reveal the figure of a full-length man who seemed to be made out of sheaves of wheat, all rendered as a crusted bread. The baker laughed at the sergeant's surprise.

'What is this?' asked Howie sharply.

'The life of the fields – John Barleycorn!' said the baker.

Howie grunted and, snatching up a knife from the counter, approached the large bread figure. His intention was to slice into it to see if there was anything in the way of a body inside it, but he heard the baker gasp as he poised the knife, ready to cut into the figure.

'If you want to look inside . . . that is it . . . isn't it?' asked the baker nervously.

'Yes, what about it?' asked Howie, wondering if the man was frightened of what would be discovered.

'Please let me. I'll slit him down the side like a French loaf. Then you can have your look inside him and it won't . . . deface *him* so . . .'

Howie found nothing inside. He went through the butcher's shop and found nothing except for a rather sickening mask fashioned from a real bull's head, which its owner proudly put on for Howie, explaining that in it he, the butcher, became Old Brazenface.

The fishmonger had nothing in his ice storage room either except, predictably, fish. He, too, was anxious to show off an elaborate costume in which, he explained, he represented 'the salmon of knowledge'.

'You can't eat enough salmon, y'know, Sergeant,' said the fishmonger, as if anxious to improve the sales of this expensive and scarce fish. 'And for why, you'll be asking. Because it is said that it acquired mystical lore through eating the nuts of the divine hazel trees, which fell into a well beneath them. These nuts conveyed to the salmon knowledge of everything that was in the world, and, by extension, those who can catch and eat of its flesh acquire supernatural sight. But maybe you've known all that since you were a babby?'

The sergeant left before being exposed to any more fishlore. Exhausted, Howie made his way slowly back up the hill. It was well past noon and he had found nothing so far. All he had were two almost equally ghoulish theories, one of which must soon prove to be correct. As far as preventing a crime or having enough hard evidence to start making any arrests, he was hardly closer than he had been when he'd risen at sunup.

# CHAPTER XI

## *May Day –*
## *Afternoon*

A BUXOM YOUNG WOMAN WAS WHEELING A BARROW UP
the High Street selling jellied eels, fresh shellfish, and cool
apple juice. The rosy-cheeked young woman cried aloud:

'Cockles and mussels. Alive, alive . . . oooh!'

Sergeant Howie suppressed a reflex instinct to ask her
for her street-vendor's licence. He knew she would have
none and he was extremely hungry. He bought a half-pint
of jellied eels, sprinkled some vinegar over them, and
munched thoughtfully as he trailed the barrow up the High
Street. People ate shellfish alive because the shellfish were
nonvertebrates, and also, he had to admit, buying himself
a half-pint of cockles, because they tasted better that way.
His final purchase was a half-pint of apple juice with which
he washed down his impromptu meal.

The girl continued to utter her cry as she trundled her
barrow, and Howie, who was slightly paranoid about being
poisoned by these people, was relieved to find a good many
folk came out of their houses, in varying stages of readying
themselves for the procession, and bought from her.

He paused at that point on the hill of the High Street
where the undertakers, carpenters, and coopers had their

courtyard. His digestive system was pleading with him to stand still for an instant and give it some rest from all this ceaseless activity, while it was busy coping with eels, cockles, vinegar, and apple juice.

'Alive, alive . . . ooh!' shouted rosy cheeks.

Howie considered her cry and, by extension, another possible fate awaiting Rowan. For the first time that day a thought crossed his mind so horrible that he had to dismiss it because he refused to believe that these people, credulous, superstitious, and misguided though they might be, would be capable of inflicting such a fate on a fellow human being. Whatever else they might do they would not attempt to eat the poor, wee girlie *alive*, surely? Eating her dead (even cooked), he had already accepted as a remote but hideous possibility.

He had been on the point of returning to the Green Man to glean what he could, when he realized that the undertaker's shop could not be ignored. It was such an obvious place to put Rowan, if they'd already killed her, that he had assumed that the idea would never have occurred to people as devious as they. However, they could have wished him to *assume* that. So he went about searching all the buildings around the courtyard. Everyone had left for the day and he searched undisturbed. The carpenter's shop was innocent of anything unexpected. The cooper's shop was naturally full of barrels into which Howie peered only to find them all empty except an old cracked one in a distant corner, from which came a plaintive cry. The sergeant had to climb over a stack of barrels to get near the one from which the sound seemed to come. But his hopes had so risen at this strange cry that, as he set about climbing towards it, he made too much haste and caused a kind of barrel avalanche. As it turned out a tabby cat had given birth to kittens in the old cracked barrel and she hissed at Howie's deeply disappointed face as he peered down at her.

He left the undertaker's parlour till last (it seemed so obvious a place as to be the least likely). There were coffins in various stages of construction. Two were laid out on trestles. In one of these he found the body of a drowned man of about sixty. Pennies covered his eye sockets and what looked like a Saint Athelstan's pippin held his jaws open. Curious, Howie removed the pennies to find the eyes gone. The skull beyond seemed as hollow as an empty nut. Howie shuddered and thought he felt a sympathetic prickling in his own brain, or perhaps it was only the involuntary tightening of the scalp as he fought back an urge to be sick. He replaced the pennies hurriedly. He wondered if they were a bizarre cosmetic notion to spare the relatives.

When he opened the other coffin it was after a count to ten. It was as if he half-feared he was going to find a dismembered Rowan and half-hoped he *would* find her if only to know she was safe from further pain or fear. There was a man's body inside. Not Rowan's. But the corpse *had* been mutilated.

Sergeant Howie took all this in almost simultaneously with a strange mixture of shock and relief. He peered at the arm from which the hand seemed to have been severed just above the wrist. The sergeant knew enough about pathology to be certain that the hand had been removed sometime after death. He remembered the old gravedigger's tale of the Hand of Glory.

Perhaps it was Dr Ewan's curious idea of a post-mortem, in which case there would have to be a report to the Department of Health about it and, in the event of anything suspicious, a report would have to be made to the police. Howie looked at the man who had lost his hand, who, like his fellow cadaver, bit on an apple, and slowly realized that he recognized him. He was a man he'd seen dancing licentiously with Willow on the first night of his visit to the island. The very same man he'd seen in the library the day before. A man who would say shush no more.

He left the place hurriedly, anxious to get to the inn and have a rare drink of whisky. He very seldom felt that urgent need, but now he almost ran across the green in his hurry to get to the bar.

To his considerable surprise the bar was empty except for Willow and Alder MacGregor. Both were still drying glasses from the morning's celebration.

'Give me a whisky, please,' said the sergeant peremptorily as he strode into the bar.

Alder MacGregor looked at the sweating, dishevelled sergeant with wry amusement and went behind the bar to pour a dram of malt whisky, 'Summerisle's Inheritance', the only name brand available on the island. Willow was more welcoming.

'Hullo!' she said cheerily enough. 'You're back early! Where are the other coppers?'

'I didn't go,' said Howie. 'My plane wouldn't start!'

Alder MacGregor set the dram of whisky down in front of Howie, who drank it off at a gulp, letting the aftertaste slowly come to him, feeling his jangled nerves relax a little. Alder MacGregor watched him with amusement.

'So he spent the time, instead, turning the whole village upside down!' said Alder. 'No wonder he's worn out. Did you find the girl?' asked the innkeeper.

Howie shook his head and finished his drink.

'I can't say I'm surprised,' said Alder MacGregor matter-of-factly.

Howie set down the empty dram glass with a bang.

'I think I'll rest in my room for half an hour,' said Howie. 'And I don't wish to be disturbed,' he added meaningfully to Willow.

'I'd stay there till tonight if I were you,' said Alder MacGregor. 'We don't relish strangers much today!'

Howie was already on his way from the bar and up the stairs towards his bedroom. He lay down on his bed and closed his eyes. A plane was flying somewhere in the distance.

*

A bomber from the Royal Air Force's Scottish Coastal Command was making a routine flight out over the Atlantic. The special radar equipment it carried was part of NATO's early warning system. On this first of May, the squadron leader flying the plane had been instructed by his commanding officer to veer off course by nearly sixty miles and overfly Summerisle, thirty-six miles southwest of Stornoway, to see if he could sight a police seaplane in the harbour there. He had been told that there had been a breakdown in radio communications, and a positive sighting would reassure the West Highland Police.

The squadron leader wheeled his ungainly flying radar station over the island at about thirteen forty-five hours, British summer time, at a little under two thousand feet. He and his crew could see the police seaplane quite clearly as it rode at anchor near the quay. They radioed this news back to their headquarters, received an acknowledgement, and set their course northwest in the general direction of Greenland.

The weather report was for a fine unclouded day. The crew of the plane was particularly relaxed. It was the received wisdom from the powers-that-be that May Day was the most unlikely day of the year for the Soviet Union to start World War Three. 'Of course,' the squadron leader was saying, 'if one May Day the bigwigs of the Soviet presidium do *not* turn up on the reviewing stand in Moscow for the great annual parade, then we might as well start bombing, rocketing, and cruise missiling the hell out of them, cause sure as "God made little apples" their ironware is already on its way.'

'D'you think our ambassador'd have the sense to signal us?' asked his flight lieutenant, who was watching Summerisle lazily as it started to recede. Suddenly he craned his neck and stared back for a full ten seconds, then tapped his squadron leader's arm.

'I could have sworn I saw a huge man standing on a cliff back there. Gigantic he was!'

'What kind of man?' asked the squadron leader. 'One of those rude drawings on hillsides left by our horny Celtic ancestors?'

The flight lieutenant had looked back again, for an instant, but then relaxed, settling down to do his duty and fiddle with the expensive machinery bought for him by the British taxpayers.

'No, sort of three-dimensional. Anyway, too much cloud now to see,' he said.

*

Sergeant Howie lay on his bed, his eyes closed. Suddenly he became aware of a whispering outside his door, which he seemed to have left ajar. He lay straining to hear, ready to feign sleep.

'I don't like to use it on him!' Willow was whispering.

'The laird said we must take no chances, didn't he?' whispered Alder MacGregor irritably.

'Yes, but with the Hand of Glory,' whispered Willow with a little squeak, 'there's no telling when you wake. He might sleep for days.'

'All the better!' said Alder MacGregor in an almost normal tone of voice. 'We don't want him butting in! Light it up!'

Howie heard some scuffling and the striking of a match. They were now approaching his door. He closed his eyes and could hear Willow's dress rustling as she crossed the room and stood beside his bedside table.

'That'll make you sleep, my pretty sergeant!' she whispered putting something down with a metallic click. Howie could smell an unpleasant sweetish, pungent odour. Willow was on her way back through his door, stifling a laugh.

Howie could tell that they were outside on the landing and that his door remained open. So that he didn't, for the moment, dare open his eyes, but continued to listen carefully.

'What's the time?' asked Alder MacGregor in a low voice.

'Nearly quarter to,' Willow replied.

'Well, I'll go and change!' whispered her father. 'We can't do without Punch. You'd best get on ahead. They've given you girls five minutes' start, haven't they?'

'All right! 'Bye,' said Willow, and she was on her way, tiptoeing downstairs. Alder MacGregor walked down the corridor to his own room. When all was silent Howie cautiously opened his eyes and looked in the direction of the noxious smell, then stifled a scream.

The Hand of Glory – the hand almost certainly of the man in the library, amputated at the wrist, was stuck on the spike of an old-fashioned candlestick, with each dead finger aflame, like five frightful candles. It loomed over Howie, from his bedside table, as if it were going to gag him with its flesh-singed, flaming fingers.

Half-fainting from fear and horror, Howie took a side-swipe at the candlestick and knocked the whole thing to the floor. Somehow he managed to stop himself vomiting although the cockles and apple juice surged, so that he tasted them again, but bitter and bilious. Gritting his teeth, he knelt on the floor beside the amputated hand that had come loose from the candlestick. Wetting his finger and thumb with his saliva, he extinguished the flaming digits of the dead hand, nearly retching again at the smell. Then, at the far end of the passage, he heard, and then saw, Alder MacGregor walk from a corridor closet to his own room carrying his Punch costume, including an elaborate mask with the traditional hooked nose and jutting chin on a grinning face.

There was no other sound in the inn.

Howie did not even wait to work out, in his normally legalistic policeman's mind, what justification he could have for his next action. Whether attempting to lull an officer into deep and lasting sleep with the Hand of Glory was simply 'impeding him in the course of his duty' (God knew, a serious enough offence), or something far worse, hardly mattered for the sergeant now. He was determined on action, and violent action at that, because he had seen the perfect way to shadow the procession. He was going to take part in it! But masked, as Punch!

Creeping on stockinged feet, the length of the passage, he reached Alder MacGregor's bedroom door. Peering inside he could see the fat man straining into the costume like a plump insect attempting to re-enter its chrysalis. Howie measured the distance he would have to travel before he reached the innkeeper, selected the exact place on the back of Alder's neck where a karate blow with the side of the hand could make him unconscious without any lasting harm.

When he did it, when he hit Alder, it was so swift and with such economy of motion, that the innkeeper could hardly have spent more than an instant being aware of his assailant before he slumped to the floor, a breathing lump of matter, but otherwise inert. The Hand of Glory had, in a manner of speaking, boomeranged.

After he had bound and gagged Alder, it took several minutes for Howie to dress himself up as Punch. The hunchbacked jacket had to be wrestled off the limp but lumpy frame of the innkeeper without tearing its fine, cream-silk material. Where it had the scarlet medieval slashes on the sleeves it tended to catch on things and start to rip. When the sergeant saw the trousers, his resolve nearly failed him. Where the zip or fly-buttons of the trousers might otherwise have been was a huge, waving codpiece, cross-gartered in cherry-coloured silk. Howie was about to rip this obscene protuberance off the garment when he realized that to these dreadful people this orna-mental phallus was an expected part of Punch. As a fairy might be thought incomplete without a wand!

He donned the whole costume and examined himself in the looking glass. There was something wrong. Then he realized that he looked more like a Pierrot than a Punch, because the costume hung on him in folds. A minute or so later he had stuffed a pillow into a quite convincing facsimile of Alder's beer belly. Then he donned the mask and Punch's three-pointed cap with a bell hanging from each corner.

Howie had closed the door on the unconscious inn-keeper when, walking past the still-open closet from which Alder had taken his costume, he saw a short, thick stick attached by a string to an inflated pig's bladder. Alder MacGregor must have momentarily forgotten it, thought Howie. Even if it was not a normal part of the costume he couldn't risk leaving it behind. If he wanted to avoid having to talk to anyone he must arrive late for the procession's start so that his silence could be taken as embarrassment. To be sent back for the bladder might be disastrous! While he was sure that the costume totally disguised him, he had no illusions that he could imitate the boozy, leprechauny tones of the man he was impersonating.

The sergeant rushed across the green towards the already formed-up procession like a recruit late on parade.

'Come on, MacGregor!' roared Lord Summerisle's voice. 'The girls are five minutes ahead of us. They'll think the old boss isn't going to catch them this year if we don't hurry!'

Howie, who was only just learning how to squint through the eye slits, suddenly realized that a commanding female figure with long black hair, wearing a mauve lace dress that looked as if it had been discarded by an impoverished governess, was the person addressing him in the noble lord's voice. When he saw the sneakers the figure wore he realized it was, indeed, Lord Summerisle. The Teaser himself.

The procession was facing so that it would have to pass down the High Street and then along a coast road, that Howie'd never so far travelled, in order to reach the stones. At their head, the Hobbyhorse plunged about like a temperamental racehorse before the start. Behind 'the hoss' Lord Summerisle capered about in his Teaser's costume, and behind him Howie took his place in his disguise as Punch. Then came the swordsmen whom Howie/Punch had wanted to follow, but who obstinately fell in behind him.

There followed crowds of men dressed in animal masks – otters, badgers, foxes, eagles, stoats, and rats predominating. A ram carried the effigy of John Barleycorn held aloft, and the Salmon of Knowledge was there, and Old Brazenface. Flanking the procession were the musicians – carrying drums, tambourines, hornpipes, bagpipes, whistles, and fiddles.

Three loud beats on the drum started the procession, at five past three p.m. The drum then continued to throb while the men who had previously heated the hot tar barrel rushed up to the Hobbyhorse with big brushes dripping tar, and proceeded to paint its vast hooped skirt while it plunged and whirled like a beast in mute pain. The hornpipes and three-holed whistles took up the beat, followed by the fiddles and, at last, the sustained drone of the bagpipes. Slowly the melody emerged as the men, for they were all men, launched themselves into the ancient Morris Dance Hornpipe, 'Hunt the Squirrel'. The procession moved off down the High Street led by the great, plunging, prancing Hobbyhorse, dripping warm tar from its skirt and clacking its hinged jaw.

With a dance-drama on the move the best view is reserved for the birds. A bird's-eye view of the procession, as it danced its way down the High Street, would have shown an extraordinary pattern of varying activity. At the rear, many of the dancers peeled off, and entered the houses on either side of the street, going out by the back doors to enter the next house by adjacent doors, and so emerge on the street again, to rejoin the procession. Many of these dancers carried branches of blossom and green leaves, which they left in the living rooms of the empty houses. At the end of the High Street nearest the harbour, the procession wheeled and headed for the open country along a road that led them into the open fields and orchards.

So fast did they move, once they were clear of the

township, that they could soon see the dawdling, laughing women ahead of them.

As the men approached, the girls' delighted shrieks of anticipation floated back to them on the wind. The procession surged forward, with the monstrous Hobbyhorse fair flying down the road, followed by the whirling Teaser, and the lumbering Punch.

The women and girls, who included every female of child-bearing age or over, were walking at no great pace, and continually looked back over their shoulders towards the advancing procession of men. The giggling and hysteria mounted the nearer the Hobbyhorse came, until suddenly with a darting, leaping run it was upon them, clacking at their heels, and swinging its skirts to smear their clothes with tar. Sometimes he managed to seize a girl and put her under his great skirt, only to release her a few seconds later squealing and blushing. Behind the foraging Hobbyhorse, Lord Summerisle, in his Teaser dress, danced wildly in counterpoint, his long black hair flying in the wind. But at his side Punch laboured badly. The disguised Howie's performance plainly infuriated Lord Summerisle who had presumably rehearsed elaborately with the Alder Mac-Gregor he supposed to be his Punch.

'What's the matter with you, MacGregor?' he complained. 'Call that dancing? Cut some capers . . . Use your bladder . . . Play the Fool, man. That's what you're here for.'

Howie/Punch flicked his bladder feebly at a couple of girls who easily eluded him.

'I suppose you've gone and got drunk at your own bar

again!' shouted Lord Summerisle, looking rather like Poca-
hontas's aunt in a rage.

Suddenly the ranks of the retreating women broke, and
Willow and Miss Rose danced forward. Both wore valen-
tine masks, one of silver, the other of gold. They carried
two long tong-shaped castanets in their hands which, to
much laughter, they aimed at Punch, nipping at his codpiece and his bladder. Finally, to a roar of applause, he
attacked them furiously with his bladder, driving them
back to disappear into the crowd, now mixed more and
more with the men.

'That's more like it! ... Good!' shouted Lord Summerisle. 'Enjoy yourself, MacGregor! Today's the day you play
the Fool!' The procession wound on its way: the Hobbyhorse snapped and darted; the women screamed and were
sometimes 'covered'; the Teaser pirouetted on his sneakers;
Punch was mocked and retaliated; the sword dancers whif-
fled their swords from side to side and clanked them ritually
together; the horn dancers advanced, retired, and crossed
sides; the men in the animal masks danced and imitated
the sound of the creatures they represented; the musicians
banged and blew and scraped with gusto.

Howie had been kept so continuously busy, since his
mad dash to join the procession, that it had given him
little time to think and less to observe. He welcomed their
mistaken notion that he was drunk. It made his clumsy,
studied movements more plausible. He gathered from Lord
Summerisle's urgings and the actions of the women, when
the procession reached them, that he was supposed to be
the butt of everybody's fun, and that he too was supposed

to bait the girls with his bladder, driving them under the flying skirts of the Hobbyhorse. He disliked doing this intensely because he'd noticed, as Oak's great quilted skirt flew, that the man's buttocks were as bare as the day his mother bore him, and that he'd clearly been chosen for the grossness of his 'kidney-wiper', which almost made the extravagance of Punch's own codpiece seem paltry by comparison. The lewdness of it all sickened Howie but he kept his temper and went on gazing around for any sign of Rowan.

From the point of view of the great stones the music and screaming came to the hallowed circle faintly but clearly. Wood pigeons and jays and an occasional cuckoo flew up out of the oak trees to wheel overhead in the clear late afternoon sky, and hares bounded away from the dancers' path into the undergrowth.

Inside the mask Howie started to feel a restriction that was other than purely physical. Not just the difficulty of seeing anything, save a kind of peephole view of his surroundings, but the fact that he was playing a role that demanded much of his concentration. The result, which he had not foreseen when he had decided to take on Alder's part, was that he had no leisure to look carefully at every female islander in the procession to try to measure who might be under which mask. However, he did have the opportunity to start identifying some of the people he had met by the creatures they had chosen to represent.

It was easy to see that the thickset Boar was Dr Ewan, and his companion, the Red Fox, was clearly Mr Lennox. If Rowan was here, Howie wondered, would they have disguised her in so obvious a mask as that of a hare?

Nevertheless, he looked for hares, and to his dismay saw that there were at least three of them, and while one was a man, Howie realized that there was sufficient duplication of bird and animal masks in the crowd to make this a doubtful means of recognition.

The oak woods were now behind them and the stones loomed ahead. The mood of the procession had undergone a subtle change as they approached the hallowed circle. Lord Summerisle now led, and he used the sickle and the mistletoe he carried in his hands like the conductor of an orchestra uses his baton. The music was quietened to a monotonous tuck-a-tuck of the drum. The Hobbyhorse was tamed to a gentle prance. The men and women had largely paired so that the whole gathering advanced in a double column behind the six swordsmen.

In this way, Lord Summerisle finally halted under the pediment of the principal portal stones that seemed like the natural entrance to the circle. Everyone behind him stopped while he held the mistletoe and sickle high above his head.

Howie wondered what he was supposed to do at this obviously prearranged signal. The swordsmen began slow marching, like soldiers at a funeral, to surround the dolmen stone at the centre of the circle. The Hobbyhorse hurried to the side opposite the Teaser and, in response to Lord Summerisle's slow lowering of the mistletoe, the horse's head bowed until it almost touched the ground. It then reared briefly and was still. The musicians took up a position just outside the circle while everyone else formed a single line behind Lord Summerisle. The swordsmen were watching the Teaser and waiting, but Lord Summerisle was staring at Punch, who had simply wandered into the circle as if he were a spectator and not a participant. Howie saw that he was in the wrong place and hurried to join the single line that was still being formed behind the laird. He watched Lord Summerisle's back anxiously. Had he given himself away? Or was his presumed drunkenness going to save him from suspicion? What he dreaded was that it would become part of the ceremony for everyone to remove their masks before he had time to identify Rowan.

Lord Summerisle was making another ritualistic signal. He swept his sickle in a semicircular movement in front of him, as if he were miming the cutting of something. The watching swordsmen reacted instantly. The swords leapt up and were thrust together, forming a faultless knot. They held this laterally between them so that it was parallel to the dolmen stone that lay at their feet, flat with the ground. The swordsmen looked back at the Teaser expectantly.

'Here comes the chopper to chop off your head!' intoned Lord Summerisle.

The musicians started, at once, to play the opening bars of a tune that Howie was amazed to remember as a nursery rhyme: 'Oranges and Lemons said the bells of Saint Clement's . . . Here comes the chopper to chop off your head.' At school he'd been told that the song dated from the great plague of London in the seventeenth century. He thought there had been a line that went 'Bring out your dead said the Bells of Shoreditch.' But with the melody over, Lord Summerisle and the whole congregation started to chant:

'Chop, chop, chop, chop, chop, chop . . .'

If the words were naïve and childlike or repetitive, the atmosphere in and around the circle of stones certainly wasn't. Howie, who was trying desperately to see and search the masks of the people for any trace or hint of Rowan, believed he saw signals of fear from the tense body language of the crowd.

'. . . Chop, chop, chop, chop,' they all chorused continuously.

Now the knot was raised and the Teaser, Lord Summerisle, ran forward and stood on the dolmen. The swords descended, in time to the music, until the knot rested gently on Lord Summerisle's shoulders. The crowd watched the swords intently now. After a double beat of the music, they were raised again and Lord Summerisle stepped briskly away from the dolmen to have his place taken by the next person in the line, a deer-man. The knot descended around the antlered figure's neck; a double beat followed and the knot was raised. The deer bounded off the dolmen stone as if released from a pen.

This process was repeated with each person as their turn in the line came. Howie noticed that there was a sense of growing tension in the people ahead of him as their moment to have the knot about their necks approached. Even more remarkable was the way they nearly all cringed as they stood on the dolmen stone. Howie's mind raced back to the children's game that went with the nursery rhyme. It had been played often at Christmas parties for the kids back on the mainland.

Two people faced each other, he remembered, their hands clasped to make a sort of knot. They raised and lowered the knot to the rhythm of the music and when the sound stopped clasped the child they'd caught and he or she was then considered out. Howie supposed it represented what was once the apparently random choice of the plague for its victims. Perhaps it had, itself, been adapted from some earlier pagan practice such as he was now witnessing . . . but *here* the music hadn't stopped, *yet!*

Howie tried to think it through step by logical step. The game here was not, as originally in the children's version, simply one of elimination, until the remaining person was the winner. Perhaps the music would only stop *once* in this 'game' . . . and that was how the sacrificial victim was chosen? But if Rowan had *already* been selected, why go through all this? Love of ceremony and charades? That was possible, given Lord Summerisle's extraordinary imagination. It occurred to Howie that perhaps only a small clique knew that Rowan was the 'chosen one'. Hence, the apparent fear of some as they came under the knot. He strained to see who was ahead of him, in case there was some risk of Rowan being among them, but it was hard from his in-line perspective to see. By this time a great many spectators who had already braved the knot stood about inside the circle watching. Howie decided to risk getting out of line and mingling with these people, the better to look out for a possible Rowan.

Once he had edged some ten yards from the line he could see that the next fifteen persons in line for the knot were mostly men and the few women among them, people whom he easily recognized like Miss Rose and Willow and Old Swallow. No teenage girls, not even any hares. But there were at least a hundred people still to come.

Howie was wondering if he dare wander down the line

looking for Rowan when he felt a hand come and grab him by the nose. He hung onto the Punch mask fearing he was about to be found out and unable to see whose hand it was through the eye slits. A deep voice in his ear soon told him:

'Everyone must go through, MacGregor. It's a game of chance. Remember?' breathed Lord Summerisle.

Howie felt himself being pulled back to the line and inserted into it about three people from the knot. What will happen when the music stops? Could it, Howie wondered, possibly stop when he was the one on the stone? The answer was of course it could. He was still trying to follow his line of deductive reasoning. Since he knew for certain that Rowan was the intended sacrifice, was it possible that the person who was about to be chosen here was *the person who would carry out the sacrificial act*? After all, being the executioner was never a popular role. That would explain the whole community having to go through the knot so that the killer would be chosen by pure chance, but still represent the whole community in whose name he killed. The actual sacrifice was to be made on a beach. Lord Summerisle had already announced this so the sergeant still believed he had a little time.

It was Howie's turn next, after a frog whose head was a particularly bilious green. The sergeant knew now what he would do if the music stopped while he was under the knot. Since it seemed practically certain he would have to unmask, he was determined to make his speech then and there, grabbing the knot so as to disarm the swordsmen. He would appeal to them all in the name of their sovereign, the Queen of Scotland, whose crown he wore on his uniform under the Punch costume. He would offer to intercede for them with the authorities in return for their immediate handing over of Rowan Morrison. He would explain the 'conspiracy law' and the law relating to being 'accessories to attempted murder', if, please God, he was now proved wrong in his wild thought that they intended to devour an already slain sacrifice. If a ritual killer was being chosen by the chop chop game, it pointed to the fact that he or she must have a live someone to kill. Rowan, of course.

The frog had not been chosen.

Even as Howie stepped under the knot himself he was sure his theory was correct. Here *comes* the chopper clearly referred to the candidate to *play* the role of chopper . . .

The knot had descended over his shoulders. Howie could see the tense, excited expression of the baker-swordsmen who stood almost opposite him.

A beat-beat of the drum and the knot was raised. Howie found himself bounding forward, relieved at his own reprieve. Now he could be free to go down the line to look for Rowan, because the people who had been through milled about, just watching.

Then the music stopped.

Howie spun around to see who the knot had caught and was aghast to see that it was a young girl in a white robe with the garlanded head of a hare. He hadn't remembered seeing her in the line. She was so obviously Rowan that he actually felt a surge of relief that at last she was going to be revealed alive.

The steel of the swords screamed as the knot was pulled suddenly tight, decapitating the little hare.

The headless body fell to the ground while the head itself flew some six feet in the air before falling among the gasping, screaming crowd. But then there was total silence as Lord Summerisle, Miss Rose, and Dr Ewan, the Boar, rushed towards the body.

For almost a complete moment Sergeant Howie was too stunned to move. He had stood and *watched* a murder. He had never seen the feat of 'pulling-the-knot-tight' so he had never dreamed it might be done. With the swords knotted he'd assumed them unusable.

He stared at the headless body and was disgusted to see it move. Like the proverbial chicken, he supposed. He was gathering his energy for the gargantuan task of arresting these people, and was about to take off his mask, when from the chest of the headless body a wicked laughing girl's face appeared. Howie immediately recognized the brown-haired girl who had fallen headlong from the cupboard.

'Well done, Holly!' said Miss Rose. 'You can come back to life now!'

Howie's first reaction was one of relief mixed with bewilderment, then 'back to life' suddenly made him remember another phrase: 'Death and Resurrection'. Howie wondered if that game he had just witnessed could be all they had meant by it. But it still left the sacrifice that had been announced for the beach and answered none of his questions about Rowan's whereabouts.

The whole congregation was applauding and laughing and crowding around Holly, while the bemused sergeant examined the hare's head. It was beautifully made so that it sat on the head of the child, who had obviously been given false shoulders in her cleverly made white dress.

'To the beach, friends!' Howie heard Lord Summerisle shout.

The crowd remained masked and streamed along a path that led to the cliffs and from there down a serpentine route to a pebbled beach. Howie went with them avoiding anyone, like Willow, whom he thought might want to talk to him. Miss Rose did speak to him as they waited to walk, in Indian file, down the cliffside path.

'We'll have to put you on the wagon next year, Alder. Or find a new Punch. It sets such a bad example for the young people to see you not taking your role as seriously as you ought. Shame on you, man! What have you to say for yourself?'

'Nothing,' Howie ventured in a low voice, from within the mask.

'You're incorrigible, Alder. Anyway I won't scold you any more. This is a happy, holy day!' said Miss Rose, preceding him down the path.

This left Howie relieved but, in the wake of the charade played out in the circle of stones, still utterly bewildered. He wondered if he dared hope that everything was to be symbolic. Yet he had a strong feeling that it was not to be. For the time being, however, his mind refused to grapple any further with the problem. He decided to abandon deductive reasoning in favour of simple, vigilant observation. Particularly since Punch appeared to have no role to play at the moment.

Glancing down at the beach, he noticed that the Suffolk Punch carthorses stood by the water's edge, their dray loaded with the coffin and the huge barrels that he'd seen being wrestled up the ramp in the courtyard off the

High Street. The ramp was in place again but this time it led down to the water's edge. There must, Howie thought, be some other access to this beach, for they had certainly never got the horse and dray down the path they were all descending.

Howie noticed that the entire congregation, as soon as they reached the foot of the cliffs, walked hurriedly towards the horses and cart, falling on their knees in a semicircle around it. He joined in this movement keeping his eyes on Lord Summerisle, who appeared to have exchanged his mistletoe and sickle for a hefty axe. The laird climbed up onto the cart while two of the swordsmen wheeled one of the barrels so that it was poised on top of the ramp.

Lord Summerisle swept his axe through the air commanding complete silence, and everyone faced out to sea.

'Shoney, God of the Sea!' he declared in a voice so loud that he may have hoped it would be heard in the depths. 'I give you this ale as a libation, that you may, in the year to come, bestow on us the rich and diverse fruits of your kingdom!'

Then with a mighty blow he stove in the side of the barrel with his axe. Beer and foam shot forth but Lord Summerisle was already kicking the barrel down the ramp where it whirred round and round spewing forth ale, until it fell into the sea with a great splash.

'Hail Shoney! Accept our offering!' roared the crowd.

Lord Summerisle was meanwhile dispatching the other barrel. Howie watched with the others as the barrel broke upon the incoming waves spreading a spume of foam and froth over a wide area. It really was a very childlike religion, he thought. Charades and giving their mythical gods goodies, like beer. As if a sea god would be thirsty, thought Howie, really smiling for the first time under his ceaselessly grinning mask.

Perhaps they were simply to be pitied as they played these apparently harmless games. Howie half-dared to hope that Rowan would appear, in the end, to be crowned carnival Queen and that everyone would go home, rejoicing, and he would find his fears had all been just a nightmare. Lord Summerisle turned to face the congregation, the lowering sun making him an awesome silhouette with his flying mane of black hair.

'And now,' he said, 'for our more dreadful sacrifice. To those who command the fruits of the earth.'

Some distance away a horn sounded. The congregation turned to look down the strand to where the cliffs met the sea in a pile of enormous rocks. Upon these boulders stood four men with lighted flambeaux. Behind and beyond the rocks was a cave. In the mouth of which stood Broom, the piper, blowing a conch horn.

Not far from Broom, standing, in a white dress, her hands apparently tied behind her back, was a girl with reddish-coloured hair and a garland of flowers around her neck.

Howie recognized her at once.

It was Rowan Morrison.

## CHAPTER XII

# May Day –
# Evening

THE HORN SOUNDED AGAIN. IT ECHOED SONOROUSLY in recurring waves, as if it were running along great subterranean passages and then returning.

The congregation had given a gasp that was the kind of sound a crowd makes when it has been waiting to see a great movie star, and there suddenly she is . . . in the flesh.

Howie was already running towards her. If MacGregor was a drunken disgrace maybe this is what he'd have done anyway, he thought. He could hear the congregation on the move behind him, but no one was actively pursuing him, yet. He watched for some movement from the flambeaux-carrying men standing on the rocks, who seemed to serve as sentinels to the cave.

'What is it, Mr MacGregor?' shouted one.

'Alder's had a snootful too much; let Broom deal with him,' called another.

Sergeant Howie couldn't believe his luck. When he got that close he'd *deal* with Broom. He so wanted to take his mask off now, to see a little more easily, but he didn't dare. Having everybody think he was Alder MacGregor was winning him time. Now he had travelled along a path that led between the rocks. All that remained between him and Rowan was a steep slope of slippery shingle and then came the flat rock that was at the entrance to the cave. Howie could see, as he started to scramble up, that Rowan was tied by a rope around her waist, that also bound her hands. Her wrists, in turn, were tied to a piece of stalactite rock. Light shimmered on the roof of the cave, leading Howie to hope that it might have another exit, perhaps to the next cove along the coast.

'Wo-up there, Alder,' Broom called down to him as if he were talking to a rogue carthorse. 'This isn't the night of the virgin springs, y'know. Have you no respect for the sacrifice, man?'

Howie scrambled up onto the rock and got his balance. Now he was ready.

'I'll blow an alarm if you don't get down from here at once, Alder!' cried Broom sounding suddenly scared.

Howie hit him so fast and hard, on the point of the chin, that Broom just crumpled. There were screams now from the congregation. Then a roar from Lord Summerisle.

'Get him! *Get him!*'

Looking around at the strand and the nearby rocks, Howie could see he had about a minute and a half to loosen Rowan and start to try to get her away. The whole congregation was stampeding towards the gap in the rocks. The men with the flambeaux were jumping from boulder to boulder before scrambling the eight feet or so down to the foot of the shingled slope.

Howie meanwhile was with Rowan. The child was very pale and had tears in her eyes.

'Oh, please get me away from here, Mr MacGregor,' she

gasped out to Howie, who, having lost fifteen seconds getting at his police knife by ripping through the Punch costume, was cutting her bonds one by one.

'I'm not MacGregor. I'm a police officer in his costume. I'm going to get you away,' he said, trying to reassure her.

'You know what they're going to do to me?' she asked wonderingly.

'I know. I know. C'mon, let's get going,' he said.

'There's a way out through the cave,' she said.

The first flambeau bearer was on the rim of the rock. Howie kicked him square on the jaw, sending him sprawling to the bottom of the shingled slope.

'Run, Rowan! Run! Run!' he shouted, measuring ten yards between them and the next nearest pursuer. She was away and Sergeant Howie ran after her, flinging off his mask as he went.

They were inside a huge cave lined with stalactites and stalagmites. Through an opening to one side of the cave the sea ebbed and flowed, leaving a fluorescent, flickering light within. Rowan beckoned Howie to follow her and soon they were having to flatten themselves to crawl through a floor-level gap to another chamber beyond. It was pitch black in this other cave and very clammy. Only the echoing sound of Rowan's voice, as she called out to him to hold the sleeve of her dress, told Howie that he was in a large enclosed space.

'If we try to run we may fall into one of the rock pools,' she said. 'I can feel my way around the edge.'

'What happens when one of them gets in here with a torch?' asked Howie, feeling as vulnerable as a rat in a trap.

'The bats,' said Rowan, giggling. 'Listen! It's a game we

always play on kids who come here for the first time, sending them in with a torch.' Howie could just hear a very high-pitched twittering coming from above them.

'We have to start climbing here,' said Rowan. 'Can you make out some light up there?'

Howie, whose eyes were becoming accustomed to the dark, could see both the distant gap through which he'd come and a small hole above and beyond him, through which came a phosphorescent glow. He could also see that a man with a flaming flambeau was trying to edge his way into the cave by the way they'd come.

The added ambient light this gave enabled Rowan and Howie to clamber quickly to the yard-wide hole that led to the next cave. Rowan insisted on looking back as the flambeau carrier struggled to his feet. A thousand bats were swooping from the roof at the unfortunate man who was finding that, although some of the bats were immolating themselves in the flames of the flambeau, others were in his hair, on his face, everywhere. Screaming, he threw the brand into a rock pool and all was inky blackness once again.

Howie had now clambered into the next cavern and, before Rowan could warn him, found himself falling. Fortunately for him, the hump on his Punch's costume caught and wedged him between some rocks lower down. Moreover, there was a great deal more light in this cavern. Howie could see a huge glittering green pool below him, which was clearly connected to the sea itself for a soft glow flooded in from a cave entrance below the ruffled surface of this pool. A small waterfall showered gently down from the roof of the cave far above.

Rowan was appalled at Howie's mishap and hurried down the rock face to try to extricate him. Once' again, when their eyes were accustomed to the new level of light, this didn't prove too difficult. The child, who struck Howie as remarkably resourceful, used his police knife to cut off part of his upholstered hump. Then, with her help, they were climbing again, this time up, up, up inside a vast fissure in the cave's ceiling. There were enough toeholds on either side and it was possible for both of them to brace themselves between the two walls of the fissure.

'The really hard bit's just ahead,' panted Rowan, 'but it leads out to the top of the cliff.'

Howie looked up and could see what she meant. The fissure closed ten yards or so above them. But before that there was a three-foot-high tunnel, from which the small euphonious waterfall sprayed down to the pool far below. The tunnel, which was the conduit for this stream, seemed to run at a forty-five-degree angle upward, and looked like a slanting hole in a petrified sponge.

'"The mouth o' the womb", it's known as hereabouts,' said Rowan.

'Don't the adults know these caves just as well as you kids?' asked Howie, a note of concern in his voice.

'Oh, yes. But not the males, of course,' she said.

'Not the men? Why on earth not?' he asked.

'Well, we're in the Grotto of the White Goddess, dedicated to the Earth Mother,' she added, by way of explanation. 'Miss Rose is the one we'd have to worry about, but at her age she's not much of a climber, naturally. Also she's terrified of bats and only comes in by the sea entrance at very low tide. I bet they're hunting for us in the next cave. We could have swum out, y'know. But I didn't want to risk you drowning.'

'Thank you, Rowan,' said Howie, touched to be the rescuer rescued. But he was still curious about the cave.

'You mean men aren't allowed in here?' he asked, as he was struggling up towards the waterfall, led every step of the way by Rowan, who showed him where the footholds were.

'Allowed?' Rowan didn't seem to understand.

'Permitted,' said Howie.

'Oh, yes, of course. It's just that they wouldn't want to, would they? Men are a bit squeamish about revisiting the womb. Miss Rose says our female magic comes from there. It's why I've always looked forward to becoming a woman. So that I'll have my own magic. In a few months it would have been too late to sacrifice me.'

Howie, who was taking a short rest before crawling into the funnel-shaped tunnel, behind Rowan, wondered whether she meant that by then she would have reached her maturity, or lost her virginity. On this island the two events were probably almost concurrent, he thought bitterly.

He took a last look down into the phosphorescent cave with its rippling green pool and the white spongy-looking rock around it. For the first time his head reeled from vertigo as he realized that he was perched above a hundred-foot drop.

He scurried at once into the tunnel, finding that he could only move along it by crawling up the incline, his hands and knees and feet in the trickling water.

Five minutes later, after sometimes having to edge

forward on his belly to make it under the overhanging rock, he could see that Rowan was silhouetted against bright light ahead. The tunnel along which the stream flowed, went straight on, but another fissure, in the cliff-top this time, now made it possible for Rowan to stand upright, largely disappearing from Howie's view.

'It's an easy climb from here,' he heard her say.

Then he too was standing, looking up at the late evening sky. The scudding clouds were tinged with pink and the gulls hung lazily into the wind. It *was* a fairly easy climb except that Howie was quite exhausted from the painful journey he had already made. Three minutes later, they both emerged at the top and lay for a moment breathless on the coarse grass of the cliff-top heathland.

'I'm sorry,' gasped Rowan apologetically, 'it was worse than I remembered it.'

'Never mind,' said Howie. 'I think we've lost our torch-bearing friends.'

Even as he was saying this, Howie noticed a kilted swordsman, silhouetted against the sky on a nearby pro-montory.

He stood up quickly, as did Rowan. The sergeant protectively took Rowan's hand in his. He was looking around to see who else might have caught sight of them when he heard a familiar voice.

'Born again, eh, Howie?' said Lord Summerisle. 'How *very* propitious!'

They had emerged some fifteen yards from the cliff's edge. In a dip nearby stood three figures. Howie saw them all at once and his heart sank. Lord Summerisle, Miss Rose, and Willow stood together like figures from a conversation-piece painting. All appeared to have changed from their costumes into clothes more suitable for a respectable stroll in the cool evening air. All gazed up at Howie and Rowan with unblinking recognition.

The sergeant completed his hasty three-hundred-and-sixty-degree survey of the horizon. All six swordsmen were posted where they could most easily intercept any attempt to escape. He looked quickly back to Lord Summerisle who stood, now, with his arms stretched wide open and a smile of quite beguiling sweetness on his face, looking straight at Rowan.

Howie felt the tug of her hand leaving his, and saw her running towards Lord Summerisle.

'Did I do it right?' she cried.

'Dear little Rowan,' said Lord Summerisle gathering her in his arms, 'you did it excellently.'

The women kissed her warmly too, and Miss Rose pointed to a rotund figure that had appeared in the distance. Mrs Morrison beamed, a picture of maternal pride.

'Mummy!' shouted Rowan happily and ran to her mother's arms.

The sergeant walked quickly to the cliff's edge to see if any path down existed. *His* was the principal and only danger. Now at last, too late, he saw it. He found himself gazing at sharp oblong rocks pointing up, like the stone fingers of a drowning man, from the turbulent sea below. Once again the feeling of vertigo suffused him and he swayed at the cliff's edge. He felt a girl's hand pull him back and glanced around to see Willow looking up at him with an expression of tender awe on her face. Remarkable, he thought, there's not a trace of sexiness there now. But what the look that had replaced it boded he could not, as yet, tell.

Lord Summerisle walked over to him. He spoke carefully and, although his words were, as ever, patronizing, his manner wasn't.

'Welcome, Fool!' said Lord Summerisle. 'You have come of your own free will to the appointed place. The game is over.'

'What do you mean? What game? Which game?' asked Howie, who was sick to death of games.

'The game of the hunted leading the hunter,' said Lord Summerisle. 'You came to find Rowan Morrison. But it is we who have found you, just as we intended to do.'

Sergeant Howie was now roaming the immediate cliff area to see if there was any possible route down. If he could evade them till dark he knew he had a chance. There was no danger that police would *not* be sent from Stornoway if he failed to make some contact in the morning. Lord Summerisle followed him, explaining what Howie had already understood, in a wave of bitter realization, the moment Rowan had said 'Did I do it right?' They had all done it right. But this insufferable madman must rub the salt in, as if it made any difference, now Rowan was safe, whether he, a simple police officer, understood all their complex mumbo-jumbo or Summerisle's ludicrous rationale for it.

'You see our research had told us that you were just the man we wanted, and we were determined to get you here. Of course we were equally determined to control your every action and thought once you had arrived. We were rather successful, don't you think?' Lord Summerisle seemed to be asking this question quite seriously.

'Successful?' shouted Howie. 'If you call wasting two days of a police sergeant's time with an elaborate game . . . yes, very successful!'

'Specifically, we persuaded you that Rowan was being held as a sacrifice because the crops failed last year.'

'But they did fail last year,' retorted Howie. 'I saw the Harvest photograph.'

'Oh yes, they failed all right,' agreed Lord Summerisle. 'Disastrously so, for the first time since my great-grandfather came here. The blossom came, but the fruit withered and died on the bough. That must not happen again this year.'

Sergeant Howie was only half listening. There was no way down the cliffs. His mission, in a sense, was completed, however unsatisfactorily, and he knew he had to get away from these people, and back to the mainland, as fast as possible. The certainty that they would try and hold him was reinforced by the appearance of the Oak, the Hobby-horse man, now dressed simply in a roll-necked sweater and his kilt, but standing, arms akimbo, looking quietly determined. He added to the ring of swordsmen.

The sergeant knew he could not possibly run the gauntlet of so many armed men. He could, however, try to walk through them, defying them to attack or hold him, and acquaint them of the potential gravity of any such actions.

He'd read his Kipling. How, he asked himself, would a Highland sergeant have faced a similar situation in India in the old days? Looked the natives straight in the eye and never faltered. At the slightest threat he'd have promised them the vengeance of the Great White Queen. But all these men were *Scots*, like himself, and they appeared to have a White Goddess of their own. His Queen was far away in London and here he was all alone, standing right on top of *their* White Goddess's limestone womb. He didn't fancy his chances but he was determined to face it out with dignity.

Howie squared his shoulders and prepared to try to march quickly out of the trap. But Lord Summerisle stood in his path.

'*Listen* to me, Howie. I don't think you've quite understood our position on *sacrifice*. And it's vital that you should,' said Lord Summerisle urgently. 'Animals are fine, of course, but their acceptability is limited. A child would have certainly been excellent . . . but we hold them all far too dear. These people are very sentimental. Besides, the sacrifice of a child wouldn't be nearly as effective as the sacrifice of the right kind of adult.'

'What right kind of adult?' Howie snarled the question at Lord Summerisle and stepped right past him without waiting for an answer.

He started to walk towards the swordsmen who held positions on a series of raised ridges, where the cliffs sloped upward to the evening sky. Even as he watched, the long, tireless horizon line came alive, and the whole congregation of the islanders came into view. They wore their masks still, and stared down at him. He stopped in a mixture of wonderment and fear. Then they all took off their masks and seemed to bow to him.

Miss Rose and Willow now came and held him gently by the arms.

'You see, Sergeant,' said Miss Rose, 'we needed a stranger who would come of his own free will – who would come here with the power of a king, as you have power, by representing the law . . .'

'. . . Who would come here as a virgin, as we have good reason to believe you still are,' added Willow.

'Get out of my way!' said Howie brusquely, brushing them aside. He walked with a measured step, looking up at the islanders. No one ran to intercept him. Oak, whom he was approaching, bowed low like the others.

'You are a fool, Sergeant Howie,' shouted Miss Rose in her clear, lilting, Scots voice.

The sergeant glanced back at her, heard a footfall behind him, and recognized the trap too late. His left shoulder was twisted, and his right leg kicked from under him by the enormously strong Oak. Howie found himself spinning, rolling like a log down the grassy slope till he came to a halt at Miss Rose's feet. His arms were ready to thrust himself up into a standing position, but Oak was too fast for him and had him pinned from behind. It was the big man who brought Howie to a standing position again, his huge forearms wound back under the sergeant's biceps, and with his big fists locked, holding the back of Howie's neck.

The wretched sergeant found himself again facing Miss Rose and Willow, with Lord Summerisle watching from a few yards away. In Oak's grip he was as helpless as if he had been in a straitjacket.

'You, Punch, are a fool. One of the great fool/victims of history,' Miss Rose instructed him, 'for the role of Punch is to be the King for a day . . . and who but a fool would want that?'

Lord Summerisle, like Miss Rose, ever the pedant, ever the teacher, patiently explained it all to his agonized prisoner.

'Punch got his hump, you see, to protect him from the traditional scourging that purified him. You are happily already pure so there will be no need to scourge you, Howie. Punch, in the shadow of death, was also always offered the most sumptuous of women. We offered you Willow, a 'dish' indeed to set before any king, but you, in defence of your virginity, rejected her, as we hoped you would. For it makes you doubly acceptable to the gods.' Lord Summerisle made it sound as if Howie had just won an Oxford blue in rowing.

Willow was holding a gleaming dirk in her hand, the kind of ornamental dagger Scots wear in their knee-length socks. This was obviously no toy, but honed and sharp, and she was pointing it straight at his throat. Howie could hear the trampling of hundreds of feet behind him as the congregation made its way to surround him – to touch him, if they could. But the swordsmen protected 'the King' from the people's 'reached out' fingers and hands.

A small basin and a jug of water were now being held before Howie by the hairdresser.

'Sergeant Neil Howie, you will be anointed and revered as a king,' said Miss Rose in ringing tones. 'You will undergo death and rebirth. Resurrection, if you like. The rebirth, sadly, will not be yours, but that of our crops.'

Howie feared his death, and he thought it was Willow's

knife that might bring it to him at any moment. But he answered defiantly:

'I am a Christian and as a Christian I hope for resurrection, and even if you kill me now it is I who will live again, not your damned apples!'

He looked over his shoulder at the congregation and shouted so they could all hear him.

'No matter what you do you cannot change the fact that I believe in the life eternal as promised to us by our Lord Jesus Christ!'

'That is good,' said Lord Summerisle when Howie's gaze had returned to Willow's knife. 'For believing what you do we confer on you a rare gift these days. A martyr's death. You will sit at the right hand of your God, among the elect!'

Howie heard the sound of a Celtic harp, somewhere in the crowd, start to play a refrain. Both women unpinned their long, fair hair and Willow now plunged her knife deftly forward, but it was not to cut his throat, as he had feared, only to slit his Punch costume from the neck to the codpiece. She and Miss Rose hummed a kind of lullaby as they undressed him. When he stood entirely naked they took the basin and the water and washed his body, drying him tenderly with their hair. Miss Rose used some ochre to anoint him in four places upon his chest and also upon his forehead.

They were punctiliously gentle with him. Having washed him and anointed him they presented a deliciously scented oil for him to smell and then rubbed it into his thighs and his back, into the places where, by some strange prescience, they seemed to know he ached. Yet their knowledgeable caresses were as painful in their way to poor Neil Howie as if they were the arrows that had struck Saint Sebastian. If death really faced him he valued his purity as never before. He felt defiled by their very touch.

Then they rinsed their hands of the oil and, taking a plain, white, raw-cotton shift, pulled it over his head and tied a cord loosely around his waist.

They stopped their humming and ended their strange task singing these words:

'Sleep, close and fast!'

In the silence that fell upon the entire congregation, Howie wondered what ghastly charade they now had planned for him. What was to be their next terrible game, and when would they stop playing with their 'mouse' whom they mocked with the name of 'king'?

Lord Summerisle gazed around at his islanders with the look of a visionary who has seen his own prophecy come true.

'And now,' he said to Sergeant Howie, 'it is time to keep your appointment with the Wicker Man.'

CHAPTER XIII

## Sunset –
##     on May Day

HOWIE REALIZED THAT HE WAS NO LONGER HELD BY Oak, that he stood among them unconstrained. Now might be his chance to speak to them all, to persuade them. He turned suddenly and walked straight into the crowd that opened before him. He was horrified to find that part of their indifference over his progress was because they were still engaged in tearing his clothes and even his shoes into minute pieces and haggling and quarrelling over the distribution of them.

But as he spoke they gave him their attention. Yet the quality of the hearing they gave him seemed to resemble more that of people listening to an old Caruso phonograph record than a crowd trying to comprehend a speech from the unjustly condemned. He spoke. They watched his lips intently and tried to memorize the cadences and timbre of his voice. They drank in the manna they seemed to think his closeness to them conferred.

'Wrap it up any way you want,' shouted Howie, so they could all hear, 'but you are committing murder. All of you. Each and every one of you will be *guilty*! Before the law of the land. Guilty! Your punishment will be a lifetime in prison. Why suffer that punishment for *no reason*? For there is no Sun God. There is no Goddess of the Orchards. Your crops failed because the strains failed. Fruit is not meant to grow on these islands. It is against nature. True, for a while, due to the science of the laird's great-grandfather, the fruit grew. But their failure means exhausted strains, worked-out soil, or a quirk in the weather. You must go back to the laboratory for the answer. And back, perhaps, to the true God that no amount of science has yet disproved. Killing me won't bring back your fruit. Summerisle,' he called out to the laird who stood listening on the fringe of the crowd, 'tell them that you know it won't.'

'But I know it will,' said Lord Summerisle in his deep, confident voice. 'The sacrifice of the willing, kinglike, virgin fool will be accepted!'

The people had looked at their leader more to hear the incantation of this dedication of the sacrifice than in expectation of any other answer to the sergeant's exhortation. Howie understood this and shouted at them again, in desperation, trying to get through the religious trance he sensed in them, to the reasoning machinery of their brains. But they had all started to hum like a vast swarm of bees, as if in response to the laird's words.

'But don't you all see,' Howie desperately reasoned with them, 'if the fruit fails again this year you will need another blood sacrifice, and it will have to be a more important one than me! Next year no one less than the King of Summerisle himself will do. D'you hear me, Summerisle? If the crops fail, your people will kill *you* next May Day!'

Howie pointed a prophetic finger at the laird.

On Lord Summerisle's face there was a flicker of anxiety

at these words. Only Miss Rose seemed to notice this, however, and she glanced at Lord Summerisle speculatively. The rest of the congregation was humming louder and louder now, more like the approach of a swarm of locusts than the mere buzzing of bees.

'Don't you see I'll be missed?' yelled Howie in sudden extreme panic, elbowing his way through the crowd. 'They'll come looking for me!'

But Lord Summerisle was shouting in a peremptory tone:

'There will be no traces! Come on! Bring him *up*, Oak.'

Howie felt himself seized from behind by the familiar hands of the huge Oak. Dozens of other strong arms tossed him aloft, so that he rode along on the sea of their upstretched hands.

'No! Just think what you're doing. In the name of God, just think what you're doing!' he kept shouting to them until the moment when he had reached that point where the sloping cliff-tops met the plateau at their summit. Here they tied his hands behind his back, holding him, the while, up in the air, his face to the setting sun.

Gently they lowered him to the ground and turned him so he faced east.

Then he saw the Wicker Man. Standing alone on the plateau, looking as if the very oak wood itself had been metamorphozed into the shape of a gargantuan man.

'Oh, God!' cried Howie. He still could not quite see its purpose. Only knew his terrible fear of it.

'Sweet Jesus, no!' he cried.

What Howie *saw* was a figure over sixty feet high, constructed of segmented wicker cages lashed together to form the shape of a man, and topped by the huge eyeless wicker head that blindly faced the sun. The cages that made up the arms and shoulders and pelvis of the man were filled to overflowing with goats, sheep, pigs and calves, chickens, and sundry other edible birds. The central partition of the giant's stomach and chest was an empty cage, its door open to receive the principal victim, a ladder leading up to it from the ground. Heaps of brushwood were piled around the legs of the Wicker Man.

'Sweet Jesus, no!' yelled Howie to his Saviour, who, for a moment, he was sure had forsaken him. 'No, Christ, *no*!' Sergeant Howie screamed as only a man can who has not really believed, until now, that death awaits him inescapably and right away. He had been so sure that gentle Jesus, whose name he praised day and night, would (it was his innermost conviction) take him, Howie, his servant, only in his lean and slippered age, hopefully in his sleep. Now here was a cage built specially for him. Here were people who openly proposed to burn him alive. There stood the four torchbearers close to the brushwood kindling at the feet of the giant. This, at last, was no charade. But the whole meaning of their May Day. He was their sacrifice. He the Host. He the body and blood of *their* sacrament.

The tuck-a-tuck of drums reminded him now of his dream of Lord Summerisle's ghostly army. Oak half-led, half-pushed him, barefoot, across the open heath to the Wicker Man. Thistles stung his feet and several times his legs refused to carry him further and he fell to his knees, only to be lifted to his feet again by Oak. Looking back in wonder at the awful congregation and the small band of balladeers, he saw that they all followed Lord Summerisle, first Miss Rose and Willow, then, in orderly twos and threes, the rest of the islanders, stretching half a mile back to the cliff face, to the spot where he and Rowan had emerged from the White Goddess's womb such a short while ago.

As he got nearer and nearer the monstrous structure and could hear the lowing of the calves, the snorting of the pigs, and the occasional anguished clucking of the birds in their constricted draughty baskets, he was struck with a terrible remorse at his doubt of his Saviour. These innocent, unknowing victims of the islanders' ignorance and cruelty were to be his companions in death. Summerisle was right that they had conferred upon him one great gift, for what was a comfortable demise abed in comparison to the glory of a martyr's death? It was not that he had given up all intention of escaping if he could, or all hope that help, at the last, would somehow, from somewhere, come. He simply discovered that his manhood and his faith were indivisible. He would live as long as he could as a man, he would certainly die, if it was God's will, with the dignity of a Christian and, if they saw him as such, yes, as a king. Pride was one sin his Maker would have to forgive Sergeant Howie. That, as they no longer had to push him towards the steps of the Wicker Man, became certain. He turned and walked backwards now, looking his executioners in the eyes, showing them his lack of fear, his faith. Allowing Oak to simply guide him.

Then came the one event of that memorable day that no one had planned exactly as it happened. Howie could hear shouts from the throng. Then someone was running towards him. An instant later a man was grovelling in front of Howie and Lord Summerisle had quickly moved forward raising his hands to halt the procession, before the man should be trampled underfoot. Howie recognized him almost at once as Beech, the self-styled guardian and king of the sacred grove.

Lord Summerisle seemed excited at what had occurred and as Sorrel, the gillie, hurried up to lead her brother away he restrained her and gently raised Beech's head so that the poor deluded man could look up at Howie. What Beech saw in the sergeant was a man transfigured by pride and dignity. A man absolutely confident that if he was not to be saved here, then he would shortly be in heaven. Beech's lips moved wordlessly as he gazed at the sergeant.

'Perhaps he is trying to say *ecce homo* to you, Howie!' said Lord Summerisle, fascinated by Beech's conversion.

'God forgive you your blasphemy!' said Howie, simply, to Lord Summerisle.

'The King. There is the real King!' shouted Beech, getting to his feet and pointing out Howie to the congregation.

'The real King's name is Jesus. Go and read about Him!' said Howie quietly to Beech, planting the seed of a new faith in the man.

Sorrel was now able to lead her brother away. He went meekly with her, back to his place in the procession. The drum started its beat again and Howie now led them with a firm tread right to the foot of the Wicker Man. The islanders had spread around the edifice in a great circle.

Oak carried the trussed Howie up the stairs of the Wicker Man, holding the helpless sergeant upon his shoulder. Having laid him upon the floor of the central cage, Oak hastily left and padlocked the door, which had three one-foot-square windows in it, through which Howie was able to look out at the throng of islanders more than forty-five feet below him.

Lord Summerisle stood at the foot of the steps facing the tangerine sun. An irreverent and silhouetted flock of gulls, momentarily all but eclipsed the deity but then the laird cried aloud the Lord's Prayer of Summerisle.

> 'Nuada, Great God of the Sun
> Hear Summerisle!
> Giver of all life
> Ender of night
> Accept this our anointed King
> Our sacrifice.
> Give us music, love
> Health, crops and joy.
> Nuada, make our island fruit!'

Then the islanders all turned and faced the sun and, bowing their heads, responded.

'Nuada, mighty God of the Sun, accept our sacrifice!'

'Reverence the sacrifice,' said Lord Summerisle.

The islanders turned once more to face and reverence Howie, who was searching the darkening sky for any sign of an aircraft – the ocean for any sighting of a ship. There was none. Not that he didn't realize that it was far too late to save him now, but he still was policeman enough to hope that the blaze they were about to make would attract some attention. For he could understand, now, what Lord Summerisle had meant by 'There will be no traces!' Also he'd been waiting for a chance to focus the attention of the islanders on one last message he had to give them. He must, before it was too late, tell them the absolute truth of their situation in the Word of the true God, as the Scripture had told it.

Therefore, while Lord Summerisle had the ladder taken down, Howie sought, in his memory, the fire and brimstone passage that the minister had addressed to them at times when he felt that Portlochlie had so far sunk into iniquity that the fate of Sodom and Gomorrah might soon overtake it. It was odd how apposite it was, as it came back to him.

'Hear ye the words of the Lord,' he shouted. 'Repent ye heathens! And howl! For it is the Lord who has laid waste your orchards.

> It is He who hath made them bare.
> Because the truth is
> withered away from . . .
> the sons of men.
> Desire shall fail . . .
> . . . and ye shall all die accursed!'

He looked at them now that he'd spoken his last words, or rather God's words to them. They gazed up at him with an implacable curiosity mixed with awe. He realized that they were not killing him because they hated or feared or despised him, rather the reverse, but mainly because it was expedient. More, in their eyes, his death was vital. Beech alone, of the whole congregation, applauded his words and seemed to be weeping for him. The others ignored Beech,

tolerant in their acceptance of a single, mad individual as
an aberration to be expected in any flock.

Lord Summerisle gave a signal to the torchbearers and
they stepped forward and lit the piles of brushwood. Howie
could smell the burning long before he could see any
smoke, let alone the flames. At the same time as the
lighting of the brushwood at the feet of the Wicker Man,
a drum gave four enormous beats, and, led by Lord Summerisle, the entire congregation started to sing:

> *'Summer is acumin' in*
> *Loudly sing Cuckoo*
> *Grow the seed and blows the mead*
> *And springs the wood anew.*
> *Sing Cuckoo!*
> *Ewe bleats harshly after lamb*
> *Cows after calves make moo*
> *Bullock stamps and deer champs*
> *Now shrilly sing Cuckoo . . .*
> *. . . Cuckoo . . . Cuckoo.*
> *Wild bird are you! Be never still Cuckoo!'*

The poor animals were in a pandemonium of screaming
and cackling and honking as they could hear and smell the
fire mounting the edifice towards them. Howie looked out
at the individual islanders as they all stood swaying and
singing with a communal joy. Willow's expression was
indistinguishable from Old Loam's expression, in spite of
her beauty and his hideousness. Lord Summerisle's exult-
ant look was exactly mirrored by that of Rowan and Sorrel
and Miss Rose and May Morrison and Cuckoo and Lark

and Swallow and the rosy-cheeked girl who had so pro-
phetically called 'Alive, alive . . . oooh!'

Howie was reminded of having seen, one night on BBC
television, the replaying of a famous documentary about
the Nuremberg Rally. It had been called *Triumph of the
Will*. Lots of well-scrubbed blond people with expressions
just like this congregation. Of course, they hadn't burned
anyone there, as far as he could remember. That had come
later.

He realized he still didn't know if he was the first of
their human sacrifices, but he knew, looking at their faces
as they sang, that he wouldn't be the last.

Some pigs below him were meeting their death with the
most frightful shrieks, and Howie could see that the whole
of the trunk of the edifice around him had taken fire, while
his feet were already blistering in the extreme heat.

The inactivity of waiting for death was almost as dreadful as listening to the sound of it all around him.

In one patch at the side of his cage the flames were
already intruding, leaving a hole through which he could
see one of the arms of the Wicker Man – in which wood
pigeons, plovers, ducks, and geese were incarcerated, but
whose cages had not yet caught fire.

Poor Howie had to hop about on the now burning floor
but he was able to get his wrists to the flames where they
were coming through the wicker side of the Man. He
remembered, as he deliberately burned through the ropes
that tied his wrists, how much more painful a burn was a
little time *after* the actual burning process had singed the
flesh. Painful now, but not yet the pain that was to come.
With God's grace it might consume him entirely, this fire,

before that lingering agony ever reached him. Meanwhile the sight of the birds in the as yet unburned arm had given him an idea. He looked at his lacerated wrists and blackened hands and experimented with his fingers. The tendons worked well although the pain of working them made him shout. He kept on shouting now, for shouting he could keep moving. And moving he could still take action.

His mission in coming to this infernal island had been to find a child. If he could only *save* some of the increasingly terrified birds he could see in the Wicker Man's arm he might not count his police mission here an entire failure. For that aspect of what was happening to him he kept quite separate in his mind from the witness he'd been able to give to his faith, and from which he felt a growing exaltation, as his death crept closer. He kept Mary Bannock deliberately from his thoughts for he knew he could not think of his grief for her and act, at the same time, to save the birds. He was certain that his soul and Mary's soul were both assured an eternity of bliss. Earthly bliss was not God's will for them.

'Amen!' he shouted.

He had noticed that there were big joists of wood in each corner of his cage. If he could tear one of these away from the burning fabric of the wicker, he might be able to poke it through the hole and so force open the cages in the Wicker Man's arm. First he took off the white garment, the hem of which was already on fire, and stood naked in his cage, bellowing at the pain of his burning feet, but determined still to try to free the birds. He pulled and yanked at the joist with his bleeding, blistering hands, until it came away. Then he rushed to the hole in the side of his cage.

Looking down he could see the swirling, twenty-foot flames from the tarred tree trunks that were the Wicker Man's legs. The wickered fingers of the arm were already burning. He could see that each group of birds in their small cages was enclosed by a door with a latch and pin mechanism, and that he had only to use his joist to lift the pins. Wiping the sweat from his eyes, he tried to aim the end of the joist so that the pin could be knocked up and out of the latch. It worked. But with the door of their cage open, the pigeons were too frightened, at first, to move. Howie used his remaining strength to resist his mounting agony and to open three more cages that were within his reach. By that time the pigeons had started to flutter out in ones and twos. Soon the other birds, scared into motion by the sudden roar and crackle of the 'hand' below them catching fire, started to take wing. Howie watched them in triumph, even as he screamed again.

'Jesus!' he shrieked. Then he committed the last conscious act the ebbing span of his life permitted.

In his flaming, smoke-filled cage, he spoke direct to his God in words it had been his pleasure to learn and remember as a child. He took a deep breath from a corner of the cage unfilled with smoke.

'O, God,' whispered Sergeant Neil Howie in his last moment, for only by whispering could he keep his lungs clear of smoke, 'Whose nature is ever to show mercy and forbearance, I humbly entreat Thee, for the soul of this

Thy servant, Neil Howie, who will today depart from this world. Do not deliver me into the *enemy*'s hands or put me out of mind forever, but bid Thy holy angels welcome me and lead me home to Paradise. Let me not undergo the real pains of hell, because I die unshriven, but establish me in that bliss which knows no ending . . .'

The floor collapsed before he had time to say 'through Christ Our Lord. Amen'. But he thought it as he fell into the thirty-foot bonfire between the Wicker Man's legs. He was immediately unconscious, and dead only ten seconds later. To the remaining animals God showed less mercy, but that was part of a riddle Sergeant Howie was now spared from the solving, for one must suppose he already knew part, or all, of the answer.

The congregation sang on. Their eyes shone and the heat of the fire flushed their faces as they watched the whole sixty-foot man ablaze. In the mounting wind that was coming off the sea, the flames tore upward till the figure seemed to breathe and stir like a vast living thing.

The watching sun settled its rim, just kissing the ocean, and the escaped birds wheeled high above the huge graven image of that creature of whom it was once said, 'If animals could conceive of a devil his image would be man's.'

A few minutes later, as the sun was setting on the horizon like a spreading, melting clot of cream, the Wicker Man collapsed, and the voices of its victims were mercifully hushed at last. The good people of Summerisle wandered home tired after their holy day. The flambeaux men stayed with the bonfire to see it was all reduced to ashes. Carts were arriving for a collection of the residue;

it would be diligently spread in the wake of the plough when the time came for the new fruit tree planting that year.

Summer was acumin' in.

And as for Howie, it would be good to think that all the trumpets sounded for him on the other side.

*Follow the phenomenon and get the inside
story of the classic cult horror film*

# ALLAN BROWN

## Inside the Wicker Man

### *The Morbid Ingenuities*

With the cooperation of Christopher Lee, Anthony Shaffer, Robin Hardy, Diane Cilento, Edward Woodward, Britt Ekland and Ingrid Pitt.

*The Wicker Man* (1973) is a classic from the golden age of the horror film; along with *Performance* and *A Clockwork Orange*, its *Exorcist*-like history makes it one of the most controversial British films ever made, and widely hailed as the greatest film made in Scotland. Twenty-five years after its release, *The Wicker Man* is at the centre of an enthusiastic cult hooked on its enduring enigmas, psychological twists and its compelling fascination with pagan ritual, ensuring that the film's popularity and exposure grows every year, overshadowing its desultory release as *Don't Look Now*'s B-feature.

This is the full story of *The Wicker Man*'s conception, production, release and reception, including full details of the infamous lost footage, interviews with the film's participants, rare stills, and a serious exploration of the film's themes and roots in Scottish paganism and culture, to position it rightfully in the film pantheon.

Allan Brown is the award-winning Chief Writer of the *Sunday Times* in Scotland. He has regularly investigated the trail of *The Wicker Man*, and helped produce a documentary on this hidden classic for BBC Scotland in December 1998.

ISBN 0 283 06355   £14.99

256pp trade paperback 16pp rare black and white
and 8pp colour pictures, stills and documents

Sidgwick & Jackson and Pan Books are available from all good book-shops, or can be ordered direct from the publisher. Indicate the number of copies required and fill in the form below.

Send to:    Macmillan General Books C.S.
                Book Service By Post
                PO Box 29, Douglas I-O-M
                IM99 1BQ

or phone:    01624 675137, quoting title, author and credit card number.

or fax:      01624 670923, quoting title, author and credit card number.

or Internet:  http://www.bookpost.co.uk

Postage and packing free.

Payment may also be made with order in sterling by UK personal cheque, Eurocheque, postal order, sterling draft or international money order, made payable to Book Service By Post.

Alternatively by Access/Visa/MasterCard

Card No.   ☐☐☐☐☐☐☐☐☐☐☐☐☐☐☐☐☐☐

Expiry Date  ☐☐☐☐☐☐☐☐☐☐☐☐☐☐☐☐☐☐

Signature _____

Applicable only in the UK and BFPO addresses.

While every effort is made to keep prices low, it is sometimes necessary to increase prices at short notice. Pan Macmillan reserves the right to show on covers and charge new retail prices which may differ from those advertised in the text or elsewhere.

NAME AND ADDRESS IN BLOCK CAPITAL LETTERS PLEASE

Name _____

Address _____

_____

_____

_____

Please allow 28 days for delivery.
Please tick box if you do not wish to receive any additional information.  ☐